D0396027

CAGED EAGLES

ERIC WALTERS

ORCA BOOK PUBLISHERS

Library and Archives Canada Cataloguing in Publication

Walters, Eric, 1957–
Caged Eagles
Sequel to: War of the Eagles.

ISBN 10: 1-55143-139-4 / ISBN 13: 978-1-55143-139-0

1. Japanese Canadians—Juvenile fiction. I. Title.
PS8595.A598C34 2000   jc813".54   C00-910192-6

PZ7.W17129Ca 2000

First published in the United States, 2000
Library of Congress Control Number: 00-100927

Summary: A young boy learns to take pride in his Native heritage, but can he accept his country's betrayal of his best friend.

Orca Book Publishers gratefully acknowledges the support for its publishing programs provided by the following agencies: the Government of Canada through the Canada Book Fund and the Canada Council for the Arts, and the Province of British Columbia through the BC Arts Council and the Book Publishing Tax Credit.

Cover artwork by Ken Campbell

ORCA BOOK PUBLISHERS
PO Box 5626, Stn. B
Victoria, BC Canada
V8R 6S4

ORCA BOOK PUBLISHERS
PO Box 468
Custer, WA USA
98240-0468

www.orcabook.com
Printed and bound in Canada.

17 16 15 14 • 11 10 9 8

To those who endured.

. 1 .

Kairn Island, British Columbia
March 17, 1942

"You know you can't take all your dolls with you," I said softly to my seven-year-old sister Yuri.

"But I can't just take one and leave the other two here," she pleaded. "It wouldn't be fair to pick one over the others. And who will take care of the ones I leave? I can't just leave them here ... alone ..." She blinked her eyes quickly to try to hold back the tears that were starting to form in the corners of her eyes.

"There just isn't room on the boat for all of them. Maybe you could just tuck the other two dolls into your bed together and that way they wouldn't be alone," I reasoned.

"But there'd still be nobody to take care of them. They'll be scared," she whimpered.

I didn't know what to say to her. I was scared right now. Maybe it would have been better if we at least knew where we were going. All we were told by the RCMP was that we had to be out of our homes within twenty-four hours — by noon today. Since then every family in the village had been working to put their things on their fishing boat. And I'd heard that the same was happening up and down the whole coast. All families of Japanese heritage had been ordered to leave their homes and assemble at Prince Rupert. For some families, farther up the coast, that was a trip of over a hundred miles. For us it was about fifteen miles to the outer reaches of the Prince Rupert harbor.

My father said that once we were at Prince Rupert we'd be told where our final destination was. There were rumors — there were always rumors — that our boats were going to be pulled out of the water and stored in the boatyards in Rupert, and then we'd all be sent by train down to Vancouver. And what then?

"Tadashi ... I just can't leave them ..." Yuri continued.

"But father said you could only take one," I answered. I'd been surprised that he'd allowed her to even take the one. There really wasn't much space on the boat — at least, space in the cabin — and that space was already filled with pots and pans and dishes and food and extra clothing and bedding ... things we'd need. The only non-essentials he'd allowed anybody to take were the family photo albums and two delicate vases that had been brought over from Japan thirty years ago when my father and his family first came to Canada.

"Are we just going to be gone for a few days?" Yuri asked.

"I don't know." That was at least partially truthful. I didn't know how long we were going to be gone for. Nobody knew. All we did know was that every person who had Japanese blood in them had been ordered to leave an area within one hundred miles of the coast now that Canada was at war with Japan. Why couldn't they just leave us alone?

"I just can't choose one of my dollies over the others," she said, clutching all three to her chest, tightly wrapped up in her arms. She was no longer even pretending that she could stop the tears and big, fat drops started to leak out of the corners of her dark eyes, tracing a path down her cheeks.

"Maybe I can help," I said. "Let me see your dollies."

Yuri hesitated and then reluctantly released her grip on one and handed it to me.

"What's her name?" I asked.

"Mollie."

"She's a very pretty dolly," I said, grateful there was nobody in the room to overhear my conversation. At fourteen, I was far too old to be playing with dolls.

"She's my prettiest doll," Yuri said. "Doesn't she have lovely hair?"

I ran a hand over her hair, stroking it gently. It was soft, red yarn that formed the doll's hair. The hair matched the freckles spread across her face. Bright blue eyes stared back at me as I looked at the doll.

"And what do you call these two?" I asked as I reached out and took the other dolls in my hands.

"Their names are Nabuko and Sachi."

"They're very pretty dollies too," I offered as I looked at them.

Although I hadn't known their names, I knew the dolls well. They'd been in our house for longer than Yuri had been — actually, longer than I'd been around … a lot longer. They were dolls my mother had when she was little. Sent to her by a grandmother she'd never met — a great-grandmother I'd never known. My mother was born in Canada just one year after her parents — both dead now — came from Japan.

The two little dolls were almost identical: straight black hair, dark slanting eyes, slight in build and powdery-white faces — little Japanese girls. Of course, the traditional Japanese dresses had long ago been replaced by dresses that looked like those worn by my two sisters, like those worn by any other girl in my school.

My mother was a wizard with a needle and thread and could make anything. She sewed almost all our clothes. Sometimes Yuri or my other sister, Midori, who was eleven, would come to her with a picture of some Hollywood actress and beg her to sew them a dress like the one in the picture. If mother thought it was a nice dress, she'd make it. If she didn't like it, she'd give some excuse about not having the right material or say. "maybe later." My mother didn't like to say no, but I knew what maybe later really meant.

I looked at the dolls. They were wearing Western clothes, but that still didn't change what they were — little Japanese dolls ... still Japanese dolls after being in this country for forty years. And I looked over at my little sister and saw the same delicate features of the dolls and realized that being born here hadn't changed her appearance either ... or mine.

"Why do we have to leave our house anyway?" Yuri asked.

I didn't know what to say. "It's because ... because of the war," I stammered. "They want to make sure we're ... safe."

That was nothing but a lie and I knew it and felt bad. Our safety had nothing to do with it. Instead, it was to make sure that they were safe from us. They were afraid that we'd help the Japanese — be spies or blow up bridges or kill people or I don't know what. Did they believe my grandmother was dangerous? Or my mother, or my two little sisters? Or me? I was born in this country. Did they really think I was going to help Japan? I'm Canadian.

"Will my doll be safe if I bring it where we're going?" Yuri asked anxiously.

"Are you a little scared like your dolls?" I asked, realizing what she really meant.

A trail of tears started again. I reached out and wrapped an arm around her shoulder.

"Everything is going to be okay. We're all going to be

together. Do you think Father or Mother, or Grand-mother, or Midori or your big brother here would ever let anything happen to our little Yuri?"

She shook her head, and I squeezed her a little bit tighter. If only I believed what I was saying.

"Tadashi!"

I turned around at the sound of my father yelling out my name. "I'm in here with Yuri!" I yelled back.

He appeared at the door to her room. "No time to waste. Come and help — now," he ordered.

"I was just getting the bedding from the girls' room," I explained. There was no point in mentioning the dolls to him.

"Hurry. There is much still to be done."

"Yes, Father."

"I will help old Mrs. Koyanagi. She is alone and needs assistance. You finish loading our boat while I help with her belongings," my father continued.

"Is she coming with us on our boat?" Yuri asked.

"No," he answered, shaking his head. "Traveling with others."

"I'll get the bedding down to the boat and come right back to the house," I offered.

My father gave a curt nod of his head in response and then he was gone.

"Here," I said, handing Yuri one of the Oriental dolls — I didn't know if it was Nabuko or Sachi.

"But what about the other two?" she pleaded.

"They'll be just fine," I said.

"But I can't leave —"

I put a finger up to her mouth to silence her. "You're not leaving them." I took the two dolls and stuffed them into the bedding, folding them in so they were lost but safe within the folds of the material. Yuri's face erupted into a smile.

"But I want them to stay deep down in your bedding. I don't want to see them, and you better not let Father see them. Do you understand?"

She nodded her head obediently.

The bedding filled my arms and I walked out of the room. I held it tightly, knowing that I had two little secrets locked away inside. My mother and Midori were nowhere to be seen, but I could hear my grandmother in the kitchen, humming loudly to herself. How she could be humming I didn't understand. Throughout this whole ordeal — the bombing of Pearl Harbor by the Japanese, the declaration of war against Japan by Canada, Great Britain and the United States, all Japanese-Canadians having to get registration cards and not being allowed to leave our village, and now, finally, being forced to move — she'd seemed almost happy. No, that was wrong. Not happy … just not upset. All she kept saying, over and over and over, was *shikata-ga-nai*. That was Japanese for "it can't be helped." She somehow saw this as being almost like fate — our fate — and there was no point in fighting it.

I wanted to fight it. Or fight something. Or somebody. But there was nobody to fight. I just felt so angry and hurt and confused and it was all so tightly balled up together inside of me that it made my gut ache when I thought about it too much.

I opened the front door and walked out into the cold March air. Walking down our front path I couldn't help but be amazed at the sight before me. Everywhere I looked were the people of our village, either burdened down with possessions and headed for the boats at the dock, or walking back toward the houses empty-handed. Regardless of the direction they were moving, they all looked the same: heads down, moving silently, serious expressions etched on their faces. I wondered what would happen if I called out to somebody, or yelled or laughed out loud. Would anybody even turn my way? Would they pretend that they even heard or noticed? Probably not.

I hurried along the path to the dock. Our boat was just one of more than a dozen little fishing vessels tied to the wooden dock. There were another two dozen sitting out in the harbor, already loaded, anchored and waiting for us to join them. It wasn't unusual to see them all bobbing up and down together in our little harbor, except at this time of year. All the fishing boats had been taken in for the winter, their hulls scraped and repainted, fishing nets mended and stored. Then came the order that the fishing boats had to be turned over to the government. Did they really think that somebody would chug their little boat out into the ocean and then lead the Japanese Imperial Navy to the coast? I didn't know what was more stupid, the thought that any of us would help the Japanese, or that they'd need our help to find the coast.

So all the boats had been put back in the water, waiting to be turned over. And now that we had to leave as well, it only made sense to pile our things onto the boats and go to Prince Rupert. If the boats had been turned in before this, then how would we ever have gotten our possessions to the town? We couldn't very well walk to town with our things on our backs.

I looked at the line of waiting boats. While they were all different, they weren't very different. Each was a wooden vessel with a small cabin to shelter the captain and crew — usually one other man. The deck was mostly open to accommodate the gear and nets. Near the back was the hatch, which opened to the hold where the catch was stored.

Most of our deck was covered by an enormous, gray, oilskin tarp. Underneath it was large pile of wood — fuel for the woodstove in the cabin. My father's worst fear was that once we got to Prince Rupert, they'd make us live on the boat for some time, and he wanted to make sure he had enough wood to keep us warm.

I danced between the other people along the length of the dock. A couple of them nodded their heads at me, but nobody said a word. It was an eerie silence. The only sounds were of the wind, the waves washing against the shore, the boats rubbing against the tires lining the dock and our footfalls against the wood.

Shifting my load to one arm, I carefully grabbed hold of a stay and stepped onto our boat. The deck was wet, and I struggled to regain my balance as my feet almost slipped out from under me. Thank goodness the temperature was above freezing or the salty spray thrown up by the winds would have been forming into layers of ice. I'd only ever been on the boat once when it was like that.

It was a late November day when I was only nine or ten years old. A cold front had moved in without warning. Our boat had been in a Prince Rupert shipyard for a refit, and when it was ready, my father had to sail her back to our village to be stored for the winter. Although it was only about four miles through the forest from Prince Rupert to our village, the trip by sea was longer, almost fifteen miles. My father asked if I wanted to come along. Back in those days I wanted to be a fisherman, just like my father, and I never turned down an opportunity to join him aboard. Of course, we weren't fishing that day. The nets were already in the storage shed. I remember how calm the water was when we were in the Prince Rupert harbor. But what had been calm in the harbor changed fast as soon as we hit open water. The waves were tremendous — bigger than I ever remember seeing. When we were in the trough between waves, I could look up through the windows and see the crests of the waves on both sides rising high above the tallest part of the boat.

I wasn't scared, though — at least, not at first. I knew my father knew everything about the sea and he'd never let anything bad happen to me. So we were rocking and rolling and bouncing and bucking. I closed my eyes and imagined we weren't on a boat but were riding a wild bronco. I used to love reading western paperbacks and thinking about what it would be like to be a cowboy, but that was as close as I'd ever come to actually riding a horse.

Of course, everything in the cabin was tied down — that is, everything but me and my father. We were bounced around pretty good. I tried my hardest to hold on to something all the time, but I was thrown right out of my seat by one wave.

The waves were bad, but what was worse was the wind. It screeched and howled and rattled the small windows of the cabin. And with the wind came the spray, and, while there was no danger of the ocean itself freezing, that spray froze solid as soon as it touched anything. Soon the deck, all the windows except the one out the front that was constantly cleared by a hand-cranked wiper, and all the lines were coated with ice. I thought it looked pretty, and I mentioned it to my father. He said there was nothing pretty about something that could kill you. I didn't understand how some pretty ice could kill anything. He then told me that he'd heard of boats that got so caked with ice that they became top-heavy and then "turned turtle" — flipped over.

I can remember that first rush of fear when he said that, and I think he saw it in my face. He told me not to worry, that he'd never let anything like that happen. And I believed him, and I felt better.

After that he turned to me and said, "Take the wheel," and before I even knew what he was doing, he left the cabin and went out onto the open deck and started to chop away at the ice and throw chunks overboard. He was probably only out there fifteen minutes, but it seemed like forever. And I knew we'd be okay because my father said so, and he was never wrong. At least, that's what I thought back then. Sometimes I wish I was still back then, instead of here and now, loading the boat to leave our home.

I pushed through the door into the cabin. It was crammed full of things, and the tiny space seemed even smaller now. Pots and pans and dishes protruded out of boxes piled against one wall. I knew they'd have to be stowed differently before we left or they'd come tumbling down when we hit the first decent wave. Bedding and clothes were piled against the other side. Three mattresses — my parents', Grandmother's and Midori's — were propped up on their sides. At night, when they were laid flat on the floor, there wouldn't be any space left over to move. I could hardly imagine how the six of us were going to fit in here. I guessed if the waters were calm enough I could go out on deck. Of course, that was a big question mark. How calm would the waters be this time of year?

I looked out through the side window, across the harbor, and tried to see beyond the finger of land that protected it from the open ocean. It was hopeless. Whatever awaited us wouldn't be known until we got out of the harbor … but what did it matter anyway? Rough or calm, we were going out there.

"*Shikata-ga-nai* … it can't be helped," I thought out loud, and then couldn't help but smile at my grandmother's words escaping from my lips.

As I watched, a boat rounded the outstretched finger of land and entered the harbor. Who would be coming to the village at this time? Maybe it was a fishing boat from farther up the coast, also heading for Prince Rupert, but forced in by bad seas … no, it wasn't a fishing boat. It was under a good head of steam and quickly crossed the calm of the harbor. It looked like it was going to try to put in at the dock. Whoever it was would need some help getting in.

Carefully I laid down the bedding, making sure that the dolls remained safely hidden within the folds. I hurried out of the cabin, securing the door behind me. I climbed up onto the dock. There was now plenty of space. In the short time I had been on our boat, two other vessels had moved away from the dock. I waved my arms so the captain of the vessel would be able to see I was offering my assistance. Partially I was trying to be helpful, but I was also anxious to hear what the conditions were out on the open ocean.

I still couldn't see who was inside the cabin, but I could clearly tell it was no fishing boat. Who was it? Who would be out there? As the boat came about, positioning itself to come into the opening at the dock, two men came out onto the deck. The flashes of their uniform jackets answered my question; it was the RCMP. They were probably coming to make sure we were following the orders to leave our homes. And I was going to help them dock to do it.

.2.

One of the officers moved to the bow of the vessel while the other strode to the aft. They readied ropes to secure the boat. It looked like it was going to overshoot the space along the dock, and the captain threw it into reverse and gunned the engine noisily to try to draw it back into the opening. The waves pushed the vessel toward the dock while the engine strained to pull it away from the last fishing boat. Just as it looked like they were going to bump together it swung into the spot. The officer in the bow tossed me the line. I grabbed it, pulled hard and then secured it, tying it in place. I looked down, expecting somebody else to have taken the aft line, and realized nobody was there. That was strange. There were so many people here I was surprised that no one else offered to help … I slowly turned around. There were at least a half dozen men from the village who were close at hand — close enough to help; you're always supposed to help other boats — but nobody had made a move. Maybe I shouldn't have given them any help either … I probably wouldn't have if I'd known who it was.

An RCMP officer leapt from the aft of the boat, bridging the small gap of open water, and secured the other end of the boat.

"Thanks a lot, son," called out a voice. It was the officer from the bow. He climbed onto the dock beside me, while a group of four other police officers exited the cabin.

Maybe I'd helped when I shouldn't have, but at least I'd get to know about the conditions. "What's it like out there?" I asked.

"I've seen worse. Winds weren't bad, waves about five feet. We got tossed, but not much." He laughed. "A couple of the guys, not used to the ocean, had green faces. I'd hate to be aboard with them if it really got rough." He paused and looked at me thoughtfully. "I know you," the officer said.

"What?" I sputtered.

"I know you. You go to school in Prince Rupert … Prince of Wales Public School. Right?"

"Yeah, I do … I mean, I used to," I answered. We hadn't been allowed to go to school for the last six weeks.

"What's your name?" he asked.

I wondered if he was going to check my registration card, the one that all Japanese over sixteen years of age had to carry. I was fourteen, which meant I didn't have to have one, but because I looked older I'd been asked for one before.

"My name is Tadashi Fukushima. I don't have a card because I'm only fourteen," I explained before he had a chance to ask me.

"Tadashi, that's right. I thought I recognized you."

Recognized me from where? I thought.

"You play baseball," he said.

"Yeah … I do," I stammered in reply. That certainly wasn't what I'd expected him to say.

"I saw you pitch for your school team last September."

"You did?" I asked.

"I was there to watch my son, Toby, play."

"Toby Johnson? You're his father?"

"Yep. He's the oldest of my three boys."

Of course, I knew Toby, as well as his two younger brothers, Raymond and Kenny. That was no surprise, though, because I knew everybody in the whole school.

Toby wasn't really a friend, but he was friendly.

Toby had only been in our school for the past year. He'd once mentioned that his dad was with the RCMP and had been transferred up to Prince Rupert. I knew the RCMP detachment had almost tripled in size in the past year to match all the growth in the town.

It wasn't that many years ago, before all the talk of war, when Prince Rupert only had five thousand people. Now it was home to over twenty thousand. People were flooding into town because there was so much work. The dry dock, railroad yard, oil refinery and all three canneries had all taken on more men.

Then there was all the building being done by the military. There were three bases being built just outside of town. I'd had a job after school, along with my best friend Jed and his mother, at one of the bases, and they were throwing up buildings so fast they could hardly get enough lumber to keep up with the demand.

I'd heard somebody say that war was good for business. And I guess that was true enough, even for us at first. Lots of the men in our village had taken on second jobs, working at the cannery on weekends or with one of the lumber mills, felling trees or working right in the mill. There was more money working in the cannery then there was pulling fish out of the ocean.

Of course, all of that stopped when we were all told we couldn't work anymore. Just after Canada declared war on Japan, all those men whose families were from Japan — no matter how long ago they came to this country — were let go. No jobs in the factories or at the bases or in town or even fishing.

My thoughts were broken as I watched the other police officers climb off the boat and start toward the village.

"We were sent up to see if anybody needed assistance," the officer, Toby's father, said.

And to make sure we all followed orders, I thought, but didn't say.

"Loading the boats, moving things, making sure the homes are all locked up tightly," he continued.

"We don't have a lock on our door," I said.

"You don't?" he asked in surprise.

I shook my head. "Nobody does. I don't think there's a locked door in the whole village."

It was his turn to shake his head slowly. "Things will be all right. You're pretty isolated up here. I can't see anybody coming around and bothering anything."

Up until him mentioning the possibility of somebody doing that, I'd never given it any thought whatsoever. It would never have occurred to me that we would need to lock our doors. Every single person in the village knew everybody else, and it wasn't like there were ever any strangers around. Who would watch the village?

"You'll be making patrols up here, right?" I asked hesitantly.

"Yeah … I'm sure we will," he answered. There was a pause. "Maybe we'll send a patrol out by boat every week or two."

"Not more often than that?" I blurted out without thinking.

"I don't think it could be more often than that, what with all the business we have right in town. With all those soldiers and sailors in town it's like the wild west, especially on Saturday nights. But don't worry, I'm sure everything will be okay."

I wasn't so sure. I just wished I'd thought to mention to Jed to come by and check the house.

Jed was my best friend, and he lived in the next village up. We'd known each other since we were little. Jed was half Native Canadian and half white — which meant he was no part Japanese, so nobody made him go anywhere. When the war started, his father, who was

English, enlisted and was now over in Europe flying fighter planes and battling the Nazis. His mother was Tsimshian, and she and Jed had moved into his grandmother's house. Just like everybody in my village was of Japanese descent, everybody in that village was Tsimshian. I thought we were at least lucky that the nearest village was Native. Indians are like Japanese and show respect for people — and their property. Nobody from that village would bother our houses, and anybody who wanted to come here from Rupert would have to go right through Jed's village to get here ... unless, of course, they came by boat.

One of the first things I'd do once we got to where we were going was write to Jed — like I'd promised to do anyway — and ask him to come and look in on my house as often as he could. I knew he'd be busy, between school and continuing to work part-time at the base, but not too busy to do that for me. Best friends are like that.

"I'll say hello to Toby for you," Constable Johnson said.

"Thanks, that would be good."

"Is your family all packed?" he asked.

"Um ... almost," I said, pointing to our boat. "We just have to put a few more things on board — some more clothes."

"Are most of the families ready to go?"

"I'm not sure," I answered. "I guess."

"Good," he said, and let out a big sigh. "That'll make it easier."

Easier? Easier for him, maybe, but not for any of us who had to move.

I watched as he started up the path away from the dock and toward the houses. In the distance I could see some of the other officers. They had already started, in pairs, to go from house to house, checking to see that people were gone or getting ready to leave.

"Wait!" I yelled.

Constable Johnson stopped and turned around. But it wasn't just him who responded to my call. More than a dozen people, my neighbors, all turned for an instant and looked in my direction. I knew that while they wouldn't be staring at me, they'd be watching me out of the corners of their eyes, and listening. I started up the path and Officer Johnson waited.

"You're here to see that we all get out, right?"

He nodded his head ever so slightly.

"What if we didn't leave?" I asked, surprising even myself with my question.

Officer Johnson looked taken aback by my question. "Are there some people who aren't going to leave voluntarily?" he asked. There was a hint of worry in his voice.

"There are *no* people who are leaving voluntarily," I said.

Now he looked genuinely worried, and confused.

"We're being forced to leave. Nobody's going voluntarily," I continued.

"I understand," he said almost apologetically, his face suddenly relaxed. "What I meant was, are there some families that are refusing to follow the orders?"

"I don't think so …" I paused. "What would you do if somebody refused to go? If they refused to leave their home behind?"

He didn't answer for a minute, and I could see by the expression on his face that he was struggling to come up with any answer.

"That is a good question."

I turned around. It was Mr. Yano. He was one of the most respected men in the village. His grandfather's family had been the first to settle the village, and he was born here — making him one of the first Japanese born in

Canada. He had been standing silently behind me and must have heard my question. I looked around. There were others standing within earshot, waiting.

"You have your orders," the constable said.

"And if we don't follow those orders?" Mr. Yano asked.

"Then … then, I have *my* orders, sir." Constable Johnson took a deep breath. "And those orders are for this village to be cleared by noon — and we will arrest anyone who does not comply with that order. I certainly hope that will not be necessary, sir."

"It will not," Mr. Yano said quietly. "We are law-abiding Canadian citizens. How long have you been a police officer?"

"Um … nearly eight years."

"And how long in Prince Rupert?" Mr. Yano continued.

"Just over a year."

Mr. Yano nodded. "And in that time have you ever had to arrest a Canadian of Japanese descent?"

"No, never," Constable Johnson answered.

"I didn't think so," Mr. Yano replied. "And it will not start now. We are good citizens, good Canadians, and we will follow the order to evacuate."

I could see the relief in the officer's face. "We were hoping for your cooperation. We are here to offer any assistance we can in helping with the evacuation. Thank you, and good day, sir," he said as he turned and walked up the path. Silently I watched him walk away.

"He knows it isn't right," I said softly.

"Everybody knows it isn't right," Mr. Yano agreed. "That makes it even worse. You be careful, Tadashi. People don't like it when you point out their errors. There is no gain in refusing to do what they ask."

"I wasn't trying to resist," I blurted, shocked that he thought I was going to offer resistance. "I just wanted to know."

"Don't ask questions. Just do as your father orders

you to, stay close to your family and we will survive all of this. Understand?"

"Yeah … I mean, yes, sir."

"Good boy. Now go to your house and finish preparation."

"Yes, sir," I answered, and hurried away.

I moved quickly up the path. There were far fewer people on it now than there had been earlier in the morning, when everybody in the village was out and moving things down to the boats. Now, most of what was being taken was stowed, and many people were already on board, waiting. I slowed down as my house came into view, and then stopped, looking at our home … my home.

It was funny how I'd never really given it much thought before. It was just a place I lived with my family. My father, assisted by our neighbors, had built the house when they'd originally settled in the village twenty years ago. And then when I was born another bedroom was added, and then another when Midori was born two years later.

It sported a brand-new coat of blue paint, sky blue. My mother loved the color of the sky. The path leading up to the front door was made up of flat stones, some of them three feet wide, that my father had hauled up from the water. Spaced at intervals on both sides of the path were shrubs, delicately shaped by my grandmother's pruning shears. On one side of the path was a large garden, neatly furrowed, waiting for the spring planting. We'd always had a garden, vegetables in the center, ringed by two rows of beautiful flowers, but over the last month we had worked the soil so the garden would be more than double its size when we planted again.

That was just one of my father's projects — and the projects he's made me do. Since he wasn't able to fish, and there was no school for me, there was time. First we started with the boat. It was repainted, refitted, any questionable planks replaced, the nets fixed and rechecked. Then he turned his attention to the house. He repaired and repainted — even things that didn't need to be painted. I think he would have put an addition on the house if lumber hadn't been so scarce. That was when he decided that the garden had to be enlarged. As he explained it to me, it might even be something we needed to survive. If we weren't allowed out of our village by summer, we'd have to survive on what we could grow, catch in the forest or harvest from the sea. That thought made putting in the garden a more meaningful task than most of the others he'd had me do. How much satisfaction is there in painting something that doesn't need to be painted? With the garden, each row of planting might be the difference between eating and going hungry.

Of course, it wasn't just my father who was insisting on us doing all this work. About the most Japanese thing I could think of was working. Wasting time was something that wasn't even considered. There was always some job that needed to be done — even when there really wasn't.

As I stared up at my house, the front door opened and my sisters emerged, followed by my mother and grandmother. Each had a few items in their arms. I walked up and offered to take something from them to relieve their loads.

My mother shook her head. "Your father is waiting … inside."

They filed past me on the path. Yuri flashed me a smile and winked — or at least tried to wink — as she passed. I entered the house and closed the door behind me. I unbuttoned the top few buttons of my jacket and removed it, but left my hat on. The only fire started this morning was for cooking, and the house had already cooled down so much that I could see the faint outline of my breath.

I was startled at the sight of my father sitting unmoving in the faint light, at the head of the low table in the dining room. I slowly walked over, trying not to make a sound, trying not to even breathe, as I moved to his side. He didn't seem to notice my approach and continued to stare into the distance. I cleared my throat to signal my presence.

"Sit," he said quietly, still not looking at me.

I sat on the floor in my space, to his right-hand side, folding my legs under the table. I knew he had something he wanted to say to me. I also knew that he wouldn't speak right away, and that we'd sit in silence for a while. The longer we sat without talking, the more serious what he had to say.

Finally he spoke. "It is a good house."

I nodded.

"It has kept us warm and dry and safe." He paused. "It has been a good place for our family."

He was right, of course. It was a good place ... although I'd never thought about it much before all of this.

I didn't know what to say back, but realized there wasn't any reason for me to talk anyway. I was here to listen.

"This house ... and everything in it ... everything I own ... is yours."

As the oldest male, I knew that — but that wasn't what he'd sat me down to tell me.

"I do not know how long we will be gone."

Of course, he didn't; nobody did.

"Or what will remain when we return."

"What do you mean?"

He didn't answer right away, and with each passing second I became more alarmed. Did he know something that he wasn't saying?

"I never thought any of this would happen," he said softly as he continued to stare into the distance. I realized that during this entire conversation he had never looked at me.

"Not the registration ... not when they did not let us leave our village or work in town ... not having my boat taken away ... not leaving our home. Nothing."

"But ... but ... how could you? Nobody could have known this was going to happen."

He nodded his head ever so slightly in agreement. "You are right, Tadashi ... nobody could have known. But that only makes the future even more uncertain. We cannot predict what will come next ... we just must deal with whatever fate is before us." His voice had faded to a whisper. "Whatever ... family is all that matters ... family."

.3.

All around us were the other boats from our village. Traveling together like this reminded me of the times when we'd be heading to the mouth of the Skeena for the salmon run. We'd find a place by the mouth of the river and set down our nets and then wait for them to fill with fish. Every hour or so we'd pull them up, remove the fish and wash down the nets. They'd get covered with dirt flowing down the river, and that dirt would make them visible to the fish, and they'd move around them. Some of the local fisherman — people who weren't Japanese — thought we were crazy, hauling the nets up like that to clean them. They just left their nets in the water. I had to admit that it was a lot of work, but our catches always did seem bigger.

We crashed through a wave and spray was thrown up into the air. Thank goodness Constable Johnson had been right and the sea wasn't too rough.

The first boats up ahead in our procession disappeared as they followed the RCMP launch around the point that led to the entrance of the Prince Rupert harbor. We were almost there, and that made the last of that lump in my stomach disappear. I had been afraid that somewhere along the route the waves were going to kick up and really give us a ride to remember.

We rounded the curve, and the water was pinched into a narrowing gap leading into the harbor. The seas almost instantly flattened out. Up ahead I could see the first of the military installations protecting Prince Rupert. Two towers, one on each side of the inlet, housed men with artillery and field glasses. They scanned the surface of the water for any submarines that might try to prey on the boats in the harbor.

Just beyond those first two towers I could make out the stations that controlled the submarine net. Strung across the entire width of the inlet was a thick net, supported by steel cables. It extended from just below the surface right to the bottom. It was like a heavy curtain designed to stop any submarines from entering the harbor. When ships — friendly ships — were sighted, the net was lowered just enough to allow the ship to pass, but not enough to allow a sub to sneak in with it. I wondered what they thought about the sight of sixty-five little wooden fishing boats sailing up into the harbor — fishing boats that belonged to Enemy Aliens. That was what they were calling us: Enemy Aliens.

I couldn't even think that term without my stomach starting to churn. Born and raised in Canada ... most of us were either Canadian-born or naturalized Canadians, but we were all the same to them; "Once a Jap, always a Jap" — that's what they were saying.

I guess the only difference they mattered to them was the color of our registration cards: pink if you were born in Canada or naturalized, and yellow if you were a Japanese citizen. They must have thought that was pretty smart, yellow for the "yellow peril" from the Far East. Either way, though, regardless of the card's color, it meant the same. Each man and woman over the age of sixteen had to carry around those cards, and on those cards it said ENEMY ALIEN in big letters, and if the police caught you out in public without that card, they could throw you in jail.

Some people had been thrown in jail. Nobody from

our village, but I'd heard about some businessmen and writers and people like that down in Vancouver who were locked up the day after Pearl Harbor. And I don't know, maybe they *were* people who would have been dangerous, who would have passed on information to the Japanese army. After all, there were around twenty-two thousand of us in this province, so I guess maybe a few of them would be cheering for Japan, and maybe even helping out a little ... maybe.

Rumor was that those people taken prisoner were shipped out to someplace the other side of the mountains and were being kept in some sort of prisoner-of-war camp. If they *were* spies, then the government did the right thing in rounding them up ... at least, that's what I'd thought when I first heard about a few men being taken away. Now that we were all being rounded up too, I had some different thoughts in my head.

"There sure are a lot of boats," Yuri said as she appeared at my shoulder and peered forward out the windscreen.

I nodded my head in agreement. Looking beyond the little convoy of fishing boats, I could easily see the outlines of at least a dozen big supply ships at anchor in the middle of the harbor, waiting their turn to dock and unload. And I knew that because of the shape and size of the harbor, there were probably just as many others at anchor and half as many again at the docks being loaded or unloaded — and it was going on twenty-four hours a day, seven days a week. Men, supplies and equipment. Either being unloaded to supply the growing military bases that ringed Prince Rupert or being loaded after being brought in by rail to be taken by ship to the Queen Charlotte Islands or further north to Alaska.

My eyes scanned the shore. The only things that took up more space in town than the docks were the rail yards. The entire western part of the town's shoreline was dominated by the railroad tracks. There was a big freight yard that must have had twenty or even thirty sets of tracks that came off the main line. There weren't enough men to unload the ships and railroad cars when they arrived, and they were backing up more and more. I shook my head in disbelief. There were some Japanese who'd worked the freight yards before the orders came to fire them. Did they think that stopping all the Japanese-Canadians from working would make things run better?

I walked over to my father's side. "Are we putting in at a dock?" I asked, although I realized as soon as I asked that there wouldn't possibly be space for all the boats to dock.

Without looking at me he shook his head. "At anchor with all the other boats ... those from up and down the coast." He pointed up ahead.

My eyes widened in surprise at the sight. There were fishing boats — hundreds and hundreds of them — at anchor, bobbing up and down on the waves. I had never seen so many fishing boats in one place, not even clustered around the mouth of the Skeena during the salmon run, and it was hard to believe there were that many boats along the whole coast.

My father turned the wheel and brought our boat around, looking for a spot to anchor. He found a patch of open water amidst the clutter of other boats, and I could hear the engine become quieter as he throttled back. He cut the engine even further, took it out of gear and motioned for me to go out. I knew without asking that he wanted me to put out the anchor.

Zipping my jacket and jamming my hat on my head, I went out into the cold air. I moved carefully around the side of the cabin to the bow. Quickly I grabbed the anchor, lowered it over the side. I released the gear on the winch and stepped out of the way as first the chain and then the heavy line paid out of the anchor hatch. Once the anchor reached bottom, I fed out some more line and then signaled to my father. He put the engine in reverse and the boat slowly back up until the anchor set and the line went taut. I went back into the warm cabin.

"I must go ashore," my father said. His words were so soft that I had to strain to hear them over the noise of the wind and the waves. "I am to be told what is planned for us."

"Can I come with you?"

He shook his head. "This is only for the head of each family. You have a job." He paused and I waited wordlessly. "While I am gone you are in charge ... in charge of the boat ... and those on the boat. Do you understand?"

"Yes ... yes, sir."

He turned his head slightly in my direction and gave a slight nod of acknowledgment. I followed him out of the cabin.

"Your mother is putting on rice. I'll be back before too long."

I had noticed that a rowboat had been put out from one of the fishing boats. It was moving between vessels like a water taxi, probably picking up men to bring to the town for the meeting. My father raised his hand in greeting as the boat came toward our vessel. It contained three men already, people I knew from our village. As it came alongside our boat, my father nodded to me, then climbed into the rowboat, and it started away. I watched as it stopped at another fishing boat, picking up one more passenger. With the weight of the five men in the small boat, only a few inches of gunwale showed above the water line. I was grateful it was calm in the protected waters. A big wave would have washed right over the edge. The little boat bobbed up and down gently, quickly becoming smaller and smaller as it moved toward the shore. I followed it with my eyes, watching as it disappeared and reappeared from behind other boats, until I saw it put in safely at the dock.

I wished more than almost anything that I could have gone along. The only thing worse than knowing our fate was being decided somewhere on that shore was not being able to be there to hear what was being said. Instead I sat out here, the deck rocking under my feet … waiting … waiting … waiting. My grandmother has often said that the Japanese are the most patient people. I guess I must be more Canadian than anybody knew.

My attention was caught by the sound of the cabin door opening. I turned to see my sister Midori.

"Tea is made," she said.

"You know I don't like green tea," I answered.

"I know," she said apologetically, "but Mother said I should tell you it's made."

"What I'd like is a coffee or even a soda."

"There's none of either on board," Midori said.

"No surprise there. If I wanted a good cup of coffee, the only place I could get one would be up at the base."

There was always a big urn of coffee on in the mess hall at the military base. And since I'd often worked right there in the kitchen, a steaming-hot cup of strong, black coffee was never more than a few feet away. I closed my eyes and I could almost smell it.

"Do you miss working at the base?" Midori asked.

Her question surprised me. Nobody talked much about what had happened to us, including me having to stop working at the base.

I shrugged. "The work wasn't that hard … so, sure, I guess I miss it."

"And Jed."

"Jed?" I asked.

"You miss him too, right?"

"I just saw him," I said, being careful not to say just how recently we'd been together. It had been only ten hours earlier. In the middle of the night.

Jed and I had met at a spot between our two villages. From there, under cover of darkness, we'd snuck by the guards and gone to the base. We were there because of the base's mascot, Eddie the eagle. He was a full-grown bald eagle who had been found injured in the forest and been brought back to the base months earlier. He lived chained to the flagpole in the center of the parade ground. He was cared for — a vet looked at his injuries, and he was fed and everything, mostly by Jed and his mother, and sometimes by me — but he was still a prisoner. So Jed and I had snuck onto the base to where Eddie sat on his little house. We cut him loose and then watched as he flew away. We hoped his injuries had healed enough to let him survive in the wild. Either way, though, free to live or die in the wild was better than alive and chained to a flagpole.

"But you're going to miss him," she continued.

"Of course, I'll miss him," I said abruptly. Why was she trying to make this harder?

"Do you think Jed will miss you?" she asked.

"What do you think?" I snapped.

"I guess Jed will miss lots of things."

"What has he got to miss?" I demanded. "It's not like he had to give up his home or school, or leave his village, or ..." I looked at Midori and suddenly remembered her feelings about Jed. "And I'm sure he'll miss other people as well."

Her expression brightened noticeably. Of course, Midori had known Jed all her life, and she'd always liked him. But over the last year or so it had been increasingly obvious that more than just liking him, she had a crush on Jed. She was always laughing at his jokes — and they weren't even very funny — or asking about him, or hanging around us. It had gotten embarrassing for both me and Jed. He liked her — the way he liked my whole family — but there was no way he was going to be serious about some kid who was three years younger.

"Are you going to write letters to him?" Midori asked.

"Yeah … why?" I asked hesitantly. I hoped she wasn't going to ask to write to him too. I wondered what Jed would think about that … but, even worse, I knew what our father would think.

Father had also noticed the way Midori had been acting toward Jed and put his foot down. He was like all the Japanese. He didn't believe that people should marry outside of their kind. Japanese should marry Japanese, whites should marry other whites, and Indians other Indians.

"When you write to him —"

"I'll say 'hi' from you," I interrupted, hoping that would be enough to make her happy.

"I guess that would be okay," she said quietly.

"Did you say there was rice?" I asked, trying to change the subject to something safer.

She nodded.

"Good, I'm hungry. Let's go inside and eat."

•••

I looked up at the sound of the cabin door opening and was surprised to see my father. I'd been so lost in my studies that I hadn't seen or heard him come back on board. Despite the fact that I hadn't been in school for almost two months, the school work hadn't stopped. Most of the parents in my village had insisted that school work and studying had to continue even if there wasn't school.

My father squatted down at the small table we had used for our meal earlier. Without having to be asked, my mother immediately set before him a steaming bowl of rice.

I closed my books and glanced at my watch. He'd been gone for less than two hours. Did that mean the meeting hadn't taken place, or that it was short and pleasant, or that they didn't really have any answers to give as to where we were going? But of course I couldn't just ask. It wouldn't be respectful to question my father. I'd have to wait. "Be patient," I heard in my mind, my grandmother's words and voice inside my head.

I studied my father, looking for some sort of telltale sign. He sat expressionless, sipping his tea. I wasn't surprised. I would have been shocked if his expression ever revealed anything. It never did betray his feelings or emotions. He always looked the same — calm, serious and determined. It wasn't that he couldn't laugh, or scowl or get angry. It just wasn't his way to show his feelings on the outside. Yet, while he could keep his feelings off his face, you could occasionally look into his eyes and see his emotions leaking out.

I looked hard. His eyes were closed! What did that mean?

I turned my gaze to my mother. She too was staring at my father. And off to her side stood my grandmother, also watching him, as was Midori. Only Yuri wasn't studying our father. She was lying on her bedding, snuggled down under the covers. I knew that one or both arms were tightly hugging those dolls. I couldn't help but smile at our shared secret.

"Vancouver," my father said quietly.

"What?" I asked, almost not sure if I'd even heard him speak.

He opened his eyes but didn't look at me, instead staring straight ahead. "We are going to Vancouver."

"When? When are we going?" I questioned.

"Tomorrow."

"But we won't have time … will we be able to even take all of our stuff?" I was thinking about the limited space on a train. "And what about our boat?"

My father raised a hand to silence me. "It will not be taken out of the water. We are traveling to Vancouver on board our boat."

"But that's over eight hundred miles!" I exclaimed. "And there are some stretches where we'd have to leave the coast and travel across open waters. And what about the weather and the ocean? It could get rough, really rough. I don't think it's very —"

I stopped in mid-sentence as my father spun his head toward me and caught me in his gaze. This time I had no trouble reading his emotions and his wishes; he wanted me to close my mouth. I looked down at the floor.

"All the fishing boats will travel together," my father began. "We will be escorted by a naval ship … it will be towing the boats."

"Towing. I guess that'll be good," I acknowledged.

He nodded again. His expression remained calm and reassuring.

"A few men are going to send their families … wives and small children … down by train," he said. "They will meet in Vancouver."

"I don't want to go by train!" Midori exclaimed. "I want to stay with everybody else!"

"Midori," my mother hissed under her breath.

We all knew it wasn't her decision to make or even comment on.

"You will not be going by train," my father said. "We are going down together. A family needs to be together."

Midori smiled, pleased with the decision. If she only knew what this trip could possibly be like, she wouldn't be so happy.

•••

In the distance I could see the faint outlines of the tall buildings that made up the skyline of Vancouver. I'd read that some of those buildings were over twenty stories tall. Looming behind the buildings were the mountains, which stood so many more times taller and wider and dwarfed the skyscrapers.

I'd always wanted to see Vancouver. I guess it's like my grandmother always says: "Beware of what you ask for, because you may get it." This certainly wasn't the way I'd wanted or expected to see Vancouver, but then again, I couldn't complain. There'd been times on this trip when I didn't think we'd ever make it this far. It was almost over, but it had been without a doubt the longest and hardest two weeks of my life.

I knew how those buildings felt standing against the mountains, the feeling of being dwarfed. Our little boat had been nothing more than a speck on the ocean. Moving along with the other specks, sometimes towed by the navy frigates and sometimes chugging along under our own steam as we moved down the coast toward Vancouver.

We'd travel during the day, sometimes for fourteen hours and sometimes for only a few hours, depending on the distance between safe harbors. Each night we'd all put in at a protected spot along the coast, someplace where we could anchor out of the worst of the waves. There was small comfort in being a speck amongst many, tucked in with all the other boats. But I knew that no matter how many of us were there, we were all equally powerless. The same way we were powerless against the government.

Twice on the journey down we didn't leave our safe harbor in the morning. The wind and the waves were too strong and we stayed at anchor, bounced and buffeted by the storm, but safe … at least, safer than we would have been if we'd have put out to open ocean. Once we had to stay put for three nights, waiting for the weather to clear enough for us to make a break for the next safe haven.

I didn't know what was worse: staying at anchor, which meant having to stay on the boat one extra night; taking to the ocean and risking the elements; or finally getting to Vancouver to find out what they had planned for us next. All the options were bad.

I took a last breath of cool air and headed into the cabin. The door stuck a little — all the steam from the cooking had warped it slightly — and I gave it a big push to open it. I was immediately struck by both the heat and the smell. The heat I welcomed. The smell I didn't. The smell was a combination of odors that swirled together into a pungent soup. It was the cooking — the last two weeks' worth of meals; the wisps of smoke that escaped from the little stove — we'd been forced to burn wood that was green or wet; the smell coming from us and our clothes — we hadn't been able to wash since we first took to the boats; and the sickening smell of the chamber pot.

"Food?" my mother asked as she extended a bowl toward me.

I wasn't hungry, but eating was one of the few ways to pass the time.

"Thank you," I said as I took the bowl from her. I slumped down on a mattress beside Yuri, who was asleep. I started to scoop in the rice. It tasted good.

My mother gave me a big smile. Watching us eat was about the only thing that seemed to bring a smile to her face. Ever since we'd started down the coast there'd been something simmering or cooking on the fire. It was almost as if, because she couldn't make us our *regular* meals, she had to make up for it by making us *more* meals. There was a constant supply of food.

"It looks big," Midori said as she stood staring out the front window at the approaching city.

I nodded my head. "I was just thinking about getting off the boat."

"Me too," she said, nodding her head. "I'm so tired of being trapped in this little cabin." She paused. "Maybe I shouldn't be so eager," she said quietly.

I knew what she meant. This was awful, but at least we knew it.

"Don't worry, everything is going to be okay," I offered reassuringly, hoping she'd believe me, even though I didn't even believe myself.

She cast her eyes down and I instantly knew that she didn't really believe me either.

"Tadashi," my father called.

Both my sister and I looked over at my father. I handed her my now empty bowl, rose to my feet and went to my father's side. Looking past him and through the windshield, I was shocked to see our position. We were closed in on all sides by the land — by the city. Wharves, warehouses and roads lined the waterfront, and behind them were tall buildings.

All around us were dozens of other fishing boats — the boats that were filled with our neighbors who had traveled with us down the coast. And as the waterway continued to narrow, the spaces between the boats became smaller.

I looked over at the closest boat and saw Toshio, another boy from my village, staring back at me through the window of his family's vessel. He nodded his head and I nodded back.

That was more than I would have expected from him. He and I didn't get along. Not ever, really, but things got much worse after the fist fight he had with Jed. Of course, it hadn't helped much that partway through that fight — when Toshio was winning — Midori had come up behind him and hit him in the back of the legs with a tree branch.

My father turned the wheel and we moved to the side. He throttled back the engine and the chugging of the motor died down to a dull rumble. Up ahead was a gigantic wharf that seemed to go on forever. All along the wharf were the fishing boats of our village, already tied up or in the process of docking. I took a deep breath. For better or worse, this part of the trip was finally over.

.4.

The sun came up and the first bright rays came through the windows and found me lying on my mattress on the floor. I could have rolled over and pulled the covers up over my head, but there wasn't any point. Whatever was going to happen was going to happen. And besides, it wasn't like the light had woken me up anyway. My sleep had been so broken and interrupted and disturbed that I doubted I'd put together any more than fifteen consecutive minutes of sleep through the whole night. And while I was worried about what was going to happen next in our lives, it wasn't just worry that had kept me awake. It was the sounds of the night.

I had become more than used to the noises of the boat — sounds of rubbing ropes, water and waves, and creaking boards. What I wasn't accustomed to were the sounds of the city that surrounded us. There seemed to be a constant rumble that filled the air: car engines softly purring, the deep growl of trucks, the occasional backfire of a motor, military airplanes with their landing lights glowing in the darkened sky as they roared overhead, and the long, low, call of ships' horns, announcing their locations as they passed each other in the dark and foggy narrows.

I'd drift off for a few minutes then be awoken by one of the sounds. Sometimes I'd just lay there listening. Other times I'd be so startled that I'd sit bolt upright.

And twice I got right up and, carefully stepping around the sleeping members of my family, went over and stood by the windows, looking out, trying to attach a sight to the sound.

The planes were easily visible — actually, impossible to miss — as they glided across the night sky, their lights blazing out a path for them to follow as they passed overhead and then touched down, somewhere just out of sight, but not far away. The sources of all the other sounds were lost from view, hidden by the buildings, darkness and fog.

I'd heard that fear heightens your senses. I didn't know for sure, but it did seem like every little noise registered deep inside my skull.

My father provided his own background noise — a high-pitched whistling sound as he breathed in and out in his sleep. He always seemed to sleep solidly through the night. The first few nights on board, the sound had disturbed me, annoyed me. Now it wasn't just that it didn't bother me anymore, but that I found it reassuring. The whistling made me feel better, safer, knowing he was close. It was good to know he was right there when I woke in the middle of the night, in the pitch black, and for a few brief seconds couldn't remember where I was. Or, worse still, woke up and knew exactly where I was.

Both my mother and grandmother were light sleepers and I was sure that they would have been woken up last night too. But neither got up or moved around or even made any sounds. They wouldn't have wanted to risk waking anybody up.

Once, just as I was getting ready to climb back under the covers after gazing out the window, I was startled to see Yuri sitting up in bed, staring at me. Just enough light trickled into the boat from the lampposts on the wharf for me to see her. Silently she waved to me and then held aloft two of her dolls. I saw a smile crease her face, white teeth glowing in the dim light, and couldn't help but smile myself. I gestured for her to stuff the dolls back under the covers and she instantly responded.

That certainly wasn't the first time she'd flashed the dolls or said something to me when she thought nobody else was around. She tried to be subtle, but she was only seven years old, and wasn't so good at keeping secrets. I knew my grandmother was aware of the dolls and suspected my parents knew as well. But I also knew that if things weren't too obvious — if she didn't pull them out right in front of my father's eyes, so that everybody would know he'd been disobeyed — he might just pretend he didn't know they were there. That way we were all okay.

My father yawned loudly, sat up and stretched his arms. That was the signal to everybody that the day had begun. Instantly my mother got to her feet and began to prepare morning tea. Midori was soon at her side to help, and even my grandmother got up on unsteady feet and went to offer assistance.

Activity had also started on the wharf. A half a dozen men, a couple of whom I knew, were gathered together, talking and smoking cigarettes. My father had noticed them as well. He pulled on his jacket and went over to the door, removed his slippers and put on his boots.

"Tadashi," he said, motioning to me with his hand. "Come."

I didn't need any further encouragement. I grabbed my jacket and pulled it on as I rushed over to the door. I kicked off my slippers and pushed my feet into my boots. I didn't even bother to tie them up, just stuffed the long laces back into the boots. Opening the door, I was hit with a blast of cold air. The bright sunlight, which had already burnt off the fog from the night, had fooled me into thinking it was much warmer than it was. I buttoned up my jacket quickly as I crossed the deck of the boat and bounded up onto the wharf.

My father had already joined the group of men and I quietly glided up behind them. There was an argument going on between two of the men, and I was even more determined to be silent.

"So we're here! What now?" one of the men demanded. He wasn't from our village and I didn't know his name. He was younger than the other men, maybe closer in age to me then he was to my father.

"You have to be patient," one of the others, an older man named Tanaka, said quietly.

"I'm tired of being patient!" he snapped angrily. "Patience is for old women! I want to know what they have planned for us next!"

"Mind your words," Mr. Tanaka said angrily. "You're so young you still have eggshell stuck to your bottom!"

The man's face flashed with anger as the others laughed at the joke made at his expense. He looked like he was going to say something, but thought better of it. Young people had no right to speak disrespectfully to their elders. Still, I wanted to know the same thing — what now?

"We all want to know the next step," my father interjected, breaking the uncomfortable silence. "But getting angry, especially at each other, will not help." Although the words were said quietly, they were said in that tone of voice that I knew meant business.

The younger man opened his mouth like he was going to blurt something out, but again thought better of it. "Yes," he said softly, looking down at the ground.

"We're all upset," Mr. Tanaka added. "We all want to know the answer to the question you've asked. But we must wait."

The group became silent. I imagined that each man was thinking about the possible answers — what was going to be happening to us and how long we'd have to wait to find out. They started talking in Japanese, discussing the weather and what sort of day it was going to be. I listened in for a while. The younger man, the one who had been so angry, spoke Japanese, but not very well. He continually threw in English words, or the wrong endings to words. Lots of Japanese his age didn't speak Japanese that well. My Japanese was better than his.

My parents, like most Japanese parents, insisted that we all spoke Japanese in the home. But I guess because I was in a village where everyone was Japanese, we also spoke it when we were outside, talking to the neighbors or playing with the other kids.

Not that my Japanese was perfect. Sometimes I found myself having to work harder to understand things when the older Japanese spoke. It wasn't just the dialect, or the words, but the way they put those words together.

Two of the men dropped their cigarette butts to the ground and stubbed them out with their boots. They immediately lit up two more cigarettes. A cigarette was offered to my father, which he declined. He didn't smoke. I decided I'd wait a few minutes, to be polite, and then head back to the boat. There was nobody here who knew anything, and I'd only come out so eagerly hoping somebody had some information.

The Japanese are big on things like waiting, being patient and accepting fate. I'm no good at any of those things. Maybe my blood is Japanese, but I guess having only breathed Canadian air in my lungs my whole life has made me as impatient as any other Canadian. I hate waiting. I think I'd rather get bad news and at least know than wait around hoping things will turn out. At least once you know, you can stop worrying and get on with doing. After all, how much worse could it get?

I'd started to slowly sidle away when my attention was caught by the sound and sight of a large, gray truck, an army truck. It had appeared from behind a warehouse, its engine rumbling, black smoke bellowing out of twin smokestacks over the cab. The engine protested noisily as it ground through the gears to slow down before passing through the gate that marked the entry point through the high wire fence that ringed the wharf.

I recognized the type of truck — it was nicknamed a butter box because it was used to transport supplies. It then clicked on me that its arrival, undoubtedly with a large quantity of supplies, meant only one of two possibilities: either we were being restocked to continue our journey elsewhere by boat, or we would be given more food because we weren't going anywhere. We were staying here at wharfside and going nowhere ... maybe for a long time.

My heart started to sink when my eyes caught sight of a second truck. How many supplies would we need? Then a third truck appeared, and a fourth, and a fifth ... and a sixth. The column just kept on coming, truck after truck. The second and third vehicles had already come through the gate and joined the first coming along the actual wharf.

All along the dock at each boat, people had come out of their cabins, alerted by the noise and attracted by the unspoken promise that something was going to happen. But what? My father, along with the other men, moved to the side, allowing the truck a clear passage. There was a rhythmic thumping as the wheels of the trucks passed over the rough, loosely fastened planks of the dock. The truck rumbled past us, leaving behind the lingering smell of smoke and diesel fuel. It continued down toward the very end of the wharf, flashing brake lights and squealing brakes bringing it to a stop beside the very first boat.

The second and third trucks passed by where we stood before coming to a stop farther down the wharf, spaced out behind the first vehicle. A truck came to rest directly in front of us. I looked way up into the cab and saw two soldiers, one at the wheel and a second sitting beside him. Letting my eyes run down the line of trucks I started to count. Twelve. All along the length of the wharf, the people who had been standing on their boats watching had now come onto the dock. They formed a thin line, knotted in places by groups, clumps where a mother and father stood surrounded by a clutch of children, or four or five men pressed together to discuss what they were seeing.

I was struck by the sight of hundreds of people ... children, fathers, mothers, old people ... all different but all the same ... all Japanese faces peering out from beneath hats or caps ... watching. Nobody was making a sound. It was like every single person was holding his breath. Waiting.

And then came the sounds. Heavy boots against the wooden dock, the slamming of doors, men's raised voices, the loud crash of metal as the heavy tailgates were untied and let drop.

From the back of the truck directly in front of me leapt three men in sailor uniforms. Then two more sailors jumped out.

"Attention!" screamed out a loud mechanical voice.

My head snapped around to see a man, a soldier in an army uniform, an officer, standing there holding a bullhorn.

"Attention! The head of each family and the captain of every boat is ordered to assemble to receive further instructions concerning evacuation!"

Evacuation! Were we leaving our boats now? That might explain those sailors. Were they here to pilot our boats when we left?

My father silently started to file away toward the man with the bullhorn. Other men joined in until he was lost to my view in the midst of a crowd. I was certain I could walk over and hear what our fate was going to be, but I was just as certain that I already knew the answer. Those sailors were here to take charge of our boats, and all those trucks, far too many to deliver anything, were here to move us and all of our possessions. The only question in my mind was, where?

.5.

I hurried back to our boat. Where we were heading wasn't as important as the fact that I'd have to help move all our belongings, and I wanted to eat breakfast before I did anything.

My grandmother was standing on the edge of the wharf beside our boat. I think that was the first time she'd left the boat since this trip had begun. Her expression was questioning. She was straining to try to understand what was happening. I doubted she had been able to pick up the meaning of the garbled burst of words yelled through the bullhorn.

"We're going to be leaving, I think," I explained as I rushed by her and jumped aboard the boat.

"Tadashi!" she called out, and I stopped and turned around. I could tell that she was struggling to find the right words. "Where ... go where?"

I shook my head. "I don't know. Father will find out. I just figure we'll be loading our stuff onto those big trucks." I gestured to the closest vehicle. "I need to eat," I said.

Grabbing the door, I hesitated and looked back. My father was now standing with the same group of men, away from the officer who was giving the instructions. Whatever was said certainly hadn't taken long — but how long would it take to say "load up the trucks?"

My grandmother had taken a few steps toward where

my father stood. She then stopped, rocked back and forth on her feet, and retreated. She shifted back and forth, took two steps toward him once again, stopped and retreated for a second time to her original position. She wanted to just rush up and ask my father where we were going, what was happening, but she couldn't. It wasn't her place; it wouldn't have been proper or polite for her to question my father, especially in front of a group of men. She'd just have to wait.

I smiled to myself. I had the urge to yell out to her, "Be patient! Wait. Just accept what happens." But, of course, it would have been just as wrong for me to yell as it would have been for her to chase my father with questions.

I opened the door and was enveloped by the warmth and odors wafting out. Somehow, when I was hungry the only aroma that reached me was the cooking, which overtook all the other less appealing smells.

"Well?" Midori asked excitedly before I'd even taken two steps inside. She wasn't restricted by the same ideas of politeness as my grandmother — at least, when talking to me.

I removed my hat and started to slowly unbutton my jacket. "Well what?" I asked.

"Well what! How can you —" Midori stopped herself as she realized I was just putting her on. I always enjoyed teasing her or, even better, watching Jed making fun of her.

"I don't know for sure," I finally answered. "But I did hear the word evacuation —"

"I heard that too," Midori said, interrupting me.

"And I don't think they brought those trucks just to carry the sailors. I'm guessing that we'll be loading up soon, putting our stuff in the trucks."

She nodded her head in agreement, as did Yuri and my mother, who were standing behind her, listening in.

"Before we have to load up I better —"

My mother interrupted my words with her actions. She reached out and handed me a steaming bowl of porridge.

"Thank you!"

Her eyes smiled back at me. "You are welcome."

I shoveled in the first spoonful. Thick and rich and sweetened with brown sugar. Tasty. Before I could put another spoonful in, my father, followed by my grandmother, came in. I expected that I'd have plenty of time to finish the bowl before my father spoke, so was shocked when he began to speak immediately.

"We must leave our boat today," he began, confirming what I had already guessed at. "Our belongings will be put on the trucks, which will take us to a place called Hastings Park."

"We're going to be living in a park?" I exclaimed in disbelief. "How can we live in a park?" I had a terrible vision of us in tents.

"The officer said there are buildings."

"You mean there are houses in the park?" Midori asked.

He shook his head. "Not houses … buildings … shared by families … it is only temporary. And we must be ready to leave in one hour."

"One hour!" I exclaimed. "It took us at least four times that long to load in the first place! That's not possible to do!"

There was a pause as my father waited for my outburst to fade from the air.

"In an hour more boats will be coming to take our place along the wharf. Our boats must be moved elsewhere."

"You mean you're not coming with us?" Midori asked my father, thinking he'd be sailing the boat away. She looked worried and her voice quivered.

"I will be coming with my family," he answered, and she smiled.

"Then who …"

"The sailors," I said.

He nodded. "They are taking them farther … up the Fraser and away from the ocean. They will be at anchor in fresh water."

That was at least good news. Away from the ocean waves and in fresh water, which would be less corrosive than the sea water if they had to stay at anchor for a while.

I put down my bowl, which was still steaming and full. "I'll start moving things."

My father shook his head. "Finish. First we have to decide what we are to take."

My mother shot him a look that asked without words what we were all questioning. What did he mean "decide what we are to take?"

"Some things will stay with our boat." He paused. "We are only permitted one hundred and twenty pounds for each person older than twelve. Four hundred and eighty pounds. And seventy-five pounds for each child younger. Another one hundred and fifty pounds."

"We must have put twice as much as that on board!" Midori said.

Having personally carried most of it, I knew the amount was much more than that.

"I will decide … along with your mother and grandmother … which items will come with us and which will be stored aboard the boat," he said solemnly.

My mother and grandmother came to his side and they began discussing things. They spoke in Japanese. My mother and grandmother spoke very quietly, but it was clear that they were doing most of the talking and my father was mainly nodding his head in agreement.

Yuri came over to my side and pulled at the sleeve of

my sweater, and then motioned for me to bend over.

"We can't bring everything?" she asked softly.

"No, not everything, but I'm sure we'll be able to take all the important —" I suddenly stopped as I saw her eyes tear up, and I realized what she was thinking: her dolls. I wanted to just blurt out that it would be okay, that I was sure all three dolls could come along, but I couldn't offer her any reassurance. I couldn't see any dolls being considered important by my parents when we were so limited in space, and I didn't know if I could smuggle them aboard the truck.

I reached out and put an arm around her shoulders, and I saw her bite down on her lower lip in an effort to fight back the tears. It would have been hard enough to leave the dolls at home, lying on her bed, but to leave them here on the boat where they didn't belong seemed so much worse.

I put my mouth close to her. "Your dollies are coming along," I whispered in her ear, and while I didn't know how, I knew that I was going to try. She threw her arms around me and squeezed.

"Tadashi," my father called out.

I turned around and stood up to face him.

"Sewing machine, clothing and bedding goes in the truck," he said.

Bedding! Of course! We'd take the bedding and I could just take the dolls wrapped up in Yuri's blankets like I did to get them onto the boat in the first place.

"What about other things?" Midori asked.

"Other things too," he answered. "Help your mother repack dishes and some pots to come with us."

"We could take seventy-five more pounds if we told them I was twelve," Midori said.

"You are not twelve," my father said.

"I'm almost twelve, and how would they know I'm not?" she asked.

"They wouldn't know," he said, "but *we* would know."

I understood perfectly what she was saying, but also knew what my father meant. He wasn't prepared to lie.

"We can bring what we need now," he continued, "as well as some other things. Pictures … lamps … a vase … school books."

I rolled up Yuri's bedding and gathered it in my arms. "I'll start with this," I said as I began to walk out of the cabin.

My father reached out and grabbed my arm. He shook his head. "Mattresses first. Something to sit on as well as piling on other things."

"Sure … okay," I stammered. I went to put the bedding back and two dolls clattered out noisily to the wooden floor.

Before I could react or even think what to do, my father bent down and scooped up the dolls. He held them up, turning them over slowly, examining them as if he'd never seen them before.

I looked over at Yuri. She looked scared. Midori stood silently, staring down at the ground as if she hadn't seen anything. Both my mother and grandmother looked away, pretending that they'd seen nothing.

"What are these doing in there?" my father questioned.

I opened my mouth to answer but I didn't know what to say. If only one had fallen out, it wouldn't have mattered. I shouldn't have defied my father, but I couldn't have just stood there and not helped my sister either.

"And is the third doll here too, or back at our home?"

"Here." I dropped to my knees to unfurl the blankets and retrieve the third doll. She was more safely trapped within the folds and resisted coming out for a few seconds. I wished the others had been so deeply buried. I handed it to my father. He took it, but instead of looking at the doll his gaze was fixed firmly on me.

"It was my fault," I said softly. "I just couldn't —"

My father held his hand up to silence me and I stopped abruptly.

"These dolls should not be in the bedding," he said.

"I know … but …" I looked at the ground.

"They could be lost," my father said.

"Lost?"

"We would not want anything to happen to three such important dolls." He reached out and handed them gently to Yuri. "I want you to keep them in your arms … in plain sight where they will not be misplaced or left behind … by accident."

I looked up at my father in shock. The expression I was expecting — anger or disapproval — was missing. Instead he looked almost proud. But that made no sense. I had defied him and he should have been angry … unless … maybe what I had done was the right thing and he knew it. My father subtly bowed his head and I bowed back.

"Tadashi," my father called out. "Mattresses first … unless you have other ideas."

"I don't know … maybe we could …" I stopped myself as I realized he was gently poking fun at me. "No … I mean, no, *sir*, I'll get them right on the truck."

The edges of his mouth curved ever so slightly into a smile.

•••

What had started as a gigantic empty truck bed had quickly become full. We were piling our belongings in one of the back corners, while the possessions of three other families were occupying the rest of the space. The other families, the Matsuis, Asadas and Moris, were all from our village and I'd known them forever. I went to school with the Matsui and Asada kids.

The Moris, though, were a lot older and had never had kids. It was getting harder and harder for Mr. Mori to run his fishing boat, so they'd sent word back to Japan that they wanted a member of their extended family to come and live with them and eventually take over the boat. And that was how Toshio came to live in our village. His father was Mr. Mori's great-nephew. Toshio's father seemed okay. He didn't speak much English, but he was friendly. Actually, the whole family was fine — except for Toshio. He was just different. He didn't talk much and when he did it was almost always in Japanese. And he always seemed to be scowling. My mother said that it must have been hard for him to leave Japan at fifteen, and how would I feel if I had to move so far away and leave all my friends behind. Back then I didn't understand how it would feel. Now I knew too well. Still, before he came I got along pretty good with everybody.

It was strange, but living in a village so small, where everybody knew each other, meant that while people may not have been family, they were a lot more than just neighbors. You knew everything there was to know about them, and they knew everything about you. There weren't many secrets in a village the size of ours. And, of course, all special occasions, from births to weddings to deaths, were shared with everybody.

I gently put down the sewing machine in our corner of the truck. It was now one of four machines in the back of the truck, one for each family whose possessions had to be put in this one vehicle. Of course, it had been no surprise that each family had selected this as one of the possessions that had first come on their boat and now was designated important enough for the truck. Every Japanese woman had a sewing machine. The sounds of sewing — the whirring of the wheel and the rhythmic pumping of the foot pedal, punctuated by the tapping of the needle through the material — marked a Japanese home as much as the smell of Japanese cooking.

It wasn't just my mother who knew her way around a

sewing machine. All the other woman in the village were experts as well. Little girls learned from their mothers, who'd learned from their mothers. Midori was already pretty skilled, and even Yuri had started to sew clothing … mainly for her dollies …

I had to smile. It was so much nicer to see Yuri holding them instead of having them secreted away. It also felt like a load had been lifted from my shoulders. I knew she should have her dolls with her, but I'd felt guilty the whole way for defying my father. I didn't like going against him like that. After all, he was my father and deserved my respect.

I leaped down from the truck. It was a long way to the ground. My grandmother and all the other old folks would have trouble getting up into the back of the truck. Maybe there was some way to put some boxes or something on the ground to make it easier.

"Come on, and quit lolligagging!" yelled out an angry voice.

I turned around. There was a soldier, who couldn't have been that much older than me, standing in front of a group of old women from our village. There were four or five of them, and I'd noticed them standing off to the side, talking, watching. A couple of them were old, even older than my grandmother, and not able to help any more than by offering words of encouragement to others as we'd been loading.

"Come on, get moving, there's no time to waste here!" the young soldier bellowed. "You're blocking the wharf!"

The old women looked perplexed. Not only didn't they understand what he was saying, or what he meant, but they were confused by his tone of voice.

"Don't you speak any English?" He held up his hand and pointed to his watch. "Ticky, ticky … time's wasting … move!" he said, making a shooing gesture.

A couple muttered something in Japanese, too quietly

for me to hear, but didn't move. They had no idea what he was trying to say to them, and it would have been rude to just walk away. The soldier walked even closer to them, until he was standing over top of them.

"Move!" he bellowed.

I couldn't just stand and watch. I had to explain. "They don't understand —"

"Leave alone!"

I heard the voice at the same instant I saw the person speaking. It was Toshio. His arms were full, but despite the load he quickly closed the distance to the soldier. He put the boxes down and inserted himself in the little gap between the soldier and the old women. Toshio was two years older than me, but he was a little guy and the soldier was a full head taller than him.

"Leave alone!" Toshio repeated, practically screaming into the soldier's face.

"You speak English," the soldier said, although I couldn't tell whether that was a question or a comment.

Toshio didn't answer. His English wasn't good — his family had only been here about a year — but I knew he understood enough to answer … if he wanted to.

"Do you speak any English, *Jap*?" the soldier said.

Again Toshio didn't answer, but I knew he hated that word as much as any of us — maybe more. His eyes darkened and his glare became angrier.

"Answer me!" the soldier demanded, and moved ever so slightly forward, reducing the space between them to a matter of inches. The soldier was now more over top of him than just standing in front of him.

I could see Toshio's fingers straighten into weapons. Toshio knew judo, and despite the size difference I knew he could toss that guy halfway across the deck. That would serve the soldier right, but it wouldn't end there and Toshio would find himself in trouble, maybe even in jail.

I had to do something. "He speaks English," I blurted

out, and the soldier took a slight step back as he turned to face me.

"His family hasn't been over here that long, so his English isn't that good," I explained. "And some of the older folks mainly speak Japanese."

"You speak English — good English," the soldier said. There was more than a hint of surprise in his voice.

I shrugged. "Why wouldn't I? I was born here."

"You were?"

"Almost everybody my age was born in Canada. Even some of the adults my parents' age were born here."

Now he looked as perplexed as the old women had when he was bellowing out orders. "I thought you were all, like, from Japan."

"Hardly anybody."

He nodded his head and then looked at his watch. "There isn't much time. I got orders to hurry everybody up." He motioned to the old ladies. "Could you get them to move?"

"Um ..." I couldn't very well give them orders ... but I had an idea.

"The soldier says that he thinks you all look tired and asks that you please sit down," I said in Japanese, bowing at the end.

As a group they smiled, nodded their heads and started to shuffle away. One of them, Mrs. Sakamoto, reached out, patted the soldier on the arm gently and bowed slightly before starting off after the others.

"What did you say to them?" he asked.

"To get moving," I lied. "Isn't that what you wanted?"

"Yeah. Thanks, appreciate your help," the soldier said.

"Sure," I answered.

He turned and started off down the wharf, leaving me and Toshio alone. I wasn't surprised to see that Toshio was still glaring — it always took me a few minutes to settle down when I was angry, too. But then I realized he was now aiming his angry eyes at me. Why was he mad at me? Didn't he understand that I'd stopped him from getting into a fight? Maybe getting tossed in jail or in serious trouble? He should be grateful to me.

"Whites your friends," Toshio said through clenched teeth.

"What?" I demanded.

"You think all whites friends."

"He's no friend of mine," I said. "I was just trying to help."

"Help the soldier … help the whites."

"Don't be so dense, Toshio! I was trying to help those old women and *you*."

"Toshio not need you help!" he snarled, and took two steps toward me. "Toshio take care of self. Not afraid of soldier."

"I didn't say you were afraid." What an idiot! Did he want to get into a fist fight that badly that it didn't matter who it was with?

"Don't be stupid," I said, backing away.

He kept coming toward me. Whether or not I wanted to fight didn't matter. He was going to take a run at me, so I put up my fists to defend myself.

"Toshio!" screamed out a high-pitched voice. It was Mrs. Mori. She yelled and gestured for him to come to her side. He hesitated, took a halting step toward her, stopped and then turned back toward me.

"In the end … you not be riding in front of truck with soldier … but in back with Japanese. You only white on the inside … outside is yellow like everybody else. You not hakujin."

Toshio turned and away.

What did he mean? Of course I wasn't white. I shook my head. There was no point in wasting any time on anything that idiot had to say.

.6.

Twenty-two of us, including Toshio, sat in the back of the truck, surrounded by our belongings. It was an eerie feeling when the soldiers slammed the tailgate with a metallic thud and then tied the canvas into place. The only light that entered the truck was either filtered through the canvas or entered through the small gaps.

Despite the faint light I could still see the glare in Toshio's eyes. He sat directly opposite me, staring, his gaze burning holes right through me. It was bad enough that I had to be sealed in the back of this truck like luggage, but why did I have to be locked in here with him?

We were bounced around and our possessions occasionally shifted as the truck rumbled and roared and bumped and bashed along the road. The noise of the engine was a constant, as were the fumes from the exhaust. It was a sickening smell, far worse than almost anything aboard the boat.

Periodically somebody would lean close to somebody else, put a mouth to their ear and say something. I couldn't hear anything more than an occasional snatch of words — always spoken in Japanese. Words seemed to be spoken in hushed tones to match the dim lighting. Were they afraid to be overheard? Did they think that anybody was listening ... or cared to listen?

I had a sick feeling in the pit of my stomach. I didn't

know whether the feeling was caused by the motion of the vehicle, the presence of Toshio glaring at me or the uncertainty of what lay ahead when the truck finally stopped and the tailgate was lowered.

I felt the truck slow down dramatically, and the engine's tone changed to a deeper rumble as it geared down. I had hoped that signaled the end of our ride, but the truck continued to move on. The ride, never smooth, suddenly became rougher, and we were bounced about more violently. My father reached over and placed a hand on my grandmother's shoulder to steady her. She nodded in response.

Then the truck came to a stop and the smell of the diesel fuel was replaced by dust, which percolated up through the folds and gaps of the canvas walls. I heard the doors of the truck opening and then slamming shut, the voices of the soldiers moving along the side of the vehicle, and then the men working the ropes to release the canvas and free us from the truck. The canvas loosened and then the tailgate groaned and creaked and dropped open with a thunderous crash that shook the whole truck. The canvas was thrown back and the bright light flooded in and I shielded my eyes with the back of one hand.

"That's it, last stop!" announced one of the soldiers.

I rose to my feet. My legs felt shaky and I steadied myself with a hand against the side as I shuffled toward the tailgate. I stopped at the edge, staring out anxiously. Behind us other trucks came to a stop, sending clouds of dust up into the air. Farther back, along a dirt track, was a high metal fence, and on the other side of the fence a street brimming with traffic — cars as well as more military trucks. Toshio and some of the men leaped down right after me. My father and Mr. Matsui offered assistance to the women and children, reaching up and then gently lowering them to the ground.

"This is it?" Toshio asked.

"What?" I asked. It wasn't that I didn't understand the question, just that I was surprised that he was talking to me. He seemed anxious and uneasy.

"We stay here?" he asked.

"I think so."

I looked around. There were a series of buildings, some small and some gigantic, clustered around the grounds. The biggest of the buildings looked like an enormous barn. In the distance sat a racetrack with a wooden grandstand. Strangely, in the center of the track were what looked like hundreds of trucks and cars. That seemed like a strange place to park.

My eye was captured again by the fence, which seemed to ring the entire place. It was metal and high, and as far as I could see the only gate was the one through which we'd passed. On both sides of the gate were wooden buildings, and I could make out the sight of soldiers. And each soldier had a sidearm strapped to his side.

I felt a shiver run up my spine. It wasn't like I hadn't seen soldiers carrying weapons before. Armed soldiers were always strolling or marching around Prince Rupert. And all the sentries at the base where I'd worked carried rifles, and the military police always had sidearms. But, of course, this was different. These soldiers and these guns weren't for some unseen or unnamed enemy. They were for us.

"Attention!" called out that same metallic voice over the bullhorn. "Please assemble by family and line up at the administrative building to be registered and assigned accommodations." There was a pause. "After you have been processed you are to return to claim your possessions. Thank you!"

I turned to find my family, and Toshio reached out and grabbed my arm.

"What?" he asked. "What he say?"

"Go to your family. Then they'll tell you where you'll sleep tonight."

He nodded and then went to find his parents. I followed behind him to do the same. My parents, sisters and grandmother were already standing together, and with my arrival, we started to move where the soldiers were directing. We stopped at the back of a line of families, outside the door of a small building. Quickly the places behind us were filled as family after family joined the line.

Even more amazing than the numbers was the sound — or, more correctly, the lack of sound. Hundreds of people stood or slowly shuffled forward in total silence. There was no arguing, or complaining, or yelling, or even talking. The little conversation that was going on was in whispers. People moved their feet noiselessly. The only sound to break through was an occasional cough — lots of people had caught colds on the trip down the coast — but even these were subdued.

We got to the door of the building and an RCMP officer directed us to enter. Stretched out in front of us were half a dozen tables, with a man sitting on the far side of each table and a family of Japanese huddled together on our side. One of the families moved away from a table and was ushered out a door at the other side of the building. A little man, balding and wearing a suit, sitting at the now open table, motioned for us to come forward. My father led and we all followed behind.

"Sit, please," the man said, gesturing to the two empty chairs.

"Thank you," my father replied as he sat down. My mother moved the second chair slightly aside and then took my grandmother by the arm and guided her into the seat. I stood directly behind my father, with Yuri and Midori standing beside our mother.

The table was cluttered with papers. The little man

shuffled and sorted them and made little notations with his pen. From my vantage point, standing above him, I had a clear view of the top of his head. The overhead lights reflected brightly off his scalp. I also noticed that despite the room being far from hot, there were beads of sweat visible on the top of his head.

"Number," he said without looking up from his papers.

What did he mean by that? My father didn't answer.

"Do any of you speak English?" the man asked.

"Yes," my father answered.

"Good. Then I need to list your numbers … the numbers on your registration papers."

"Ahh … yes," my father answered. He reached into the pocket of his jacket and pulled out his papers — bright pink papers. Pink meant that he was a naturalized Canadian. My mother retrieved her papers — also pink — and my grandmother's, which were bright yellow and signified that she had never relinquished her Japanese citizenship. My father placed all three sets of papers on the table in front of the man. The little man took them and studied them; first one, then the next, and finally the third. As he held them I could see that his hands were shaking, badly.

"Where are his?" the little man asked, pointing at me.

My eyes opened in surprise. I didn't think he'd even looked at me.

"I … I don't have papers," I stammered. "I'm only fourteen."

"Oh," he said, shrugging his shoulders. "It's hard to tell the age of you people."

Without saying another word he put his head back down and started writing again.

I watched as he made little notes and flipped through papers and then started to copy down information from the registration papers. We waited silently.

"Here, take these," he said, handing my father the

registration papers as well as another white sheet of paper on which he'd been making notes. "That will tell you which buildings you're assigned to. As well, I've listed your children — given them a number."

"Don't you need our names?" I asked.

He looked up at me and shook his head. His eyes looked sad. "Names aren't necessary. All we require to process people is a number. Go through that door," he said, pointing to the end of the building. "Present these papers to the officers and they will direct you to your quarters … thank you."

My father rose to his feet and bowed slightly to the little man. His head was once again down, poring over the papers sitting on the table in front of him, and he didn't even see my father's gesture. My father helped my grandmother to her feet.

As we moved I glanced back at the little bald man. I watched intently as he continued to shuffle and sort his papers. I was struck by the thought that he really wasn't doing any work — he was just using the papers to avoid having to look at the people he was processing. Was that was why he looked so sad and nervous, and why he had been sweating? He knew what he was doing was wrong, but he was doing it anyway. As the next family filed in to take our place, they blocked my view of him. I knew he would have liked that — to be hidden. I suddenly felt very sorry for him.

Up ahead, at the end of a short cobblestone path, stood two RCMP officers. In front of the policemen was a family. As we got closer I was surprised to hear angry words — an argument — between one of the Japanese and the RCMP. We stopped, down the way from where the discussion was taking place. My parents and grandmother looked away in respect.

We were too far away to understand exactly what was happening. Yet I could clearly tell by the gesturing, the tone of the raised voices and the occasional word I could hear — mostly spoken by the father of the family — that things weren't going well. Finally the family moved on and we came forward to take their place.

"Papers, please," the taller of the two officers requested.

My father handed over the three sets of registration papers as well as the forms given to him by the little bald man.

"You are assigned to the men's dormitory," one of the officers said, pointing to my father. "And the rest of the family is assigned to the family building," he continued.

There was a heavy silence. What did he mean?

"I don't understand," my father said.

One of the officers took a deep breath. "What don't you understand?" he asked, and his voice had taken on an angry tone. "*You* go to men's residence, you are a man," he said loudly, sticking out a hand and practically poking a finger into my father's chest. "And the rest of you," he said, waving a hand toward us, "are to go to the family quarters. Do you people speak English?"

"As much as you do!" I snapped. Why did people keep on asking that question?

"All of you?" he asked.

"Even my grandmother," I answered. And of course that was only half a lie. She understood a lot, but really didn't speak it very well.

"Good, that makes it so much easier to explain," the officer said.

"I'll try to explain," the second officer said. "Men, and that includes any male over the age of sixteen …" He paused. "How old are you?"

"Fourteen," I answered.

"You look older. Anyway, men are assigned to a bed in one building, and families go to a separate residence."

"But why can't we stay together?" I asked.

"Problems with space and privacy. The men's building is just one big room, filled with bunk beds three high. There's no privacy. It's not the place for women or children. The family dormitory is subdivided so each family has its own space."

"Why can't my father just live in that space with us?" I demanded.

The officer shook his head. "There just isn't space. It will be cramped enough for the five of you and all your possessions."

"But we wouldn't mind being crowded —"

"Sorry, son," the officer said, cutting me off. "Those are the orders and there's nothing I can do about it. Besides, it isn't like your old man will be far away. The two buildings are just a hundred yards apart. And you'll be eating all your meals together in the same building. I know it isn't what I'd want if it was me and my family … I'm sorry … I really am … I hope you understand." He handed my father back all the papers.

"Thank you," my father said.

My father started to walk and we silently trailed behind him. We stopped moving at the fork of the path, where it split off in the two directions.

"We will meet later at the truck and unload," my father said.

There was no emotion in his voice. Calm, quiet, steady. That was the opposite of how my sisters looked. Yuri looked like she was about to cry.

"Everything is fine," my father said in that same tone. "Everything is fine," he repeated. "Now go. Work to be done."

My mother reached over and took Yuri by the hand and started to lead her away.

"Tadashi … stay," my father said, and I remained at his side.

"You are to be responsible," my father began. "I will be close … for now."

A wave of fear washed over me. "What … what do you mean?" I asked in alarm.

"You and I must take care of the family. If I am not here … then you."

"But there's Mom and grand —"

My father silenced me with a hardened look. "They will help, but you will have to lead. You are the male and the oldest … almost a man."

I wanted to say something back, but his words had caught me so off guard I couldn't get the words out. I just stood there, a dumb expression on my face.

"Go," my father said. He started off in one direction and I hurried off in the other.

I followed the path around the side of the building. There was a large sliding door, gaping open. It was big enough to allow a car to drive inside. I slowed down at the entrance. What was that smell? Animals, maybe. Cautiously I walked up the ramp leading to the door and peeked inside. It was a barn, a gigantic barn. Animal stalls lined the aisles that extended into the distance.

This couldn't be the right place. I'd obviously walked into the wrong building. I was just about to turn and leave when my gaze fell on a Japanese woman, standing in front of one of the stalls, broom in hand, sweeping. Two small children came out of the stall. Then I saw other kids and two more women, all Japanese as well, by another stall … and there were people by the next one as well … and then my eyes fell upon my mother and grandmother standing in front of another stall.

.7.

I stood stock-still, too shocked to move. What were they doing here ... what were any of us doing here? The woman with the broom was sweeping up a cloud of dust, and it swirled around, filling the air. I sneezed, and then sneezed again. Wasn't the foul odor bad enough? I stumbled forward. Why was my family in here, anyway? And why was that woman sweeping out that cattle stall?

"Tadashi ..." my mother called out. There was a catch in her voice. She sounded all choked up, like she was trying to fight back tears.

I rushed to her side. "Mom?"

"Tadashi ... we ... we ... have to stay."

"I know," I said, trying to comfort her as her eyes started to fill with tears. "But we won't be staying here for too long. Let's go and find where we'll be sleeping."

"No! You don't understand ... this is where we're going to be sleeping ... here!"

"What do you mean here?" I demanded.

"Here! Here!" she said, pointing to the cattle stall.

"No," I said, shaking my head in disbelief. "You're wrong ... we can't ... this is a cattle stall ... it isn't for people, it's for —"

"Animals!" my grandmother said, cutting me off. "Animals."

My head swirled and I needed to sit down, but there was no place to sit. I took a deep breath, a breath full of dust and the smell of animals, and felt worse instead of better.

There had to be a mistake. Maybe my mother didn't understand, or somebody had directed them into the wrong building by accident, or —

"Here's the broom I promised you."

I turned around. There was a woman, a white woman, wearing a uniform. My mother reached out, took a broom from her and bowed her head slightly in thanks.

"Once you clean it out and move in your things it'll be … okay … for a while … it's not like you'll be here that long."

My mother offered a weak smile in reply.

"There are buckets and soap and water at the far end of the building," the woman continued. "I better go and help settle in the next group of people."

She walked away toward the large sliding door. There was a growing crowd of people — families like ours — all standing silently, waiting.

I turned back to my family. My grandmother now had the broom and she started to sweep. My mother spoke to Yuri and Midori, instructing them to go and get soap and water.

"What do you want me to do?" I asked.

She shrugged. "Meet your father, bring our things."

I nodded. That seemed like a good idea. I walked away, picking my way around the women and children who were slowly shuffling along the aisles. Stepping outside, the fresh air felt good. I took a deep breath and my head cleared a bit.

Coming along the path were more families. As I approached the first group, which was moving silently, eyes to the ground, I moved off the path and onto the grass. They were from my village, but nobody even exchanged a word as we passed each other.

I'd traveled no more than two dozen paces when I

became aware of the rumble of trucks. I stopped and the noise got louder. Within seconds a truck turned the corner of one of the buildings and came into view. It was moving slowly, following the same path as the families. A second truck, and then a third and a fourth, were close behind it. They looked like the trucks that had brought us here to the park.

People moved off the path to make way for the oncoming vehicles. As they approached, it became obvious that the trucks were much wider than the cobblestone path. The big tires dug into the grass, chewing up the wet sod and spitting out mud behind them. Silent little groups stood off to the side and watched as truck after truck moved past them.

I looked up into the cab of each truck, trying to see if I could recognize the soldiers who had driven us here. The cabs were high off the ground and the reflection off the windscreens made it difficult to see inside. And, of course, all the trucks looked the same.

The trucks came to a stop directly in front of the big sliding door. I ran back and arrived as the soldiers climbed out of the vehicles. I looked over the men, searching for the two soldiers who were driving our vehicle. I saw them almost immediately. Some of the older Japanese always had trouble telling one "white" guy from another. They said they all looked alike. I always thought that was crazy — as crazy as those whites who thought that all Japanese looked alike … or should be treated alike.

The two men circled around the back of the truck and unhooked the chains holding the tailgate in place. It dropped down with a thunderous crash. One hauled himself up into the back. Within seconds I saw an object fly through the air out of the truck. It was a box, and it was caught by the second soldier standing on the ground. He quickly placed it at his side as a second object came flying out at him. He caught it as well and dropped it to the ground with a loud thud. Didn't these guys know that some of these boxes contained plates and dishes and other really breakable things? Maybe they knew but didn't care!

"Excuse me!" I said, coming forward. "The things in the boxes … they could be breakable …"

"I haven't dropped one yet," the one soldier said.

"But —"

"We haven't got time to go slow, kid," interrupted the other soldier. "We're under orders to unload and get back to the docks. More of you people waiting to be loaded up."

He tossed the sewing machine he was holding and the other man just barely caught it.

"I could unload," I offered. "And you two could take a break, maybe go and have a coffee or something."

They stopped again. I could tell they were thinking it over. "I don't know, John," one said to the other. "A coffee would be nice, but we have to move fast."

"I'll move fast, really fast," I said. "And it won't be long until my father and the other men come to help."

"The men won't be here for a long time," one said.

"My father said as soon as he was settled in he'd be coming, and I know that won't take more than a few minutes, and I'll work until they get here."

"It'll be way more than an hour, kid. They have to all be interviewed by the RCMP."

"Interviewed? But why?"

"Checking for spies."

"Spies! My father isn't a spy, he's a fisherman."

"Doesn't mean he can't be both," the man in the truck said.

I was going to answer when the second soldier spoke. "Don't worry, kid, I'm sure he's just a fisherman, but it still takes time for them to interview them and —"

"I'll work fast!"

"Fast isn't possible by yourself. You need two people, one in the back of the truck and a second on the ground. You can't do it by yourself."

There had to be somebody who could help me … maybe my sister, or — I caught sight of a boy, Japanese, maybe my age or a little younger, standing just off to the side, watching. He was wearing a baseball cap on his head, chomping on a wad of gum.

"What about him?" I asked, pointing. The boy's eyes widened in surprise.

The two soldiers exchanged a look. "Sure, why not."

"Come here!" one of the soldiers called out to the boy. He didn't move.

"Come over here," the second said, much louder, gesturing with his hand.

Reluctantly the boy came over. He didn't look happy.

"We want you to help unload this truck," the soldier in the truck barked.

The boy slowly shook his head. "No … understand … no English speak."

One of the soldiers picked up a box. "Moovving. Understand?"

The boy shook his head.

"Too bad. I could have used a break … wait a second. You speak Japanese, don't you?" the soldier asked me.

"Of course."

"Then explain it to him in your language."

My language is English, I thought, but didn't say a word.

"Tell him to get up in the truck and start handing things down to you."

I nodded. "They want you to help unload the truck," I said in Japanese.

"And tell him it's an order, from me," the larger of the two said, tapping himself on the chest. "And if he doesn't do it he'll be in trouble, big trouble."

I'd tell him I needed his help, but I wasn't going to threaten him. "Your help would really be appreciated," I added in my best Japanese.

The boy nodded and walked to the edge of the truck. The soldier reached down a hand and pulled the boy up into the truck.

"We'll be back in about fifteen minutes, and we'll see how you're doing." He turned to his buddy still standing in the truck. "Come on, I can use a drink."

The soldier jumped down off the back of the truck and the two of them strolled away. Fifteen minutes — that would be more than enough time to get my family's things off the truck in one piece before they returned. It wouldn't work, though, for the boy to be in the truck. I knew what was ours. He could come down here and I'd pass things to him.

"Come on down here —" I started to say and then remembered he couldn't speak much English.

"Make up your mind," he answered in perfect English.

My mouth dropped open in shock. "You speak English," I blurted out.

"Better than *you*," he answered.

"But … but … why …"

"Why did I pretend not to understand?"

I nodded my head.

"Because if they don't think you understand what they're saying, they can't make you do things. Did you think I wanted to unload this truck? And if somebody hadn't started jabbering away to me in Japanese, I would have gotten away with it. Thanks a lot."

"I'm sorry," I mumbled. "But I could use your help — I'd really appreciate it."

He shrugged. "Why didn't you want the soldiers to unload the truck, anyway?"

"I was afraid they'd break something, something valuable," I said.

"I guess you're right." He paused. "What's your name?"

"Tadashi Fukushima."

He reached out a hand. "Pleased to meet you. My name's Sam Uyeyama."

We shook. "Is that short for Isamu?"

"No, it's short for Samuel," he answered.

"Samuel … that doesn't sound very Japanese."

"It isn't, but why would I have to have a Japanese name?"

"But … but …"

"Because my relatives were from Japan?" he asked.

I nodded.

"Maybe, but that was a long time ago. My family has been in this country for close to forty years. I don't even speak Japanese."

"You don't?" I asked in amazement. I knew of people who didn't speak great Japanese, but almost everybody spoke — wait a second. "But you understand it."

"A few words … names of food; I can count to ten."

"But you understood when I told you to help with the —" I stopped as I realized that of course he understood what the soldiers had said to him in English in the first place.

He smiled. "You always this quick?"

"Not always."

I did notice that he was quick, though — he spoke in rapid bursts and with an accent that was different than mine. It wasn't just that it wasn't Japanese, but that it wasn't even like the English I knew. It was more like … like how those gangsters talk in the movies I'd seen at the theater in Prince Rupert.

"So are we moving or what?" Sam asked, pushing the words past the thick wad of gum he was working around his mouth.

"Yeah, I guess we should. Maybe we could get my family's stuff out of the truck. Then I guess I can help with your family's belonging."

"We moved in last week."

Sam began to hand down items from the truck. Rather than direct him to things that belonged to my family, I simply allowed him to pass the things closest to the back of the truck. I guessed it wouldn't have been fair, either to him or to the other families, to just take our things. Sam worked fairly quickly, but just as quickly I discovered that he wasn't that much more careful than the two soldiers.

Within a few minutes a few of the women and children came out of the building and began to claim their belongings. They offered thanks to both Sam and me for helping. One very old woman tried to start up a conversation with Sam. He shrugged, shook his head and tried to explain to her that he didn't understand Japanese. And, of course, since she didn't seem to know much English, she didn't understand him not understanding.

"You must get that a lot," I said as Sam passed me down a heavy sewing machine.

"Just around here. Where I live there aren't any Japanese."

"None?"

"Well, other than my family."

"Where do you live?" I asked as he tossed me down the box.

"About twenty miles from here. It's a town just outside of Vancouver. You?"

"In a village just outside of Prince Rupert."

"Where's Prince Rupert?" he asked.

"You haven't heard of Prince Rupert?" I asked in amazement.

He shrugged. "So shoot me. Where is it?"

"It's on Kairn Island. Just south of the Alaskan panhandle."

"Alaska! I didn't think there was anything up there but Indians!"

"There's lots of different people. English, Norwegian, French, Dutch, Natives and lots and lots of Japanese. Everybody in my whole village is Japanese."

""What does everybody in the village do — you know, for a living?" Sam asked.

"Most people fish."

"And your father?"

"He's a fisherman too."

"Is that what you want to be as well?" Sam asked.

There was something about the tone in his voice and the look on his face that I didn't like. "Maybe, if I want. What does *your* father do?"

"He's in the trucking business."

"And is that what you want to do? Drive a truck?" I asked.

"My father doesn't drive a truck. He owns the business, a cartage company. He has ten trucks altogether. He brings in half the fruit and vegetables that come to Vancouver. Nine of those trucks parked in the racetrack infield belong to my dad."

"I thought you said he had ten trucks."

"He does … it's just …" He motioned for me to come closer. "He has a tenth truck; it's new and was going to be delivered next week — it's all ready except for the company name being painted on the side. My father just didn't tell them about the extra truck. You're not going to tell anybody, are you?" he asked. There was a touch of anxiety in his voice.

"Who would I tell?" I asked.

"Nobody, I hope."

"I really appreciate all your help. There's not much stuff still up there, is there?"

"Not a lot."

Sam went back into the truck to continue moving things. He returned with a canvas bag. It contained my clothing. He dropped it into my arms. As he turned back around, Midori and Yuri appeared. I was glad to see them. It meant that they could start carrying things, which would save me some work.

"Sam!" I called out, and he stopped. "These are my sisters, Yuri and Midori."

"Good to meet you," Sam said.

They both mumbled greetings.

"Since they're here now, they can help me. If you want you can stop," I offered.

"That's okay. I started, so I'll finish. Besides, I figure the faster this is all done the sooner I can show you around the place, explain the ropes to you." He paused. "That is, if you want me to."

"I'd like that ... I'd like that."

.8.

The air was now filled with the rumbling of voices instead of the cloud of dust. Colorful sheets and blankets were being draped along the bars across the front and sides of the stalls, providing some privacy. We'd moved all of our things into the stall. All that was left to do was the unpacking and then arranging things so there would be room for us to sleep tonight. It wasn't home — heck, it wasn't anybody's home, it was a cattle stall — but at least it was dry and warm.

If only it didn't stink so much. It was the powerful stench of animals, and instead of getting used to it, I was finding it getting even worse. I imagined that the years and years of animal droppings and urine had worked their way right through the wood of the flooring, and the soap and water and the scrubbing and rubbing now being done by the women was just freeing it up.

There was still more to be done, but it was mainly women's work — unpacking and arranging instead of moving or lifting. I glanced at my watch. It was fifteen minutes past the time Sam had said he'd come back and get me and show me around the camp. And my father still hadn't appeared.

It had been more than three hours since he left us and walked away to that other building. With each passing moment I was getting more and more concerned. What was going on? Maybe he had known something more was up when he said I was in charge if he wasn't there — I wanted Sam to show up. If he really did know his way around this place, then he could take me to where my father was being detained.

"Ready to go?" It was Sam.

I was grateful he'd finally arrived, but annoyed that he was late. "I was ready fifteen minutes ago."

"What's the rush? I promised you a tour, not a train trip. There's no schedule here and it isn't like the pool is going, anyway."

"There's a pool here?" I asked.

"Sorry, that's what the soldiers call it — the pool. We're all part of the pool. You coming?"

"Of course."

Sam turned and started away. I hurried after him. I waved goodbye over my shoulder to my mother and grandmother and they waved back. I'd wanted to introduce Sam to them, but he hadn't given me a chance. Too bad … although maybe it was better that I didn't introduce them right now. I didn't know how they'd react to a Japanese who couldn't speak any Japanese.

"Where are we going to start?" I asked.

"Depends. Are you hungry?"

"Not really. I had a bowl of cold noodles while I was waiting."

"Then we'll leave the mess for last. The mess is where people —"

"Eat," I said, interrupting him. "The kitchen and dining area."

"Yeah … how did you know that?"

"I used to work on a military base in Prince Rupert."

"They let a Japanese work on a military base?" he asked in disbelief.

"I'm not Japanese!" I snapped.

He held up his hands. "You know what I mean … Japanese family."

I nodded. "My friend Jed worked there, and his mother. They got me the job."

"Are they Japanese?"

"No."

"That explains it."

"And I had to leave not long after the bombing of Pearl Harbor."

"That happened to everybody, whether or not you worked on an army base," Sam said.

"I know. But why do we have a mess here? Aren't they going to let each family cook their own meals?"

"Nope."

"My mother isn't going to like that."

"I think they're afraid of fires or something. All the meals are served in the mess hall. Breakfast from seven until eight-thirty, lunch from noon until one-thirty and then supper from four-thirty until six-thirty."

"Is the food any good?" I asked.

"Nothing special, but there sure is a lot of it. You can go back for seconds or even thirds if you want. But I guess you'll find out for yourself. I'll make sure to get you there in time for dinner."

"Sure. Do you think you could bring me to the men's barracks?" I asked.

"Technically we're not allowed to be in there."

"We're not … Why?"

"It's only for the men. I heard they don't want us around there because of what goes on inside."

"What do you mean?" I asked anxiously.

"You know, gambling and playing cards. How old are you, anyway?"

"I'm fifteen — I mean, almost fifteen," I answered.

"I'm fourteen too," Sam said. "Even though we're not really allowed, they don't pay too much attention to who comes and goes in the building. I went there yesterday to see my father."

"He lives in there too?"

"All the males live there."

"What's it like?" I asked as we kept walking. "Is it like where I am?"

"No stalls. I don't know what the building was used for before, but it wasn't for animals. It smells okay. Just row after row of bunk beds."

"And your building? Where do you live?"

"It's like yours," Sam said. "And just so you know, you never get used to the smell." He spat out a big wad of gum and pulled out some new pieces from his pocket. "Want some?"

"No thanks."

He unwrapped three pieces and stuffed them into his mouth. "You know that even if we go to the men's dormitory you won't be able to see your father."

"Why not?"

"He'll still be in the restricted area until all the interviews are finished."

"The soldier mentioned the interviews. I just don't understand why they'd think my father was a spy," I said anxiously.

"They interview all the men who come to Hastings Park. There's nothing to be concerned about," Sam said. "It's just routine."

"I'm not worried."

"You're not much of a liar," Sam said. "But there's really nothing to worry about unless your father really is a spy."

"Don't be stupid! He's no spy, he's a fisherman!"

"That's right, you told me … and that means that the interview might take a lot longer."

"What do you mean?"

"Don't you read the newspapers?" Sam asked.

"Sure, sometimes, but what's that got to do with anything?" I demanded.

"I read them, every day. There's been a bunch of articles about how the Japanese fishermen know the coastal waters better than anybody, including our own navy."

"Of course the fishermen know the waters. If they didn't they couldn't survive. But I still don't understand."

"Well, the headlines in the papers said that the Japanese fishermen could lead the Japanese navy right into any harbor or cove or inlet up and down the whole coast," Sam explained.

"They could, but that doesn't mean they would!" I snapped.

"Hey, you don't have to convince me. The reason they took away my father's trucks and all those other vehicles was because they thought they could be used to transport the Japanese soldiers once the fishermen finish leading them into the ports."

I couldn't help but laugh. I hadn't laughed for a long time and it felt good.

"Let me show you the playing fields first," Sam said.

"That sounds interesting."

"There's a soccer pitch and three baseball diamonds, and —"

"Are they any good?" I asked.

"Are you kidding? They're among the best ball fields in all of Vancouver. The semi-pro league uses them — or, at least, *used* to use them. Do you play ball?" Sam asked.

"Of course I play! And you?"

"All the time," Sam replied.

"Do you think that maybe we could try to get a game together sometime?"

"We wouldn't have to try. There's been a game there almost every day since I got here. I've gotten into a few games already."

"That's great … How long has your family been at

Hastings Park, anyway?" I asked.

"Just over a week."

That seemed like a long time. I was hoping that we wouldn't be here that long, but who knew?

As we moved along all the paths among the buildings we continually passed by people. They were standing or walking or just sitting on the benches that were frequently placed beside the path. Some of the people were quietly talking, some looked solemn and serious, and others were actually laughing. People would often nod as we passed, or say a few brief words. Twice people asked us for directions. I didn't know much, but I did know where the family residence was located and told them the way.

I could nearly always predict which language people would use, even before they opened their mouths. The older people, people my parents' age or older, would always start off talking in Japanese. Kids or teenagers would begin speaking in English, and those in between might be talking in either language. No matter who it was, though, it wasn't like they could only speak the one language. Almost everybody had at least some of both.

Except Sam. Here was a kid with Japanese blood in his veins but, from what he'd said, hardly a word of Japanese in his head. I had thought he was just kidding when he said he knew virtually no Japanese, but I quickly realized that he was telling the truth. As I answered questions or greeted people, Sam would occasionally mutter one of his very few Japanese words — things like hello or goodbye. But more often than not, his one-word reply was totally unconnected to what was being said. And even then, he spoke with such an awkward accent.

Two RCMP officers came toward us along the path. Sam and I separated and moved just off the path to allow them to pass.

"Good afternoon, boys," one of the officers said.

"Good afternoon," I answered.

"Don't do that," Sam said quietly as we continued to walk.

"Don't do what?"

"Don't speak English when you're around the soldiers. Do what I did when those soldiers tried to get me to help unload the truck: pretend you don't speak English. It can get you out of a lot of work — at least, it will if somebody doesn't try to translate for you," he said, shooting me a dirty look.

"Sorry," I said, although I wasn't really sorry at all.

"Just kidding."

We left the buildings behind and made our way along a dirt path that cut through some bushes. We turned to the left when we came to a fence — stone and metal and almost twice as high as me. It was topped by three strings of barbed wire.

"This fence surrounds the whole park," Sam said.

"The whole thing?"

"Yep … other than the three entrances. And of course there are gates and guards at each of those."

"Are we allowed out?" I asked.

"Some people can get out, with permission. My father goes out for a few hours two or three times a week to take care of business. You can't stay out overnight."

"So we could go out?" I asked.

"Do you have any business in the city?" Sam questioned.

"Of course not!"

"Then you're not going anywhere." He paused. "At least, through the gates."

"What do you mean?" I asked.

"I've walked the whole length of the fence. There's a few places where it isn't so high, and two places where there's a gap underneath the fence that's big enough to allow somebody to get under. Why, do you have someplace you want to go?" Sam asked.

"Not really. I just don't like the idea of not being able to go, that's all."

"Then maybe we should go out sometime. You ever been to the Stanley Park Zoo?"

"Never."

"It's nice. Maybe we should go sometime … maybe tomorrow or —" Sam suddenly stopped talking. "Do you hear that?"

"Hear what?"

"Those bells."

I listened. I could hear the faint jingling of bells.

"Come on!" Sam yelled, and then sprinted away.

I ran after him. I was amazed at how fast he moved along the jagged and rough path that ran beside the fence. Up ahead I saw him wave his arms over his head, and he started yelling. He came to a stop and breathlessly I caught up to him.

"Over here!" he yelled, peering through the fence, still waving his arms in the air.

I followed his gaze. There was a boy, about our age, sitting on a strange-looking three-wheeled bike. Across the front of the bike, over top of a large yellow tub, was a string of bells — the bells we could hear. Slowly the bike moved along the road toward us. When it got close I could see drawings on the side and big lettering that said, ICE CREAM.

"Do you want an ice cream?" Sam asked.

"Um … I don't have any money with me."

"My treat."

"Thanks."

The boy had parked his bike over at the edge of the busy street. Behind him, what seemed like only inches away, cars whizzed and trucks rumbled by. Further beyond, I could see houses lining the far side of the street. They were little one-story bungalows with neat lawns and nicely tended gardens — flower gardens. I didn't see any vegetables growing at all, just flowers. There was a couple toiling away in one of the colorful gardens, tending to their flowers, and a few doors farther down a man was mowing his grass. It all looked so pleasant and peaceful … if only I wasn't looking at it through the links of a fence — a fence I wasn't allowed to go past.

As I watched, Sam pushed a dollar bill through the chain-link fence. The boy returned some change through the fence. The boy removed two paper-wrapped ice cream bars from the big "tub," which I could now see was some sort of cooler.

"Heads up," Sam said.

The boy pitched one of the ice cream bars into the air. It arched over the fence and came down. Sam reached out and caught it. The second one was thrown up, but not as well. It hit the top of the fence and bounced away. I scrambled off to the side and just managed to grab it with my fingertips before it plummeted to the ground.

"Nice grab!" Sam said. "If you can hit as well as you can catch, I want you on my side when we play baseball."

I smiled.

"Thanks!" Sam yelled out to the kid, who tipped his hat in reply.

I started to unwrap the paper, but Sam reached out and stopped me. "I'll show you a great place to eat these … a great place to get away to. Come on, we have to move fast before the ice cream melts."

Sam trotted off and I again found myself running to keep up with him. We were following a small path worn across a field. The field ended abruptly at a dirt racetrack. In the infield of the track sat dozens and dozens, or more likely hundreds and hundreds, of cars and trucks.

Sam ducked under the railing of the track and I followed. Boy, he was fast. He crossed the track, again ducking under the inner rail, and continued toward the vehicles, finally stopping at the first car. Just as I reached his side he was off again, weaving between the cars and trucks. He stopped once again at the side of a large gray truck. He reached up into the wheel well of the front drive's well and pulled something out.

"The key," he said, holding it up and showing it to me. He reached up, unlocked the door and flung it open. "Get in."

I hesitated.

"Don't worry," he said, reading my hesitation. "It's one of my father's trucks."

"Oh, okay," I said, nodding my head. I hauled myself up onto the running board and then into the truck. It felt hot and sticky as I slid past the steering wheel to the far side of the seat. Sam jumped in beside me.

"Roll down your window," he said, as he did the same.

I cranked it open and a breeze blew in from his side and right out my window. It felt good. Sam ripped the top part of the paper off his ice cream bar. He tossed it on the floor amongst a litter of candy bar wrappers, newspapers and other assorted garbage.

"Enjoy," he said, "but be careful you don't drip on the seat. Lean forward."

As I started to unwrap my bar I realized this wasn't going to be an easy job. It was starting to melt, and I quickly leaned forward so that any drips would fall on the newspapers lying haphazardly at my feet. I took a big bite. Vanilla — it felt very good sliding down my throat.

"I come here all the time," Sam said.

I'd guessed that just judging by the accumulation of garbage.

"It's good to just get away from everybody and have a little peace."

A little privacy had been one of the things I'd missed most since we first got on our boat.

"If you want to come here sometime by yourself, be my guest. You know where the key is, just lock it up and put the key back when you're through."

"But why is it locked in the first place?" I asked. The truck was squarely in the middle of a sea of other trucks and cars, so it wasn't like it was going anywhere.

"All the vehicles are locked." He paused. "And the RCMP took the keys."

"But …"

Sam smiled. "But not all the keys. My father always has a spare in the wheel well of every one of his trucks. When you come, though, I need you to be careful."

I could understand that his father might get angry, the way the cab of his truck was getting messed up.

"We're not supposed to be in here, and if the guards catch us we could be in trouble."

"There are guards?" I asked, looking anxiously out the windscreen. All I could see were the other vehicles.

"There are guards everywhere. They may call it the pool, but this is a detainment camp."

"Maybe we shouldn't be here," I suggested.

Sam laughed. "There's no maybe to it. We *shouldn't* be here."

I stuffed the last of my ice cream in my mouth. It felt cold but wonderful. "There, I'm finished," I mumbled. "Let's get going."

"You can if you want, but I'm staying here for a while." Sam inserted the keys into the steering wheel column, and suddenly a radio started to play.

"There's a radio in here?" I questioned in amazement.

"All my father's trucks have radios. He had them installed special. His drivers make runs really early in the morning, sometimes as early as four o'clock, and he figured the radios would help keep them awake."

Sam reached over and fiddled with the dials, and

music, big band music, started to play.

"This is probably one of the few radios in the whole camp — at least, a radio that doesn't belong to the guards. I mostly listen to music. Do you like Glenn Miller?"

I shrugged. I'd never heard of him.

"But I also listen to the news. Stuff that's happening in Europe and Asia and also what's happening here in Vancouver. It's important to know what's happening." He turned the volume up slightly.

"Should you be doing that?" I questioned. "What if the guards hear it?"

"They won't," he said, turning it up another notch. "They're old men who can't hear very well. The whole home guard is made up of men too old or fat or deaf to get into the regular army. Besides, they're way over there in the grandstand, sitting in a little office, playing cards. That's what they always do."

"And they never patrol?"

"I've seen them make a little circle around the edge of the vehicles every so often, but I've never actually seen them cut into the middle, which is where this truck sits. Right dab in the very middle, surrounded on all sides. We can't see out past the other trucks and nobody can see in to us. Feel better now?"

I nodded. I did feel better — not good, but better.

"Look, Tadashi, if you're only going to do what you're supposed to do, then this place is going to get boring really fast. Relax, cut a few corners. Just because these soldiers are in charge doesn't mean we have to do everything they say ... unless you think they're right to put us here."

"Of course I don't!"

"Good. I was just checking. I know this may sound crazy, but my father was telling us that some of the Japanese don't even seem that upset about the whole thing. He speaks Japanese and he was saying they just kept muttering something about how there was nothing that can be done —"

"Shikata-ga-nai," I said.

"What?"

"It can't be helped."

Sam shrugged. "Sounds like a pretty stupid thing to say, to me. I almost wished I'd learned some more Japanese so I'd know what everybody was jabbering about. Funny-sounding language … makes me think of little cartoon animals or something."

I felt a rush of anger and was trying to think of something to say when Sam started to talk again.

"Now that we've had dessert, how about supper?"

I looked at my watch. It was suppertime.

"We'll head back out the way we came. It's important to always come in from the same direction so the vehicles hide us from the guards in the grandstand."

We both rolled up our windows. I held the sticky ice cream wrapper in my hand.

"Just throw it on the floor," Sam instructed. "It's not like anybody is going to care."

I dropped it to the floorboards, amongst the other refuse.

"And by the way," Sam said, "there's a blanket and a couple of pillows right here behind the seat. If you want to come out here to sleep at night, be my guest — at least, if you don't mind sharing the seat."

"You sleep out here?"

"I have a couple of times," he answered.

"Thanks for the offer, but I think I'd prefer my own bed."

"So would I. My own bed in my own room in my own house. You haven't tried to sleep in that building yet. Just wait. Between the crying babies and the people moving around and the stench, you may decide to take me up on my offer."

What he was saying suddenly made sense to me. Maybe it wouldn't be such a bad idea. "And you wouldn't mind sharing the seat?" I asked.

"It's a big truck. Besides, I wouldn't mind the company." Sam looked at his watch. "They're only serving supper for another twenty minutes. Let's get moving or we won't be able to eat."

We closed the door, firmly so it would lock, but not so loud as to have a chance of the guards hearing it and coming to investigate. Sam returned the key to its hiding spot and then had me feel around up there until I found it myself. I then returned it. We moved between the vehicles. Some of the vehicles were so close together that there was no space between. Sam climbed up on the locked bumpers and I followed behind.

Leaving behind the last of the cars I suddenly felt very exposed. I craned my neck to try to look back as we moved across the track. No guards that I could see. As always, Sam was moving at a quick pace. I figured that even if we didn't need to rush, he'd still move at this speed. We cut back to the path, but instead of following it he moved off to the left. He traveled through some underbrush and I struggled to keep up.

"Come on, hurry up!" he yelled back over his shoulder.

I doubled my pace in order to close the gap. Up ahead, at the first building, Sam came to a stop and I trotted to his side.

"Well, here it is," he said, gesturing to a large open door. "Dinner is served."

We stepped inside. It was an enormous room, filled with tables and benches. Most of the tables were empty, and — I was shocked to see my mother waving to me. And right beside her was my grandmother and Yuri and Midori, and my father!

.9.

I took two quick steps toward my father and then caught myself. I slowed down and walked to where my family sat. There was an open seat at the table, but instead of sitting I stood. Each of them had a metal tray in front of them. On each tray was a metal plate and bowl and utensils. It was just like at the army base in Rupert.

"It's good to see you!" I said to my father.

"It's good to see you too. Your mother said you helped everybody unload their belongings from the truck," my father said.

"Yes. Me and my friend, Sam. Dad, this is ..." I turned around and realized that Sam was nowhere to be seen. I looked all around and then caught sight of him, tray in hand, standing in line waiting to be served.

"He's getting some food ... maybe I should get some food too."

My father nodded. "And then have your friend join us."

I went to the end of the line, but Sam waved to me and held up a second tray that he had been holding. I looked at the people who were behind him in line. Maybe I should grab another tray and wait my turn. Sam motioned more enthusiastically. I hadn't known Sam very long, but long enough to know what he'd say if I didn't join him ... maybe I should ... but what about the people waiting in line ahead of me? My stomach grumbled. I was hungry, and I really was with him. I walked past the back of the line, not looking at the people I passed, and joined Sam. Of course, nobody said anything, but I still couldn't help but wonder what they were thinking.

We shuffled forward, pushing our trays along a little shelf.

"When I was a kid we used to come here all the time," Sam said.

"Here?" I asked in disbelief.

"Every fall my father would bring me and my sister to the exhibition here. There were rides and displays, horse racing, all sorts of food — things like popcorn and candy apples, cotton candy — and of course the animal exhibits." Sam paused and his face took on a serious look, the first one I'd ever seen on him.

"Funny, when we used to come to the fair, we'd sometimes walk down the aisles in the barn, just looking at the animals. And some had all these ribbons tacked up on a board to show how many winners that farm had, and in some of the stalls there were families who slept there, right in the barn, so they could watch the animals at night. And I remember thinking, how could anybody do that? You know, sleep in a cattle stall like an animal … and now look at us."

I didn't know what to say in response. What could I say?

Sam reached out and grabbed two plates and passed one back to me. It was tarnished and didn't look too clean. Next he placed a bowl on his tray and then one on mine. We both grabbed utensils — a big spoon and a fork. There were no knives to be seen.

Up ahead three women stood behind a counter. On the counter were large vats of steaming food. I couldn't see what it was, but it smelled good. Then again, when I was hungry everything smelled good.

"Soup?" one of the women asked Sam.

"Everything."

She was holding a large ladle, and she filled his bowl with a yellowish, brothy mixture.

"And you?"

"Yes, please, ma'am."

She smiled. "You Japanese have to be the politest people in the world." She filled my bowl and some of it splattered out onto the tray.

"Thank you," I said instinctively, although I was tempted not to be polite just to show her.

The next woman stood in front of a big, steaming pot of what looked like stew — maybe beef stew, judging by the smell. Without asking she reached out and ladled out a serving. It hit Sam's plate with a loud "plop." She quickly did the same for me, with the same sound escaping as it hit my plate. Somehow, "plop" wasn't a sound I'd ever associated with something being tasty.

The last server held a pair of tongs, and as each person passed she placed a slice of bread — thinly sliced white bread — on the side of the tray.

Sam paused as she gave him his piece of bread. "Anything better in the back?" he asked.

What did that mean? She leaned over the counter and said something so quietly to Sam that I couldn't hear what she had said, but he smiled in response.

"What was that about?" I asked.

"A secret … but after we eat I'll let you in on it. Where are we going to sit?"

"I thought with my family."

"That should be fun."

"I … I just thought …"

"That I should meet your parents. I guess I have to sooner or later."

I led Sam over to the table where my family sat. As we approached, Yuri got up and pulled a chair over from another table, making a spot for Sam. My father rose to his feet.

"Father, this is my new friend, Sam …" I couldn't remember his last name.

"Uyeyama … I'm Sam Uyeyama," he said, reaching out his hand to shake my father's.

My father bowed slightly and Sam did the same.

"I am pleased to meet," my father said.

"Me too."

"And this is my mother, wife and daughters."

Each nodded in turn and Sam gave them a little wave.

"Please, sit, join us," my father said.

Sam plopped down into the open spot right in front of him, and I took the spot beside my father. Sam leaned over his tray and, using the big spoon, began shoveling in the food. He made loud chewing noises and it sounded like he hadn't eaten for weeks.

I had to admit that the way he was digging into it made it seem like it must be pretty good. I looked at the stew, poking it with my spoon. There were potatoes, lots of potatoes, some carrots peeking out and a couple of pieces of meat at the surface. I dipped in my spoon and gathered up a little bit of everything. I popped it in my mouth. It was … it was … nothing. There was almost no taste whatsoever. And it wasn't just the taste, but the texture. The carrots and potatoes were mushy and soft. It was sort of like … baby food. I remembered when Yuri was little and my mother would take food and mush it all up before she fed it to her. Why was it so awful?

Sam picked up his plate and scraped off the last of his stew. I was amazed by both how fast he'd eaten and how he seemed to enjoy it so much.

"I'm going for seconds," Sam said as he got up. "Anybody else?"

"Not yet," I answered.

"Suit yourself," Sam said as he stuffed his entire piece

of bread in his mouth and then walked off.

I looked over at my mother. Her food had hardly been touched. Nor had my grandmother's. My sisters were picking at their food, but for the most part it looked like they hadn't eaten hardly anything.

"This is not so good," I said.

"It's awful!" Yuri responded.

"I don't understand why they won't let you cook," I said to my mother.

She shook her head.

"They said it was because of the danger of fires," my father answered.

"But why is it so bad?" I asked loudly.

My mother shot me a sharp look, which left me with no doubt that I had been rude.

Sam suddenly returned. He was unexpectedly empty-handed.

"They stopped serving," he explained. "Are you finished?"

Did he want to eat what was left of mine? "Um … I guess so … except for maybe the bread."

"Good. Wanna come with me to check something out?"

"Sure," I said, rising to my feet and grabbing the tray. I hoped he was going to let me in on the secret … I stopped. I turned back toward my father. "Is that all right with you … can I go with Sam?"

He nodded.

"Thank you. I'll be back soon," I offered, although I didn't know how long it would take. I trotted after Sam and caught him just before he reached the exit.

"Where are we going?" I asked.

"Out back. I have a meeting."

"With who?"

"Be patient. Haven't you heard patience is a virtue?" he smirked.

We circled around the side of the mess hall and then around to the back. Two large army trucks were parked there, backed right up to the building. Sam squeezed by the truck and I followed, and we entered through a large door that led back into the mess hall — at least, the kitchen of the mess hall.

There were three large stoves. Atop each was a pot — the three largest pots I'd ever seen in my life. Steam rose from each pot and filled the air. There was a woman standing on a stepladder right beside one of the stoves. In her hands was a paddle, a canoe paddle, and she dipped it into the pot and began stirring. Over to the side, lined up beside a long counter, were four other women. They were peeling and chopping and slicing up potatoes.

I couldn't help but think about the kitchen back on the army base. Jed and his mom and me, peeling potatoes, getting the meals ready for the soldiers, the smell of the coffee filling the air. I wondered what Jed was doing right now.

"Come on," Sam said, grabbing me by the arm. He pulled me into a room off to the side of the kitchen. There was a woman — one of the women who had been serving us out front — waiting there.

"Hi, Betty, this is my friend, Tadashi."

"Any friend of Sam's is a friend of mine," she offered. "I got most of what you wanted," she said as she handed Sam a paper bag. What was she doing, giving him more stew? No, that made no sense.

"Thanks. How much do I owe you?" Sam asked.

"Four dollars and twenty-four cents."

Sam stuffed a hand into a pocket and pulled out some money. He held a roll of bills in his hand. He peeled off a dollar bill, and then another, and another, and a two-dollar bill. The roll still looked awfully big. He handed the bills to the woman and stuffed the rest back into his front pants pocket.

"Thanks," the woman said.

"I appreciate your help."

"Same for next week?" the woman asked.

Sam nodded.

"And would you like me to pick up some things for you?" Betty asked me.

What sort of things? What was in that bag? "No … no … that's okay," I said, holding up my hands.

"If you change your mind, let me know. It's no harder shopping for two than for one."

"I'll keep that in mind," I mumbled, although I didn't intend, or have the money, to have her buy anything for me.

We strolled back through the kitchen and again squeezed by the trucks as we left the building. Sam unfolded the top of the bag and peered inside.

"Still hungry?" Sam asked.

"Maybe a little," I admitted. Actually, I was very hungry.

"Here," Sam said as he handed me a chocolate bar. "Dessert."

"Thanks."

"Don't mention it. I have a lot of them."

"Is the whole bag filled with chocolate bars?" I asked in amazement.

"Not the whole bag. There's lots of chewing gum, and some candy and licorice and this," he said as he pulled a newspaper out of the bag. "Today's paper."

The gum I should have expected, but the newspaper I didn't understand.

"You have to know what's going on out there," he said, answering my unspoken question. "My father tells me, but he isn't allowed to bring the newspaper back in to the camp. Nobody is."

"What do you mean?" I asked.

"Just like there's no radios allowed, there are no newspapers allowed in here. They want us to know nothing." Sam paused. "Funny, I never used to read the paper at all, except for maybe the sports pages, before I came here. Now I try and read it every chance I get. Let's see what's happening today."

Sam sat down and rested his back against a tree. He opened up the paper. I looked around. There were people visible in the distance. If he wasn't supposed to have a paper, was this a good place to read it, where anybody, including one of the soldiers or RCMP officers, could see him? Sam didn't seem worried at all.

"Here, look at this story," Sam said, tilting the paper toward me.

In big bold type the headline read, "Japs A Threat." I started to read the first column, but Sam pulled it away from me.

"There's one of those on the front page almost every day. The worst, though, aren't here but in the letters-to-the-editor section. I'll show you," Sam said as he started to flip through the paper. He folded it over and started to run his finger down the columns.

"Here's one! Let me read it to you," Sam said. "'And the continued presence of the Japanese could spell the difference between freedom and slavery for Canada. Only a fool doesn't understand the danger of the yellow peril' — and now I don't understand this part … maybe he was … yeah, he was answering another letter to the editor … I'll go on. 'Would the Japanese be so kind to us? How can you expect them to adhere to Christian values when they are nothing more than heathens? I for one am not prepared to allow them to circulate on the streets amongst us.'" Sam abruptly folded the paper back up and stuffed it into the bag again.

"It's all so stupid that it just drives me crazy!"

Sam got back to his feet, and then looked at his watch. "I better get going. My parents should be coming in soon. How about if I call on you tomorrow? Maybe we can get into a baseball game."

"I'd like that."

"Good. Do you know how to get back to your building from here?"

"I think so," I said. I wasn't that sure, but I wasn't going straight back anyway. I was going to go back into the mess hall to find my family.

"Okay, see you tomorrow."

•••

I lay on the mattress beside my grandmother with all my family, except my father, around me. It was dark, but there was more than enough light for me to make out my sisters, sleeping just over from me. Behind them, the bars of the stall were still visible. Staring straight up I could make out the vague outline of the beams high above my head.

More than what I could see, though, was what I could hear. The night was continually disturbed by the sounds of the hundreds of people sleeping or not sleeping, lying in the dark all around me. The darkness was continually disturbed by the sound of coughing. Loud and low, or quiet and high-pitched. Behind that I could hear the occasional rumble of conversation — too quiet for me to make out any of the words, but loud enough to know words were being spoken. Maybe in the next stall, or the next. Certainly not coming from far away. Three ... no, four times, a baby had started to cry, and then, as if answering the call, another baby would join in the chorus and the sound would come over the walls from two directions. I'd been woken up by Yuri when she was a baby, but somehow this was different. Somewhere out there among the stalls, a baby I didn't even know was crying out and waking me, snatching away the few moments of sleep I'd managed to steal. But I wasn't angry. I knew exactly how that baby felt. Exactly.

And then I heard it again. The slow, steady, click, click, click of boots against the cement floors. I pictured them passing by, maybe one or two rows over. I knew they'd be going right past us in a few minutes. They passed right by every fifteen minutes or so. The third time they'd passed I'd gotten out of my bed, pushed back the blanket slightly and peeked out. It was two RCMP officers, walking by, patrolling. The first couple of times they'd passed by I'd wondered why they were there. But, of course, it was obvious. They weren't there to protect us, but to guard us.

.10.

I sat bolt upright, my eyes wide open, momentarily blinded by the bright light, my heart pounding, unsure where I was. Then I saw my mother and grandmother and sisters, and all our things spread around me in the stall.

"Bad dream?" my mother asked.

"The dream was okay," I said quietly. It was the waking up that was bad.

"My dolls slept well," Yuri said, holding them up for me to see.

"That's good," I answered. I hardly ever saw her now without at least two of them tucked under her arm or in her hands.

I got up and stretched. Everybody else was already dressed. How late had I slept? I looked down at my watch. It was just before eight o'clock in the morning. Almost the time I'd arranged to meet Sam. I poked my head out of the stall. I half expected him to be there waiting for me. Instead I saw stalls reaching down the aisle, each with some sort of blanket or cover blocking the bars. I climbed up onto the bottom rung of the gate so I could see over the stalls. Of course, all I could see were other stalls in other rows, stretching out in all directions. There had to be hundreds and hundreds of stalls, and in each one was a family — like us. I heard there were over a thousand people, many times more than my entire village, all together under this one big roof, all crammed together in these stalls, like cattle. No, not like cattle. They'd never put this many animals in each stall.

"I've got to go and use the facilities," I said.

"And you'll soon be ready for breakfast?" my mother asked.

"Sure, I guess. I just have to wash up and get changed and I'll —"

"Do we have to wait for him?" Midori asked.

"I'm hungry," Yuri added.

"That's okay," I said. "You should all go ahead. I'll catch up after I'm done."

My mother looked reluctant to leave, but Yuri grabbed her by the hand and started to drag her away, while Midori took one of my grandmother's hands and did the same.

"Tadashi?" my mother said, asking if it was all right.

"Sure, it's okay, don't worry," I answered. It wasn't like I was going to get lost — especially with a big fence ringing us in. "My friend Sam is meeting me here soon anyway. I'll come to breakfast with him."

As they started away my grandmother turned back to me. "Be careful."

"Be careful of what?" I asked.

Her face took on a thoughtful and serious look. "Everything."

Her answer startled me, and I watched as they walked away, weaving between groups of women and children who were standing outside their stalls or milling about along the cement corridor. They stopped to talk to a woman and her small children. I didn't know the woman. In fact, the people from our village, the people I'd lived with my entire life, were scattered. It wasn't just that they weren't occupying the stalls close to ours; they were in different buildings. It was almost as if they had deliberately separated us ... no, it probably wasn't deliberate, it was just that they didn't think it mattered.

I looked down at my watch again. It was time I got moving myself. I didn't want to miss meeting Sam. I didn't even know which building he was staying in.

I quickly unbuttoned my shirt, the one I'd worn yesterday and then to sleep, and replaced it with a second. I grabbed the small bag that contained a comb, toothbrush, a piece of soap and a washcloth. I wanted to wash up a little, at least if there wasn't too much of a lineup to use the sink. Last night there'd been lineups just to use the toilets. I'd finally just gone outside and went against the building, partially hidden by some bushes. It wasn't the first time in my life I'd ever gone to the washroom outside, but it was different being in the middle of the park, surrounded by thousands of people, instead of in a forest or out at sea.

At least I had the choice of going outside. The women and girls, who made up most of the people in the building, were in a line that stretched much, much further than the one I'd abandoned. Of course, everybody in the line stood there, quietly and patiently, waiting their turn. I'd been back at the stall, lying down trying to sleep, for more than an hour before everybody had finished and returned.

I hoped that because it was later, and most people had already headed for breakfast, the line wouldn't be too bad now.

Up ahead I spied the washroom doors. There were maybe a half dozen women and children extending out of the open door of the one washroom. The other door, to the men's, was closed. If there was a line, it certainly couldn't be too long.

I pushed open the door. There were four boys, all of them much younger than me, standing at the sinks. It looked like they'd been splashing each other, playing, but they stopped when I entered. I was sad I'd disturbed their fun. A fifth boy, no older than six or seven years of age, stood off to the side, a towel draped over his shoulder, waiting his turn. There were legs peeking out from under two of the four washroom stalls. The other two were empty and the doors gaped open invitingly. I took the invitation. Closing the door and sliding the latch into place to lock it, I slipped down my pants and sat down.

Other than the sound of splashing water in the sinks outside the stall, there was no other noise. I was suddenly struck by the thought that this was probably the first time I'd been out of sight of other people completely since we'd first got on the fishing boat to come down the coast. There was nobody with me or watching me for a brief moment. I was grateful that there was nobody waiting for the stall because I had the urge to just sit in there for a while, by myself. That certainly wasn't possible on the boat, and even less of a reality here in the park.

It would be so nice now to just go for a walk in the woods by myself. That was something I used to do all the time. Walk through the woods, or down by the shore, or maybe even climb up on the rocks that overlooked the village. I'd give anything to just get away, instead of being locked up here. Maybe I should take Sam up on that offer and head out of the park for a while. I wouldn't be alone — and being with Sam meant never having more than a few seconds of silence — but at least I'd be able to walk where I wanted to go.

Then again, maybe he didn't really know a way out, and he was just trying to impress me. I didn't know if he was *all* talk, but I did know he was a *lot* of talk. I'd never met anybody as talkative as him. I would have bet he talked in his sleep … or at least chewed gum in his sleep.

I heard the door creak open again. One of the sinks might be free, or maybe other people were lining up for it and I didn't have time to wait much longer, or —

"What are you doing in there?" called out a voice as a fist pounded against the door of my stall.

I practically jumped to my feet, my heart leaping up into my throat. Who was it and what did he want? I'd started to fumble with my pants before it struck me who it was — Sam.

"Come on, Tadashi, hurry up!" Sam called out.

I wanted to yell something back, open the door and smack him for frightening me like that, but I didn't want to let him know how much he'd actually scared me. I took a deep breath.

"What are you doing in there, anyway?" Sam asked.

"Guess." He must have seen me coming into the washroom.

"I don't want to guess. I want you to hurry."

"Why, are they going to run out of food?" I asked, as I opened the door.

"They won't run out of food, but they *will* run out of places on the field," he said, holding up a baseball glove in one hand.

"I can't play baseball until I've washed up and eaten."

"No time."

"What's the rush?"

"I told you. If they pick the teams before we get there, then we won't be able to play until somebody leaves. That could take till lunchtime. Just throw some water on your face and come on."

"I still have to have breakfast." After not eating much last night, I had woken up very hungry.

"No need to go for breakfast," Sam said. "Breakfast has come for you." He held up a paper bag. "Here."

"I don't want candy for breakfast," I said, recognizing the bag he'd been passed in the kitchen last night.

"Candy? I wouldn't get you candy for breakfast … not that I haven't had it myself a few times. Have a look."

I took the bag and opened it up. There was an apple, a hunk of yellow cheese and a big slab of white bread. The bread was so fresh it still had steam rising from it.

"Thanks," I said, taking out the bread and taking a big bite. "But we have to stop at the mess hall on the way so I can tell my mother what I'm doing."

"The mess hall isn't on the way, it's in the completely opposite direction, and you don't have to tell your mother because I already did."

"You did?"

"I ran into them on the way here and told them." Sam smiled. "Now can we get moving or do I have to wash your face for you as well?"

"I think I can handle that by myself," I replied.

•••

It was hard work keeping up with Sam, taking a quick bite, chewing and swallowing as we moved. There was no way I could eat, breathe, move fast and talk, so I didn't say a word as we trotted along. Occasionally I'd grunt out a response to one of Sam's continual questions or comments. It quickly became apparent that the only thing that moved faster than Sam's feet was his mouth. This boy could hold both sides of a conversation and still keep interrupting himself.

We cut between a cluster of buildings. There certainly were a lot of buildings here, and I wondered if I'd ever be able to find my way around. All around us there were people moving or standing or squatting on the ground, but while they seemed to be sticking to the paths, we were traveling between and around the backs of the buildings. At first I just thought that Sam was taking us along the shortest route to the field. Then, when we took a few turns that seemed to lead us back in what I felt was the wrong direction, I figured that he really didn't know his way around this place as well as he'd bragged.

We left behind the last of the buildings and cut across a field. This looked familiar. This was the way we'd come back yesterday after getting the ice cream. That meant that the racetrack was just over to the left. I peered off to that side and saw the grandstand in the distance. It was reassuring to know my way around at least a little bit.

How strange it was to be in a place you didn't know. I'd spent my whole life in the same village. The shore, the rocks, the paths through the forest were all so second nature to me. And even if I was in a part of the forest I didn't know, I still knew where the sun was in the sky and how to get back to where things were familiar. This was all so different.

"Damn!" Sam cursed, skidding to a stop.

"What's wrong?"

"Look. They've already started playing," he said, pointing up ahead.

We were coming at a baseball field, directly behind center field. There was a waist-high chain-link fence that curved around the whole outfield. Behind that was the green of the outfield, the infield glistening brightly, reflecting the sun, then a backstop and bleachers, maybe ten or fifteen rows high. On the field was a team, and a batter was in the box. The pitcher let loose with a throw and I heard the sound of the bat cracking out a hit. I couldn't see the flight of the ball at first, but watching the reaction of the right fielder I caught sight of it just before it flew into his glove. Beautiful catch!

"We might as well go back," Sam said, turning around.

"But aren't there two more fields?"

"There are, but they're not playable. They've started to store vehicles in the outfields of both. Let's go back."

"Wait," I said, putting a hand on his arm. "Let's go closer and have a look."

"What's the point?" he said with a shrug. "The game has started, and we might as well do something else. We can come back around noon when some of the guys will want to leave to get something to eat."

"How about if we stay for a while? Watching baseball isn't as good as playing, but what else do we have to do?"

I thought about suggesting to Sam that we head out under the fence, the way he'd suggested yesterday, but I chickened out. Maybe later.

"I guess we could stay and watch. Who knows, maybe somebody will get hurt and we can get into the game."

We walked along the outside of the outfield fence. I watched the game as we walked. The batter hit a little dribbler to the shortstop, who tossed it to first for an easy out. It must have been the third out of the inning, as the one side trotted to its bench while the other team took to the field. There were probably twenty or thirty people sitting in the bleachers — mainly men, but also a couple of kids around our age, who were probably waiting for a game as well. We settled into the stands, a few rows back behind first base, just as the pitcher took the first warm-up pitch of the inning. He reared back and unleashed a pitch that hit the catcher's glove with a loud smack. He looked like he had some stuff. The pitcher — and, actually, all the players I could see — were at least a few years older than me and Sam. It might be better for us to watch at first until I at least saw how good these guys were.

The first batter of the inning settled into the box. The pitcher reared back and let loose. The ball hit the catcher's glove a split second after the batter swung and missed. That ball had a lot of heat. The catcher tossed it back out to the pitcher. The second pitch came in high and tight, and the batter jumped back and hit the dirt. The batter leaped to his feet almost as fast as he'd been knocked down. He said something to the pitcher — it was Japanese, but I didn't know the word. Apparently the pitcher did understand. He took a few steps toward the batter, said some words back, also in Japanese, and while I knew what he was saying, I also knew it was physically impossible for the batter to do what he'd suggested. A few of the players, from both sides, called out for them to get back to playing. The pitcher turned and went back to the mound, while the batter settled into the box. The pitch came in hard and flat, and the batter threw out his bat, catching the ball against the end. The ball squirted out, threading itself between the shortstop and third baseman, almost as if it had eyes. The batter, his eyes only on first base, sprinted full out for the bag, not even daring to turn his head to look, not knowing that he'd lucked out a bloop single.

I had to admire the way he ran down to first, hoping that something good would happen, that maybe it would get through like it did, or the shortstop would boot the ball or fumble it, or maybe the throw to first would sail high and wide. What was he doing now?

The runner had taken a wide pass at first and had made the turn toward second. The outfielder hadn't come up hard enough on the hit, figuring it was a guaranteed single but that nobody would try to stretch it into a double. And now the runner was trying to make his dribbler into an extra-base hit. His hat flew off as he came barreling toward second. The second baseman scrambled over, covering the bag, ready to take the throw, as the outfielder ran forward, scooped the ball bare-handed and whipped a throw. It was a perfect strike, right into the second baseman's glove! He had the ball and position at the bag well before the runner got there. I expected the runner to hit the dirt and try to hook a foot to the base to avoid the tag, but instead he stayed upright, on his feet, and collided with the second baseman. A split second after I saw the collision, both bodies flying, I heard the crunch of the impact. The second baseman lay dazed in a crumbled heap five feet behind the bag, the ball loose and still rolling away, while the runner got back to his feet and placed one foot on the bag, yelling that he was "safe" and pointing to the ball on the ground.

There was a pause, no more than a second or two long, when nobody and nothing moved, and even the ball stopped dead in the long grass. Then all hell broke loose.

The shortstop came charging over like a bull and broadsided the runner, sending him reeling backwards, and all the players on the field and all the players on the bench came running together into a huddle around second base. There was screaming and swearing and pushing and shoving, and two men started wailing away at each other with their fists. And then the people in the stands, even the old men who had been sitting there in their shirts and hats and ties, scrambled off the bleachers. I stood up and Sam forcibly grabbed me by the arm.

"What are you doing?" Sam demanded.

"I was just going to —"

"Going to get yourself beaten up?" he interrupted. "It's not our fight."

"I wasn't going to fight anybody!" I protested.

"But how do you know that some anybody isn't going to fight you? Let's stay clear."

That made sense. It had already started to settle down out on the field, and what was I going to do out there anyway? The players who had wanted to fight were being separated by those who were more calm and by the old men who had waded out onto the field and were hollering out orders for everybody to behave.

The poor second baseman, forgotten in the scuffle, was still in the same spot where he'd fallen but was now sitting up, rubbing his jaw. He started to his feet, uneasily, and that brought attention to him. He was offered support and helped off the field. Players started milling around, picking up fallen hats or reclaiming gloves that had been abandoned on the ground.

"I've never ever seen a baseball game become a fight," I said.

"I have. Three times," Sam answered.

"Vancouver sure must have some tough baseball."

"Not Vancouver, Hastings Park. All those fights I've seen were on this field in the past two weeks."

"Come on," I said in disbelief.

He shook his head. "And I know for a fact it's safer to be here than down there."

"It sounds like … have you been in a fight out there?"

Again he nodded and a sly smile crept onto his face. "He had it coming. He was jabbering away at me in Japanese. I wasn't going to take any garbage from him."

"But you don't understand Japanese, so how do you know what he was even saying?" I demanded.

"I don't need to know the language to know he wasn't asking me how my mother was, so I took a swing at him."

"And then?"

He shrugged. "And then the same thing as what happened here. A bunch of people rolled around on the ground, a few punches were dished out and then … we played ball, like they are," he said, motioning with his hand.

In front of us the players had all resumed their positions either on the field or on the bench — all except the second baseman. Somebody else had taken his place on the field, and he was sitting down off to the side. He still looked a little glassy-eyed. Two of the older men were standing over him. One was barking out questions like "Where are you?" and "What is your name?" to see if he was okay. He repeatedly shook his head and mumbled out replies I couldn't hear. Somebody else brought him a canteen and he took a long drink. He seemed fine to me.

"So, do you still want to stick around?" I asked.

"We could," Sam said. "Or maybe we could try something else."

"Like what?" I asked.

"I don't know. Maybe we could go for a walk … you know, into town."

.11.

"You want to go out of the park? Now?" I asked.

"Sure ... why not?"

"Couldn't we get into trouble?" I asked.

"Only if they catch us, and I'm not too worried about the guards here at the park."

"You're not? Then what are you worried about?"

"You saw that one headline in the paper. Some of the people out there in the city aren't too happy to see Japs wandering around. I've heard stories of people giving Japanese a hard time. Being told they couldn't come into stores — even guys being beaten up."

"Maybe we shouldn't go outside," I said. Then I thought, "Wait a second. Stories." Working around an army base, I knew all about rumors and stories and how far they get from the truth.

"Have you actually talked to somebody who was beaten up?" I asked.

"No, but I've heard from people who've talked to people who —"

"Heard from somebody else who's cousin knew somebody who ..." I paused. "Just rumors. How about your father? You said he goes out all the time. Has he been hassled?"

"He said that people are looking at him funny," Sam answered.

"That I can handle. Has anything happened to you

when you've been out?"

Sam didn't answer. That meant one of two things: either something bad had happened or … "You *have* been outside the park, haven't you?"

"Sure. Three or four times."

Somehow his tone of voice didn't match the words.

"I've gone out with my father."

"You mean on passes? Through the front gate? I thought you'd snuck out under the fence."

"I didn't say that," he mumbled.

"But the way you were talking about knowing the spot to get out and —"

"I *do* know the spot," he interrupted. "I've even seen somebody go under."

The best lie is half the truth — another one of my grandmother's sayings.

He shrugged. "I can go out with my father and Betsy brings me back the newspapers and candy. I don't need to sneak out."

"So why are you suggesting it now?"

Sam spat out his gum, the wad sailing through the air. "Maybe I just need to go out," he said. "Maybe because you haven't been here as long as me you don't feel the same."

"You mean trapped?" I asked.

"Exactly! Trapped. It would feel good just to step outside the fence. I bet ya the air even feels better on that side of the fence. So do you want to go?"

"Maybe." I definitely wanted to go. The question was, did I have the nerve to go?

"Have you ever been in Vancouver before?"

"Just coming here in the truck from our boat," I admitted.

"I could show you some of it. Do you want me to show you the city?" Sam asked. "I'll keep you safe. I really don't have enough friends that I can risk losing one."

Friends … I guess that's what we'd become. My mind raced back up to Rupert and my best friend Jed. I couldn't think of anybody less like Jed than Sam and his constant talking, interrupting, gum chewing — but yeah, he was the closest thing I now had to a friend.

"I'd like to come along."

"Good. Any special place you want to go?"

I shook my head. "It would be good just to leave and walk around free, that's all."

"That sounds good. Maybe we can even get some lunch out there."

"I thought we were going to eat here first," I said.

"Not a good idea. What if we run into your family or mine and they ask what we're going to do? Would your parents let you sneak out?"

"No," I said in astonishment. "My father would never give me permission."

"Mine neither," Sam admitted. "And that's why we're not going to ask permission. They can't say no to a question they've never been asked. Come on, follow me."

As we moved toward the fence I became increasingly uneasy. I got the feeling Sam wasn't feeling so comfortable either. For once, Sam wasn't talking much. Most of the sound coming out of his mouth was from the chomping of his gum. He seemed to be chewing faster to make up for not talking. And strangely, as his mouth motored quicker his feet got slower. Sam was walking at my pace rather than me having to race to keep up with him.

"The place to get out is just up ahead," Sam said.

"Yeah," I answered instinctively. "But we don't have to go."

"Sounds like you're scared," he taunted.

"Not me!" I said defiantly. "How about you?"

"Me? It was my idea to go … remember?" Sam said, sealing off our last chance.

We were walking along a stretch of fence parallel to

the busy street where we'd got the ice cream last night. There sure were a lot of cars in Vancouver.

Sam stopped walking. "This is where we get out."

"Where?"

"Right here," Sam said, pointing down.

There was a stretch of fence, maybe ten or twelve feet long, where the ground had been washed away, opening up a gap of about eight inches or so under the fence. It didn't look like much, but I guessed we could wiggle out. Somehow I was expecting something different. Maybe a hole or a gap between posts or something. But more troubling than the small size of the gap was what surrounded it. I'd figured we'd have some cover instead of being on a busy street. There was no place to hide and no way we could get out without half a dozen of the passing cars seeing us.

"Isn't there a better place, some place where there's cover?" I asked.

""This is the only place I know where people have gotten out."

"And they didn't get caught?"

"If they had, don't you think they would have sealed off the spot?"

"I guess so."

"The nearest gate and guardhouse are around the corner on Renfrew Street, so as long as you watch out for the sentries, then —"

"Sentries! There are sentries?" I questioned, looking up and down the fence for them. I was relieved to see nobody.

"Of course. Weren't there sentries at that base where you worked?"

"Yeah, there are always sentries at a military base."

"Then why are you surprised? This is a military base — actually, a military prison."

Of course, Sam was right. That's what it was, a prison,

and we were prisoners. I looked up and down the length of the fence again, this time more carefully. There was still nobody in sight. The only people around were in the cars and trucks racing by.

"We'll be seen by the cars," I said.

Sam shrugged. "They'll see us, but so what? It isn't like they'll stop even if they do notice. After you," Sam said, gesturing to the hole.

I really had second thoughts about this, but I didn't figure there was any way to back out now. I looked at the gap and then took one more quick glance up and down the length of the fence. There were no sentries in sight. I took a deep breath and dropped to my knees.

"Your best bet is to slide out on your back," Sam said.

"I figured that," I replied, even though I had been considering going out on my belly.

If I was going to go I had to move fast. I flipped over and grabbed the bottom of the fence with my hands. I pulled myself forward, a couple of rocks trapped underneath me digging into my back as I slid along. I turned my head slightly to the side to allow my nose to slip beneath the fence. My shoulders passed next and I rotated my arms, grabbing the fence from the other side, and pulled myself through. In a quick motion I jumped to my feet.

I looked around anxiously, half expecting some guard to leap out of somewhere and grab me by the scruff of the neck and frogmarch me to the gate. But there was nobody. The cars kept racing by, ignoring me like I was invisible.

"Come on," I urged Sam, who was standing on the other side of the fence, grinning at me. "Hurry."

"Naaawww," Sam replied, shaking his head. "I don't think I'm coming."

"You're what?!"

"Not coming. Too dangerous. I'm going back to the

mess for a snack. See you later," he said. Sam turned around and started to walk away, and my jaw dropped to the ground.

Suddenly Sam spun around. Almost in one motion he dropped to the ground, flipped to his back, pulled himself under the fence and then popped back to his feet.

"You should have seen your face," he laughed. "You really thought I was chickening out, didn't you?"

"Well ..."

"I stick by my friends. We better get moving."

"Yeah, we better." I turned away from the fence and took a step forward but I was grabbed from behind.

"Watch out!" Sam yelled as a car raced by just inches in front of my face.

"I didn't see it!" I stammered as I staggered back another step.

"I figured you weren't trying to get killed. Follow me."

I nodded my head.

Sam stepped off the curb into the first lane. There was a big truck coming in that lane, but it was still a long way off.

Sam turned back. "Are you coming?"

Again I nodded my head. On shaky legs I stepped out onto the road and stopped right beside Sam. A car passed by in the second lane, and Sam started walking again. I scurried after him, bumping against him as he stopped in the very middle of the road, and anxiously looked off to the side for more oncoming vehicles. Sam mumbled something under his breath. Two cars passed by in the other direction, then there was a large gap in the traffic. I ran across the lanes, not stopping until I reached the safety of the sidewalk.

"So now that we're out, where do you want to go?" Sam asked.

"I don't know. How about if we just walk?"

"Sure. Let's get off the main street. Down this way."

Just up ahead a smaller street ran off to the side. As we walked along the sounds of the traffic faded into the distance. I found myself feeling a little more at ease. We were out, nobody had seen or noticed, and we were free.

The houses here were very similar to the ones I'd seen through the fence. They were all very neat and tidy, with carpets of thick, green grass and flowers, lots of flowers, filling the front gardens.

While there were lots of houses, there weren't many people to go along with them. There was an old man cutting his lawn, and an older couple sitting on their porch, but we didn't pass anybody on the sidewalk. Where was everybody? Then it dawned on me — it was a weekday. All the kids were in school, and many of the adults would have been at work.

"You thirsty?" Sam asked.

"Yeah, I could use a drink," I said. "But I don't see anyplace where we can —"

There was an old man right up ahead, watering his grass. We stopped on the sidewalk in front of his house.

"Excuse me, sir," Sam said. "Do you think we could have a drink?"

The man turned to face us. There was a quizzical look on his face.

"From the hose," Sam said, pointing.

"Oh ... yeah ... sure," he said as he offered Sam the hose.

"Thanks," Sam said as he walked up the driveway.

He held the hose to the side of his face and a stream of water cut across his mouth, spattering and splashing as he lapped up the liquid. Satisfied, he handed it to me. The water was cold and delicious. I drank greedily. It traced a cool path down my throat.

"Thank you," I said as I handed the hose back to the man.

"Water never tastes better than it does from a hose," Sam said.

The old man chuckled. "That's exactly what I always say!"

To my surprise the old man put the hose up to the side of his mouth and slurped away at the water. He looked up at us. "I don't see many of your kind around here anymore."

"Our kind?" Sam asked.

"You know, Japanese."

"You thought we were Japanese?" Sam asked.

I tried to keep my face blank and not register my surprise at his answer.

"You're not?"

"No, we're Chinese. Lots of people can't tell us apart," Sam said.

"I guess I'm one of them." He paused. "'Course, I don't know many of either type. My laundry man is Chinese, and I get my fresh vegetables from a truck that sits at the side of the road on Saturday mornings ... I think he's a Jap ... he's gone now ... and then there's my gardener. He's Japanese. You look a lot like him," he said, pointing at me.

"He does look a little bit Japanese," Sam agreed. "Now me, I look Chinese."

The man nodded his head. Actually, Sam did look less Japanese than I did. It wasn't his features, his nose or eyes or skin color, because they were as Japanese as mine, but more the way he walked and the expression on his face.

"You have a beautiful garden," I said, wanting to change the subject. His garden was filled with flowers.

"Thank you," he beamed. "It's my pride and joy. Although I have to tell you, it's usually even nicer than this, but since my gardener has been taken away I've been hard pressed to maintain it." He shook his head slowly. "It made no sense to have him leave."

"You mean you don't think they should have locked up all those Japanese?" I asked. Maybe it was more than just the people up in Prince Rupert who thought it was wrong.

"He was old, a few years my senior, and a fine gentleman. The man was a gardener, not a spy." He shrugged. "But I guess the government didn't have much choice."

"I don't know about that," I stated. "Maybe they could have just —"

"The government did the right thing," Sam said, interrupting me. "Everybody knows some of those Japs are nothing but spies."

Sam's words so shocked me that I didn't know what to say.

"Maybe you boys should get yourselves those badges," the old man said.

"What badges?" I asked.

"You must have seen them. I've seen a lot of you Chinese wearing them on your shirts. You know those badges. They say 'I Am Chinese' or something like that."

"Oh, *those* things. We both have one. We wear them sometimes — all our family does. We call them buttons, not badges. But we forgot to bring them today," Sam said. "Thanks for the drink, mister, we better get going."

"Take care, boys."

We traveled a few houses down the street in silence.

"Why were you saying things about the Japanese being spies?" I asked angrily.

"I had to say something to cover for you. Why didn't you just wave a big Japanese flag in front of him, so he could call the authorities on us?"

"I was just —"

"Being stupid," Sam interrupted. "Don't get caught defending the Japanese. We're Chinese, remember, and the Chinese don't even like the Japanese, so why would they defend them? Especially now with the war on and the Japanese invading China."

I had to admit that he was right about that. I didn't really know many Chinese people — there were only a couple of families in Prince Rupert — but I'd heard the things my parents and grandmother said sometimes about Chinese people, and they weren't very flattering. My grandmother, who hardly ever had a bad word to say about anybody, called the Chinese "dogs." And I guess if we felt that way about them, they wouldn't think much better of us.

"I can't believe he thought we were Chinese," I said.

"Why wouldn't he? All Asians look more or less the same to whites. Heck, they all look pretty much the same to me!" He paused. "But the old guy gave me an idea. We've got to get ourselves a couple of those buttons."

"You're kidding."

"We can slap those on our shirts and then we can go just about anywhere in the whole city."

"We can't just pretend we're Chinese."

He shrugged. "It worked with the old man."

"But that doesn't mean we can fool other people."

"Why not?"

"Well, for one thing, can you speak Chinese?"

"Of course not, but so what? I can't speak Japanese either."

"Well, what if that old man had asked us to say something in Chinese?" I asked.

"I can't think of any reason in the entire world why he would do that," Sam said. "But I could just mumble something in a sing-song voice."

"But that wouldn't work if we bumped into somebody who really is Chinese and wanted to talk to us. I don't think they'd be fooled by our pretending to speak Chinese."

"We could pretend we're Chinese who just don't speak Chinese."

"Not a word? Nobody's that stupid."

"Maybe you have a point. Then we'll stay away from Chinatown, and if we do see any other people anywhere who look like they might be Chinese, we'll take off quick and avoid them. Doesn't that all make sense?"

It did, and that scared me. "I guess it could work … if you actually had a couple of those buttons."

"Leave that to me," Sam said. "I'll figure it out."

I had the urge to argue with him, but somehow I thought that if anybody could arrange it, it would be Sam.

"Maybe we should head back," I suggested.

"I think you're right. Let's get back to the park. We can come out longer the next time … after I get the buttons."

.12.

I hurried out of the washroom. The lineup was getting bigger each morning, but that was only to be expected as the population of the park grew each day — the pool was getting deeper. I heard that they were now putting families in the old pig stalls. I'd heard they were smaller and smelled even worse than the cattle stalls. I couldn't imagine that.

I looked at my watch. It was almost eight o'clock. If I didn't hurry there wouldn't be much left to eat for breakfast. I'd agreed to meet Sam at eight-thirty, so if I hurried I could eat and get there on time. He was usually late, but I was still going to try and be on time.

As I turned into the stall I wasn't surprised to see both my sisters all dressed up. My family had washed and gone for breakfast before I'd even risen. My grandmother was carefully combing Yuri's hair while my mother helped put a clip in Midori's.

"There, you are both ready for your first day of school," my mother said.

I shook my head in disbelief. "I still can't believe that they went ahead and set up a school."

"School is important," my mother said.

I guess I really shouldn't have been surprised. I'd heard talk from the first day we arrived in Hastings Park that people were worried about their children "losing their year" at school. How crazy was that? People were forced out of their houses, had to sleep in cattle stalls, had virtually no idea where we'd all be heading, and they were worried about their children not getting a proper education. How Japanese.

"Blackboards have been found, paper, pencils. Even chairs and desks have been found and placed in a building."

"What about teachers?" I asked.

"Some of the women in the camp *are* teachers at the Japanese schools. They have volunteered to school children," my mother explained.

I'd heard about the Japanese schools. In Vancouver there were dozens of them. Places where kids of Japanese descent used to go on Saturdays to learn Japanese and about Japan.

"And some of the high school students are to assist them," my mother added.

"But we're only going to be here a few weeks," I noted.

"A few weeks that won't be wasted. At least, for the younger children," my mother said.

I tried not to smile, because of course I knew what she meant — the school had been set up only for those in the seventh form or lower. Just another reason to be grateful for being in eighth grade. Going to school was about the last thing in the world I wanted to do.

"Could you bring your sisters to school?" my mother asked.

"We don't need him to —" Midori stopped in mid-sentence when she saw the look in my mother's eyes.

"What building are they using?" I asked.

"I can show you," Midori said. "It's not far from the front gate. They call the building the Forum."

I knew which one she meant. It was big, and strange shaped. Unfortunately, it was in the completely opposite direction of where I was going — the mess hall.

"Come on, let's go now," I said. My stomach was already grumbling and I wanted to drop them off as soon as possible.

Both girls picked up a small bundle of books that they had been working on since we left Prince Rupert. They said goodbye to my mother and grandmother and we headed down the aisle and toward the big barn door. At almost every stall we passed, there were also children being readied for school. Hair was being combed, faces were being given a last scrub with a washcloth, as children, books in hand, stood waiting in good clothing, standing with their friends or playmates. They were chatting together, laughing, playing, smiling, all excited. Their mothers also clustered together at the entrances to their stalls and talked to their neighbors. I caught little snippets of conversation as I passed. They were talking about the school, and the weather and clothing, and ... all the sorts of things mothers talked about in our village as the children started off for school.

I stopped and Midori and Yuri kept walking, unaware that I had stopped. I looked all around at the scene being played out before me. If I looked at just the people, and not the place, we could have been in our village. Everybody seemed so cheerful, happy, excited. The children were skipping and playing. The mothers smiling and talking. Even the men being gone didn't seem out of place — they could just be out early working the fishing boats. If only it all wasn't being played out in a barn, cattle stalls covered with bedspreads. I closed my eyes and just listened. Soft voices, high-pitched laughter, the scuffling of feet —

"Tadashi!"

My eyes popped open. Midori was standing thirty feet in front of me, hands on her hips, Yuri at her side, looking very annoyed. That was just like our usual walks to school as well. I started walking again.

"What were you doing?" Midori demanded.

"Waiting for Jed."

"What are you talking about?"

"Nothing ... just joking. Come on."

That's what I would have been doing if we were heading to school from our village. As the girls hurried off, I would have stopped at the entrance to Jed's village and waited for him — he was always late, just like Sam. I guess they did have some things in common.

We moved along with the mothers and their children. We were just another part of an unofficial parade heading to the school. Yuri took my hand as we walked. Actually, I walked and she skipped along beside me. She and Midori held an animated discussion, hoping that they'd like their classmates and wondering if the teacher was going to be strict. I didn't say anything, but I knew she would be. After all, she was going to be Japanese. Not that I'd ever had a Japanese teacher — all the teachers in our school were white — but I just knew.

Soon the trickle of people flowing from our building joined into a bigger stream moving along the main path. As we passed each new building another trickle of children joined in. The stream was becoming a river. There were hundreds of kids going to school.

I hadn't thought about just how many children were in this camp. When we'd first arrived at the park, I was told there were over fifteen hundred people. That number had been dwarfed over the past week as more and more people arrived daily. I'd heard that there were now closer to three thousand. I didn't really know. I just knew the lineups were much longer at the mess, and even once you got your food it was hard to find a place to sit.

Along with the extra people came extra things. A small store was now housed just inside the main gate. It sold cold pop and candy and gum. Sam now only needed to get his newspapers from the outside, as these still weren't for sale to Japanese. A small infirmary, a place where people who were sick could go, had been set up in one of the buildings. Two of the interned Japanese were doctors and some of the women were experienced as either nurses or midwives, and they'd been assisting those needing help.

We stopped right outside the building that was now the school. It was large. Hopefully, large enough to hold all these kids. Outside the building were a number of tables. Behind each table sat two or three women. Over their heads were large hand-drawn signs in both English and Japanese to show students where to register for the different forms.

"Midori, you go over —"

"I know," she snapped. "I *can* read."

She walked off and took her place in a line with other kids her age. I walked Yuri over a couple of tables to take a place in the proper line.

All the kids seemed so excited and happy. For a split second I felt like maybe I was missing out on things. I usually did like school — at least, my old school.

"Hey, Tadashi!"

I turned around and saw Sam, his little sister Keiko — he called her Kay — in tow. They weaved through the crowd, waving, a big smile on Sam's face. As always, he was chewing gum a mile a minute. I waved back. They came over to us and we exchanged greetings. Yuri let go of my hand and took Kay's hand instead, pulling her into line beside her. They were the same age, and would be in the same grade. They'd gotten to know each other through me and Sam, and had played together a few times before. Like Sam, Kay spoke almost no Japanese.

We shuffled forward with the crowd, Sam and I making small talk, and the girls giggling and playing. Finally we reached the front and provided the necessary information — name, age, grade, school — for them to be put in the proper class. The girls, still holding hands, waved to us and were led away by one of the teachers, disappearing into the building.

"I can't believe how happy my sister was about going to school," I said as we walked away.

"Mine too. Kay was just upset that it was only half a day long."

"But I heard that they might make it a full day later … even add the higher grades."

"I heard that too, but I figure we'll be long gone before they get around to that," Sam said. "I can think of a lot of better ways to spend my time than in some classroom."

"Yeah. So what do you want to do today?" I asked.

"We could play baseball."

"I guess we could." We'd played baseball every day for the past two weeks. I didn't think I'd ever get tired of playing ball, but somehow …

"Any other ideas?"

He smiled. "I had something else in mind."

"What did you —" I stopped in mid-sentence as I saw Toshio, a foul look on his face, standing right in front of me. Beside him were two other boys — more like men — his age.

Toshio stopped directly in front of me, blocking the path.

"You still here … you not white," Toshio said, spitting out the word, a smirk on his face.

"White?" Sam asked, turning to me.

"You don't understand," I said.

"Yellow on the outside … white on the inside. You too!" Toshio said, aiming his words at Sam.

"Me?" Sam questioned and then burst into a big smile. "Did you hear that? I'm white!"

Toshio looked confused by Sam's response.

"Take a hike, Toshio," I said.

"Hike?" he asked.

"Go away," I said in Japanese.

"You not tell me what to do. You not boss of Toshio. Toshio stay right here."

He spread his legs apart and put his hands on his hips, freezing like a statue.

I shrugged. "Suits me. Then we'll go."

I stepped off the path to go around him but was violently spun around by a hand on my shoulder, and found myself staring into Toshio's face.

Before I could even react, Sam stepped in between us and brushed Toshio's hand off my shoulder.

"Shooo!" Sam said, motioning with his hands like he was trying to scatter some birds.

Toshio looked taken aback. He turned to his two friends and spoke to them in Japanese — he told them that he thought Sam was a monkey. They both laughed. Thank goodness Sam didn't understand any Japanese or he might have been —

"The only monkey around here is you … and probably your mother!" Sam yelled.

How did he know what Toshio had said?

"Do you understand me, you stupid monkey-faced boy? Your mother's as ugly as a monkey. Understand?" Sam demanded.

There was no question that Toshio understood. Even if the words hadn't made sense, the tone was undeniable. Toshio moved in toward Sam. They were going to fight. I'd seen Toshio in action and knew how dangerous he could be. I went to move in to do something and one of Toshio's two new buddies — he looked like he was about twenty and bigger than me — stepped in front of me.

"Leave them alone," he said threateningly.

The second guy stepped forward too and nodded his head in agreement. Unless I was prepared to fight the two of them, Sam was on his own.

Toshio and Sam circled each other, sizing one another up. Sam was holding his arms high, hands folded into fists, like a prize fighter. Toshio was gliding, falling into judo poses ... Judo! Sam didn't know!

"Sam, be careful, he knows judo!" I called out.

"Good for him," Sam yelled back. "Soon he's going to know a beating."

"Stop!" yelled out a voice in Japanese, and an older man rushed forward.

He was about my grandmother's age. He had been sitting behind one of the tables where the children were being registered for school.

"Stop, right now!" he yelled again, repeating himself in English.

Toshio took a half-step back and lowered his guard as the old man stepped between him and Sam. Sam kept his hands up. The old man turned his head toward Sam and started to question him in Japanese.

"I don't understand Japanese!" Sam snapped back defiantly.

The old man looked slightly confused by Sam's statement, but nodded his head. "You can lower your defenses, there will be no fight."

Sam lowered his arms, but his fingers remained curled into fists and his facial expression remained angry.

The old man had surprised me. His English was perfect, with not even a trace of accent. Most of the old people, people his age, only spoke halting English, heavily tainted by Japanese accents.

He then turned to Toshio. "There will be no fight."

Toshio nodded. His eyes were on the ground.

"We didn't start it," Sam said. "These big tough men," he said, motioning first to Toshio and then to the other two flanking me, "came over here to pick a fight with us. Really tough, aren't you three? Couldn't you find any girls to fight? Big brave —"

"Silence!" the old man said, cutting Sam off.

I was surprised, and grateful, that Sam listened.

The old man looked at Toshio, then at Sam, then at me and finally at the two men who stood on either side of me. His expression hardened and I could see his eyes flare in anger. I think he'd seen what Sam had pointed out. In rapid-fire Japanese he asked the three why they were here, what business they had and if they had started the fight. They practically tripped over each other answering, apologizing and groveling.

He shook his head. "We have been herded into this park like animals. Many are sleeping in places where animals sleep. Fed like animals. Fenced in and restricted in our movements like animals. And when you fight ... you are acting like animals." He paused. "We are not animals. We are people. We have dignity. Dignity is not *where* you live, but *how* you live. Understand?"

"*Hai*," Toshio said, nodding his head, and his friends echoed out agreement. All three had their eyes firmly rooted on the ground. I nodded my head in agreement as well.

"And you?" he asked Sam. "Do you have anything more to say?"

"No ... no, sir."

Sam calling him "sir" surprised me. That wasn't like him.

"Good. It is now finished," the old man said. "Now I have business in the school and then in the city. I suggest you all get on with your business. And remember, acting like animals justifies being placed here. But when we act with dignity we shame those people who have put us here. Dignity. Like Japanese."

The old man walked into the school.

The crowd that had started to gather at the first signs of trouble had long since dispersed. People had begun to leave as soon as the old man arrived. It wasn't respectful for them to stay and witness what was happening, although I wasn't sure my curiosity would have let me leave if I had been standing on the sidelines watching.

I watched as the old man walked away. There were now very few children remaining to be registered. In typical, efficient Japanese style, the seemingly impossible task was nearly complete. Turning back around I was happy to see that Toshio and the other two were walking away and were already at a safe distance.

"I didn't recognize him at first," Sam said.

"Who?"

"The old man. Do you know who he is?" Sam asked.

I shook my head. "I was thinking maybe the principal of the school."

Sam laughed. "He's a lot more than that. That was Mr. Wakabayashi."

I shrugged. The name didn't mean anything to me.

"I heard he owns half of the Japanese businesses in Vancouver."

I shrugged. "Are there a lot of them?"

Sam shook his head, and his expression showed disbelief. "There's a stretch of stores and buildings along Powell Street from Main all the way to Campbell. Most of the businesses are Japanese, and he owns half of them. Even my father calls him 'sir.' Funny, I was surprised to see him here."

"Why?" I asked.

"First off, I figured he lived right in Vancouver, and they aren't making the Japanese in Vancouver leave their homes yet."

"Good thing. They couldn't fit everybody into this park," I said. "But maybe he doesn't live in Vancouver."

"Maybe, but even if he doesn't, I just figured that somebody as rich and powerful as him wouldn't have to come here." He paused. "I guess the color of his skin is more important than the color of his money. You eaten yet?" Sam asked.

I shook my head.

"Me neither. Let's get some grub."

"Sure, let's …" I let the sentence trail off as I realized that Toshio and his friends were walking ahead of us on the path to the mess hall.

"Don't worry about them," Sam said, reading my mind. "I could tell that they recognized Mr. Wakabayashi too. There won't be a problem. Besides, if he does decide to start something, I'll take care of it."

"I'm glad you're so confident."

"I would have cleaned his clock. Let's go."

"Don't be so sure of that," I said as we started to walk, trailing behind them at what I hoped was a safe distance. "You've never seen Toshio fight."

"You've never seen me fight either," Sam said.

"You talk a good fight, I'll give you that much."

"I can do more than talk. You get good at what you do often," Sam said.

"What do you mean?"

"I was about the only Japanese kid in my whole neighborhood. Besides me and my sister, there were only two other Japanese kids in my school and they were both girls."

"Yeah?"

"So you don't think I had practice fighting?"

"Why would …" I had an uneasy feeling that I knew why.

"Jap, gook, fish-breath … heck, I even got called a chink. Stupid idiot didn't even know enough to throw the right insults at me — he thought I was Chinese. When I started school I learned to fight. Older kids, bigger kids, more than one of them … I didn't care. I fought them all."

"Every day?"

"Every day in the beginning. Then every week, then every so often. The last few years I only seemed to have to fight when some new kid came to the school. I'd lay a beating on him and then everything would be okay."

"That would be hard ... not having any friends."

"What are you talking about? I had lots of friends. Lots. It's just that none of them were Japanese!" He shook his head. "Funny ... out there I used to get in fights because I was Japanese and here, when I'm surrounded by Japanese, some guy wants to pick a fight with me because I'm not Japanese enough — or I guess because *you* aren't Japanese enough."

"He's just stupid."

"I figured that part out, but why does he think you think you're white?"

"Because of my friends. I hang out with Japanese too, but lots of my friends, like my best friend, aren't Japanese."

"Big deal; *all* my friends are white."

"Jed's only part white. His mother is Tsimshian."

"Tsimshian?"

"Native Indian." Then in a flash I remembered something that had struck me as strange. "You said you didn't speak any Japanese, so how did you know what Toshio was saying?"

"I don't speak any Japanese, but I do understand some of it. Besides, even if I didn't understand the words, I would have known he wasn't asking if we wanted an ice cream."

"But you knew exactly what he called you."

"Called me?" Sam asked.

"You know, calling you a monkey," I explained.

"I thought he was talking about *you*. Maybe I still should give him a smack in the head. Idiot!" he screamed at Toshio, up ahead of us on the path.

"Don't start anything!" I said, trying to quiet him

down, relieved that Toshio hadn't turned around. He and his friends were some distance away and maybe he didn't hear him, or didn't understand the taunt.

"I'd like to show him who's a monkey! Monkey boy!" he yelled.

There was no response from up ahead. I had to do something to distract him.

"How can you understand Japanese but not speak it?" I asked.

"I used to know how to speak it. Up until the time I went to the first form, that was all I spoke," Sam explained.

"And what happened?"

"What happened was that kids made fun of me. And once I understood enough English to understand what they were saying, then I started fighting."

"But what's that got to do with not speaking Japanese?"

He shrugged. "I don't know. It just didn't make sense to speak a language that nobody understood, so I just stopped speaking it."

"What about at home, with your parents or your family?"

"They didn't say anything about it. They just spoke to me in English from then on."

"And what about your grandparents or other relatives?" I knew that a lot of the older people had almost no English.

"All my grandparents have been dead since before I can remember, and we don't hardly have any relatives. Both my parents are only children ... well, I guess my father did have a brother, but he died when they were kids. The only relatives we have are some cousins my mother has, and they live way up in Kamloops, so we hardly ever see them anyway."

I thought of all my relatives, some of whom lived in our village. And then there were the people I'd known all my life, people who had actually come from the same village in Japan as my grandparents, who weren't family, but were more than just neighbors. Sam didn't have any of that. He had friends, but friends weren't enough. Friends!

That reminded me that I'd been putting off writing that letter to Jed like I'd promised. I'd started to write him a half-dozen times. But each time, I got no more than a few lines in and the letter ended up in the trash. It wasn't that I didn't know what to tell him; I didn't know how to say it. How could I describe what was happening to us? Regardless of how hard it was, I'd have to do more than just try.

.13.

Sam and I shuffled along with the lineup, waiting our turn to get breakfast. I looked ahead, hoping for something different, but was certain it would be the same as always: toast with butter and jam, cold cereal, coffee and apple juice. And, of course, oatmeal, or what passed for oatmeal, a thin, bad-tasting gruel that was not very filling. And while I had to admit that there was always lots of it, it was never any different, and never any better. And worse yet, never Japanese.

Some of the people, especially the older ones, like my grandmother, were upset about the meals. For people who'd lived their lives eating nothing but traditional Japanese food, these meals were not just unrecognizable, but almost indigestible. They didn't need much. Just some rice, maybe some fish, some green tea … nothing that unusual or hard to get.

But it was also the way the food was served. Somehow, standing in line, holding a tray with metal plates and having the food scooped out of a big vat, wouldn't have been the same even if they had been serving Japanese food. There was just something about the food hitting the plate with a loud "splat" that would have made almost any food less appealing.

I was becoming worried about my grandmother. She was never a big eater, but here it seemed like she was eating nothing. She just sat there looking at the food, pushing it around her plate with a spoon, but hardly any of it was making it into her mouth.

I was pleased to see that the lineup was shorter then usual. Things seemed to be moving quickly. We got our meals and headed for a table. There were more empty spots this morning, and we sat by ourselves at a table away from everybody.

"I guess with everybody at school this morning there's less of a crowd," I commented.

"That's part of it," Sam said. "But I think it has to do with people leaving."

"People have left?"

He nodded his head and continued spooning in his oatmeal without looking up.

"Are you sure this isn't just a story? You know how stories go around."

"They cleared out some people from my building this morning. They were loading their belongings into trucks."

"Where have they gone to?"

"I heard the name New Denver."

"Where is that?" I asked.

"Somebody said it's in the mountains. Sort of a ghost town. I also heard rumors that some of the men have been shipped out to work camps in the mountains."

"What do you mean?"

"They're sending men out to places where they can do work on the roads or the railway. Haven't you heard your father talking about it?"

I shook my head. It wasn't like my father to ever talk about things that he didn't know for sure. And lately he'd been talking even less. He'd sit at the table with us in the mess hall and hardly utter a word. And when he did talk, it was almost like it wasn't even him talking. He seemed tired, or sad, or maybe just distracted. I knew he had a lot on his mind, but it was almost as if his body was sitting there but his mind and spirit were someplace else.

"My father's told me there's a lot of angry people. There's talk about separating men from their families," Sam said.

"You mean like they did here, putting them in a different building?"

"No, putting them in separate places."

"You're kidding," I said, a chill running up my spine.

"Just stories. Maybe they mean nothing. Maybe they mean something." Sam continued to shovel in his breakfast, but I suddenly didn't feel so hungry.

"I've heard them say that maybe they'll ship us all back to Japan," Sam continued.

"How can they ship us *back* to someplace we've never been?" I asked incredulously.

Sam shrugged. "Also heard about families being sent right across the country … maybe have us staying at farms and working the fields."

"Where do you get all these stories?" I asked.

"My father told me some. Others I've just heard the men talking about when they're playing cards … you know, during the evening when I go over to visit my father."

"We're not allowed there, especially at night," I said.

"I go anyway. What are they going to do if they catch me, lock me up? You should come with me sometime."

"Maybe I should." I did want to talk to my father. There was always somebody else around, my mother or grandmother or sisters, and there wasn't much of a chance to ask him about things. I needed to find out what he was thinking about … where we might be going to.

"Are you going to the barracks tonight?" I asked.

"I go every night. I can't ever get to sleep. How about I drop over and get you around eleven tonight?"

"How about I meet you someplace at the same time? That's late and I don't want to risk waking up my sisters." What I really didn't want to risk was my mother telling me I couldn't go.

"Sure. We could meet on the foot path cutting toward the diamond."

"Why there?"

"The sentries stay on the main paths around the buildings."

"Are there a lot of sentries patrolling the grounds?" I asked. I hadn't counted on having to dodge soldiers to see my father.

"Don't worry, they don't seem too interested in seeing anything. Just think of it as being a little adventure."

"The only adventure I want is to get on our boat and go home."

"If we have homes to go back to."

"What do you mean, of course we'll have our …" I looked at Sam and his expression was dead serious. He'd even stopped chomping on his gum. "What have you heard?"

"Some of the empty houses have been broken into, things stolen, things destroyed."

"So a house or two has been broken into."

"Not just a few — lots. Lots of houses," Sam said.

"Yours?"

Sam shook his head. "Our neighbors are looking after our place, cutting the grass, even tending to the flowers. It's mainly happening in areas where most of the houses are owned by the Japanese and now nobody's around."

"Like in my village," I said under my breath.

Sam shrugged. "I don't know anything about up north."

"What about around here?"

"There's no problem in Vancouver — yet. Most of the people are still being allowed to stay in their homes, thank goodness."

"That is good for them."

"And for us," Sam said. "Where do you think they'd be putting us if they had to crowd in all those Japanese who live in Vancouver? That's the only reason the authorities are letting them stay in their homes until they move to the resettlement areas."

"I hadn't thought of that. Maybe I should be more grateful we have the stalls."

Sam shook his head. "How Japanese of you."

I gave him a confused look.

"Being grateful for things you should be mad about."

"That doesn't help me know about my place, but I know who would know … my friend Jed. I could write and ask him."

"You won't find out anything if you mail a letter from here."

"Why not?" I asked.

"Don't you know about the censors?" Sam asked.

"What are censors?"

"People who read all the mail that goes in and out of here."

"Somebody reads our mail?" I asked in disbelief.

"Everything, in or out. We're Enemy Aliens, remember? They want to make sure we aren't passing on military secrets to the Japanese Imperial Army."

"That's crazy. I'm just going to write about the park and ask him to check on my house."

"I've seen some letters my father got. Big black lines blotting out almost everything. I doubt your friend would even understand to check your house."

"But I promised him I'd write. Besides, how else can I found out about my house?"

"I'm not saying you shouldn't write him. I'm just saying that you shouldn't mail it from here."

"You mean …?" Of course, I knew exactly what he had in mind — leaving the park.

He nodded his head. "And these might come in handy." Sam stood up and reached into the right front pocket of his pants. He pulled something out and placed it on the table in front of me. Two "I Am Chinese" buttons stared up at me.

.14.

I scrunched up another piece of paper. It wasn't that I didn't know what I wanted to say and ask, but that I couldn't seem to arrange the words on the paper the right way. I couldn't go on like this for much longer. Not only was I running short of paper, but I was running out of time. It was almost ten-thirty and Sam and I were to meet in a little more than thirty minutes.

My sisters had been in bed and asleep for over an hour. They were both tired after being in school today. From the time they had arrived home until they finally turned in for the night, all they did was blabber on excitedly about their teachers, and new friends, and what they'd learned in class, and the games they played at recess.

It would have been nice to be that excited about something. Maybe it was being so young, or it could have been because they didn't know enough to be worried. I hadn't even talked to my mother about the things I'd heard — what was the point? Either they weren't true and not worth repeating, or they were true and there wasn't anything she could do about it anyway, except worry. And she already had enough to worry about with my grandmother.

My grandmother wasn't feeling well. She'd gone to bed even earlier than the girls. She said she wasn't "in balance." This was her polite way of saying that she hadn't been able to hold down any food for two days, and had made at least four trips to the washroom since she had first laid down tonight. There was some kind of flu going around the whole park and there were lots of sick people.

Each time my grandmother got up, my mother got up with her. She held her gently by the arm and walked her to the washroom. My grandmother looked so little, and frail. She had hardly been eating at all even before she got sick. She just hated the food … couldn't understand the whole thing … standing in line, big metal plates … eating with so many strangers all around. All she talked about was going home … home.

I glanced at my watch. I'd wasted more time. If I was going to write Jed it had to be done now. Sam and I had agreed we were headed out tomorrow to mail the letter. He'd showed me a letter his father had received from a neighbor. It was filled with thick, black stripes that blotted out more than half the letter. I didn't have any way of knowing what was underneath that ink, but the rest of the letter was just everyday stuff about the neighborhood activities and gardening. I couldn't imagine the hidden parts of the letter contained the location of allied shipping or some other military secret.

Maybe I couldn't find the right words, but I was now out of time. Whatever I wrote in this one was going in the envelope and to Jed instead of into the trash bin.

Dear Jed,

Sorry I didn't have a chance to write earlier but it's not so easy to send a letter. All mail, in and out, is read by the soldiers who guard us. I've seen what they do to letters. They use big markers and just black out anything they don't think anybody should know. They don't think anybody should know anything. I got away from the park for an hour and mailed this from

a mailbox away from the park so they couldn't get
their hands on it.

At least, that's what I was hoping to do — leave the park and mail this letter. It was a dangerous thing to do, but what choice did I have?

That's right, I'm living in a park: Hastings Park, in
Vancouver. I always thought Vancouver would be
pretty exciting. Mostly what we see are the fences
surrounding the park. You can get out if you're
sneaky, but we're supposed to stay inside. Besides, my
parents don't think it's safe to be Japanese and out in
the city. The newspapers are full of stories of the war
and they're afraid we might be attacked on the streets.

Getting attacked. That last line echoed around in my head. I had to go out to mail this letter if I wanted to find out the truth. I needed to find out the truth. Besides, the attacks were probably nothing but rumors. I didn't believe half of what I heard. I thought about the "I Am Chinese" buttons and couldn't help but smile. Who was going to bother two Chinese kids? Back to the letter.

After the trip down here I don't fear getting attacked.
Nothing could be worse than what we went through.
It took us fifteen days. All the fishing boats were tied
together behind two navy frigates. There were sixty
boats. The seas were heavy and there was a lot of fog.
Our boat became covered in ice from the spray. We had
to chip it off. The only place to get away from the cold
and spray was in the cabin. You know how small that
is, but somehow we managed to find places to sleep.
There were times I wasn't sure we'd make it.

*I heard afterwards they probably brought our boat up
to the Annieville Dyke on the Fraser River. Somebody
told me they have twelve hundred Japanese fishing
boats all tied up there. I think it causes my father
great distress to know how his boat is being cared for
— or, really, uncared for. He said if he knew what was
going to happen to it he would have sunk it himself.*

My father had said it more than once. The first time
I couldn't believe my ears. He cared for that boat almost as much as he cared for us, and he regretted not
sinking it. It took a lot for that thought to sink in.

*The boat ride prepared us for living in a small space.
My family has been given a stall to live in. I don't
mean a small place. I mean a stall. We're living in
the place where they used to show livestock. All of us
families have been given a separate stall, and we've
hung blankets and things to act as curtains. So I
guess if somebody asks me if I was raised in a barn, I
can answer yes.*

I stopped writing. I looked around. Even sitting here
in the stall, knowing that of course everything I was
writing was true, it still didn't seem real. I was living in a
cattle stall. I wouldn't be surprised if Jed didn't believe
what I had written. I was living it and only half believed
it myself. I took another quick glance at my watch.

*I can kid about it, but it really steams me to be treated
like cattle. A lot of us, mostly Canadian born, are
really angry. There's a lot of talk about a protest or
petition or civil disobedience, or something. Nothing
has come of it. My father tells me not to get involved.
None of the Issei seem to want to get involved.*

I shook my head in disbelief. How could people not

want to get involved in something that was their whole life? It was almost as if nobody cared.

My father is typical of how they're acting. He walks around with his eyes on the ground. Best I can make out he feels shamed by his treatment. Can you imagine that? These people make us leave our homes, and he figures he should feel ashamed! The people who should feel ashamed are those politicians who ordered our internment and the RCMP officers who did it. So much for democracy and the British sense of fair play. Can you tell me where the fairness is?

I almost would have liked the censors to read that! Maybe they'd obliterate the words with thick black ink so Jed couldn't read it, but at least for a few seconds they'd have to think about it, and know what I'd written was right.

I don't know for sure, but I figure there must be close to three thousand people living here. They cook big meals for all of us. There's only a couple of showers and a few more washrooms for the whole place.

There isn't much to do. When the weather changes there'll be more things. There's a baseball diamond, and a soccer field. Fortunately, or maybe not so fortunately, we probably won't be here when that happens.

I stopped and took a deep breath. Where would we be? New Denver or Alberta or where? Part of me wanted to stop the letter right there. The terrible danger was that if I asked him a question about my house he might give me an answer — an answer I didn't want to hear. But I guessed I had to. For better or worse, I needed to know.

*There's lots of rumors going around. I heard they're
going to ship us across Canada, away from the coast.
Another rumor is that we're bound for Japan. Some
other people said the war will be over before spring
comes and they'll let us go home. Another rumor is
that we don't even have homes to go to, that our
homes are being taken apart by looters. Other talk is
that we don't even own the homes anymore, that the
government is taking them away. Who knows? It
would make me feel better if you could just go by my
place and make sure everything is okay. You can write
me back at Hastings Park Exhibition Building,
Vancouver. Please tell me how you're doing and how
things are going around Rupert.*

*Your friend always,
Tadashi*

There, done! I folded the letter in two and was just
about to stuff it into the envelope when I remembered
something else Sam had mentioned, about them keeping a big book of all mail going in and out of the camp.
I unfolded the letter and picked up my pen again.

*p.s. You'll get another letter from me in a day. That's
so the censors will see me writing to you and won't get
suspicious when you write back.*

Was there anything else I should write? Maybe I
should just remind him that he had to be careful what
he wrote back to me.

*p.p.s. Be careful what you write. They read all the
letters coming in as well as going out.*

p.p.p.s. They've got me acting like I really am a spy.

I put down my pen and folded the letter for the second time, slipped it into the envelope and licked the flap, sealing it in place. For better or worse, this letter was finished. Now all that had to happen was for it to be mailed. I tucked the envelope into the front left pocket of my pants.

I got up and looked down the aisle toward the washroom. There was no sign of my mother and grandmother. They'd been gone for over thirty minutes. That probably said something about the lineup and the number of people who were also sick. I would have liked to have said something to them before I left, but I only had a few minutes until I was supposed to meet Sam. I just didn't have time to wait. They'd be back soon and they knew I was leaving. When I'd told my mother what I had in mind, I had the feeling that she wasn't too happy, but she didn't voice any objection. I think she was worried about my father too.

I took one last look at my sisters, peacefully sleeping in the darkened stall. There was just enough light still streaming in for me to see their faces.

"Good night, girls," I said softly.

"Good night, Tadashi," came back a little voice.

"Yuri ... what are you doing still awake?" I asked.

"I was asleep. I woke up," she whispered.

"Try to get back to sleep," I said as I tucked in the edge of her blankets.

"I've been trying, but I've got too many thoughts in my head."

"Thoughts about what?" I asked. I wondered if she was worried about grandmother.

"I was thinking about living here."

I was surprised. I didn't think it was something she gave any thought to at all.

"Do you think we'll be staying here a long time?" Yuri asked.

"Not long. Some people have already been moved out. Don't worry, we'll be gone soon."

"But I don't want to go," she said.

Her words caught me completely off guard. "You want to stay here?"

She nodded her head.

"But why?"

"I like it."

"What exactly is it that you like?" I asked.

"I have friends to play with and I get to go to school."

"You'll have friends wherever we go and there'll always be a school."

"I like *these* friends and *this* school," she said emphatically.

I wanted to say something about how she might not like this school so much after the first day, but I didn't.

"But what about living here," I said, motioning around with my hands, "in a cattle stall?"

"It's good."

"What could you find good about this?" I asked.

"All our things are here … it looks pretty … I have my dolls … and I like that everybody is so close when we sleep … not like in the house we used to have."

"What do you mean 'used to have'?" I demanded. Of course, I knew what she meant, but I didn't like to hear it described that way. It was still our house.

"In our old house. I used to get scared at night and there was nobody there but Midori. Now Mother's right here, and Grandmother and you."

"But not Father."

"He could come, there's enough space," Yuri said. "Do you see the way I always sleep at the edge of my mattress?"

I'd never noticed before, but she was lying on the very outside of the bed, almost balanced on the edge, as if she was trying to get as far away as she could from

Midori, sleeping with her.

"There's room. They could let him stay with us."

"It's not that simple. All the men have to stay together ... as long as we live here."

"And if we live someplace else?" she asked.

"I don't know. Maybe the fathers can be with their families. I don't know."

Yuri took a deep breath and a loud sigh came out of her. "If Father could live with us, then maybe I could make new friends."

I reached out and stroked her head. "Of course you could. But right now I think you need to get to sleep. You have a big day tomorrow at school. Do you have your dollies?"

With one hand she pulled down the blanket to reveal all three dolls tucked under her other arm.

"Good. Now all *four* of you get to bed." I paused. "All right?"

"I'll go to sleep. Can you say hello to Daddy for me?"

"Of course," I said as I pulled up her blanket and she snuggled down under the covers.

It was time to go. I got up and started off. I knew if I didn't leave now, not only would I be late for the meeting with Sam, but it would be harder to get out of the building. The soldier on duty here in the building usually began his patrols at around eleven.

I walked in the direction of the washrooms. There was a small exit at the back of the building. It didn't seem wise to go out through the big front door. As I neared the washrooms I saw the reason why my mother and grandmother hadn't returned yet. Despite the late hour there was still a lineup. Obviously, there were a lot of people not feeling well. I hurried past them and along the back corridor.

The door was far enough from the washrooms for nobody to really notice me — somehow it seemed better to leave without being seen by anybody. I pushed down on the handle and the door opened with a noisy groan that sent a shiver down my spine. I looked around. Anybody who might have heard the noise was lying in the darkened stalls. I stepped out and was relieved to find that the door was nestled amongst bushes and trees. I closed the door behind me, slowly, so that the groan would be muffled. It sealed with just a click. I looked at the outside of the door. There was no handle or door-knob. It was meant as an exit, but not an entrance. When I came back it wouldn't be this way.

Slowly I moved through the bushes. Before breaking through into the open I looked out, scanning the grounds for any motion. I couldn't see anything, but that wasn't surprising. It was dark. The only light was from the few lampposts placed at intervals along the path that ran through the grounds.

Moving beyond cover I felt very exposed. It was dark, but I didn't know who else might be hiding in the dark. I moved quickly, crossing the path at a point as far as possible from the lights. I took a deep breath when I reached the shelter of the shadows of the next build-ing. It was a large warehouse, and one of the few buildings that hadn't been converted to hold people — at least, not yet.

I moved along the side of the building. Right around the back of it was a thicket of bushes coming up almost to the edge of the building. Once I got within the cover of the bushes I'd be safe from any patrols. I started to run, not just because I was late, but to get into the cover as soon as possible. I walked along the building with the wall protecting me on one side and the bushes on the other. As I moved I couldn't help but think about the last time I'd been out on my own at night.

It was the night before my family had to leave our village, when Jed and I had tromped over ten miles through the dense forest, dodging army patrols, on our way to the military base. Just like tonight, we'd had to avoid the guards. I'd felt braver then, with Jed at my side, even though where we were — in the middle of a forest — and what we were doing — trying to free the eagle — was far more dangerous than this.

I couldn't help but think that thanks to me and Jed, that eagle was now flying around the forests on Kairn Island — free. And here I was.

I stopped at the spot where I was to meet Sam.

"Sam!" I called out, trying to be heard but not from too far away.

"Over here," came back an answer.

I saw a shadowy figure move out of the darkness. "I didn't think you were coming."

"I'm not that late. Besides, it's about time I kept you waiting."

"Maybe, but could it be someplace else than in the dark?" Sam asked.

"What's wrong, you scared of the dark?" I kidded.

"Not the dark, but what's *in* the dark."

"Monsters? The boogie man?"

"No, animals."

"Animals! It's not like you're going to find a mountain lion hiding in here, you know," I chuckled.

"I heard noises."

"Probably just a skunk or a raccoon."

"A skunk! Let's not give it a chance to come back. Let's go."

I wasn't concerned about any skunk, but I was eager to get going and see my father.

Sam almost immediately headed out of the bushes and onto a path that cut straight across the compound and toward the men's building. Shouldn't we be staying in the shadows? I looked all around anxiously. There was nobody to be seen. I couldn't help but think how nervous Sam felt about being alone in the dark, and how I felt that way about being here in the open where one of the guards could see us.

I thought I heard faint strains of music wafting through the night air. Where would that be coming from? Nearing the building I got my answer. The music was flowing out one of the doors that was propped open with a chair.

"I didn't expect music," I said.

"Sometimes it goes on for most of the night."

Sam moved through the door and I followed. I felt a huge sense of relief stepping inside the building and away from the guards.

In the dim light I could clearly make out the rows of bunk beds stretching into the distance. The music was now louder, and it was punctuated by bursts of conversation, laughter and some profanity, in both English and Japanese. Many of the beds were empty, their occupants still awake. There were men strolling down the aisles, a group standing over in the corner, talking loudly — not arguing; they sounded like they were happy.

I sniffed the air. There was a strong, almost sickeningly sweet odor. "What is that smell?" I asked.

"That's the still."

"Still?"

"It's what they use to make alcohol."

"They're making alcohol?" I asked in amazement.

"Lots and lots of it."

"How do you make alcohol?"

"I don't understand it much myself, but they make it out of things like potato peelings."

"Come on, you can't make —"

I stopped as I remembered my one taste of a strong Japanese drink made from fermented potatoes. I'd had a couple of little sips once from a bottle my father used to keep in the pantry.

There was a burst of loud voices and laughter. "People seem awfully happy," I said.

Sam shrugged. "Probably been drinking."

We followed the sound of the voices, and they led us to where six men were sitting in a corner around a table, playing cards. Each man had a drink at his side. Sam was right about the alcohol. The deck was shuffled, cards dealt and each man put some bills into the center of the table.

"Poker," Sam said. "I've never been here without seeing a game. My father said there's gambling going on twenty-four hours a day."

"My father doesn't even play cards," I said.

"Not just cards. Dice is big, and some strange Japanese games that I don't understand. The only thing all the games have in common is that money and betting is involved."

"He doesn't gamble either," I said.

"Neither does mine. He says business is enough of a gamble. I'm going to see my dad. How about if we meet back here in about an hour?"

"We don't have to," I said. "I can get back to the building by myself."

"If you want to get back," Sam said.

"What do you mean?" He couldn't want to leave the camp at night, could he?

"I'm going to sleep in the truck tonight. Do you want to come along?"

I didn't know what to say.

"That way you won't have to worry about waking up your family when you go back tonight. And, we can get an early start tomorrow."

That did make sense.

"Well?" Sam asked.

I nodded my head. "See you in an hour."

Sam smiled and then started off in one direction

while I headed down another aisle. It was funny, but Sam had hardly left my sight when I began to feel uneasy.

Moving quietly, I started down an aisle toward where my father had told me his bunk was located. While there were many bunks all made up but unoccupied, most were filled. Men were huddled under their covers, their faces often buried beneath the blankets as well. I was surprised, though, by how many men were in their beds but not asleep. They sat there on the edge of the bed, either reading in the dim light or simply staring silently into space.

I then wondered if maybe my father wouldn't be in his bunk, and I'd have to go searching for him. Or maybe he was there and was already asleep. Would it be right to wake him up?

And then I saw him. Up ahead, sitting on the edge of his bed. He was here and he was awake. I stopped just beside his bed. He was staring straight ahead. He hadn't even noticed that I was there.

"Father?" I asked quietly.

He turned and looked at me, his face showing his surprise. "Tadashi … why are you here? Is something wrong?" he asked in alarm, standing up.

"No, nothing. I just came to see you."

He looked relieved as he sat back down on the edge of his bed. "You should not be here."

"I just wanted to talk," I said.

He gave me a questioning look.

"About what's happening. About where we're going," I said.

"Who knows?"

"I heard some people have already been moved out," I said.

"Some."

"And that some are going to the abandoned mining towns and some families are going to Alberta."

"Both," he answered, without looking at me.

For the first time I noticed the smell of alcohol on my father's breath. Maybe he hadn't been gambling, but he had been drinking.

"But where are we going to go?" I asked.

He shrugged. "Maybe our family goes to the mountains. Maybe I go to a work camp."

"You mean you wouldn't be with us?" I questioned.

"Not all the time. I would come and visit."

"But if we went to Alberta, couldn't we be together?" I asked, repeating what I'd heard.

"Together, but not better. The fields, working sugar beets, is very hard. It would be better in the mountains. Better for the family. I'm not a farmer. I'm a fisherman … I was a fisherman."

"You're still are a fisherman," I said.

He shook his head slowly. "I am nothing," he said softly. "Nothing."

I wanted to say something, but I couldn't find any words.

"I was thinking about my boat," he said.

"I heard the boats aren't far from here, up at the Annieville Dyke, about thirty miles away."

"If it is there."

"Why wouldn't it be?" I asked.

"Seventy boats were sunk … by accident … when they were moved up the river."

"I'm sure our boat is fine!" I blurted out, although of course I couldn't possibly know anything.

"Maybe … maybe it would be better if it wasn't. Maybe it would be better if it had sunk."

"How can you say that?" I asked. Just how much had he had to drink?

"If it was gone, it would be over."

"But we'll get it back … once things are over."

"A few months, a few years being uncared for … what

· 159 ·

will it be like? Will it even float? Will I be able to fish?"

I hadn't thought of that.

"If I had known … I would have sunk the boat myself."

"You can't mean that," I said in disbelief.

He nodded his head. "Yes."

"But the war can't last forever. Someday we'll get back our boat and we can fix it up and it'll be as good as ever," I said.

"The war will end … but they may never return our boat," my father said.

"I don't understand."

My father didn't answer immediately. He took a deep breath. "Probably stories, probably rumors."

"What are the rumors?" I asked.

"The boats, maybe other things, will be sold."

"They can't just sell our things," I said.

My father snorted. "They can do … whatever they wish … and we can do … nothing to stop it."

"There's always rumors. They don't mean anything!" I snapped. "I've written to Jed. He can tell us about our house and —"

I stopped as I heard a rumble of conversation and shuffling of feet coming from up the aisle. My father had heard it as well and had turned to peer down the darkened aisle.

"Come," he said, getting up and starting to walk.

Other men had either woken up or simply gotten out of their beds as well and were moving toward the commotion. There was a crowd of men gathered at the end of the aisle. We pushed into the back of it. Through their heads I saw RCMP officers, a half dozen of them, moving across the floor. I ducked down slightly, hiding behind my father, remembering that I shouldn't even be here.

Between two of the officers was a Japanese man. Each

of the officers held him by one arm, and as he passed I realized that he was in handcuffs! What had he done and what were they doing to him?

The crowd parted at the far end as two police officers pushed through, followed by the pair practically dragging the man between them, and then two other officers, one carrying a suitcase. They left the building.

"What was that all about?" I asked.

A man turned around. "Angler."

"What's Angler?" I questioned.

"A camp in Ontario ... northern Ontario," he answered.

"Like here?" I asked.

He shook his head. "A prisoner-of-war camp."

"The place where they put troublemakers, people who give them problems," my father added.

"What did he do?"

"They caught him at the fence," another man said.

"He was trying to escape?" I asked in amazement.

He shook his head. "Trying to get back in. He had been out for a few days."

"But if he was trying to get back ..." I let the sentence trail off.

He shrugged. "That's the punishment for going over the fence."

Or for going under the fence, I thought. What could have happened to me and Sam if we had been caught? What would happen if we were caught tomorrow? Maybe we shouldn't go, shouldn't risk it for a letter. But maybe we should.

.15.

I opened an eye and then instantly closed it again, shielding my face from the bright sunshine that was streaming through the windshield of the truck. Sam was still asleep at the other end of the seat, snoring away. Somehow during the night he'd managed to take all the blanket. I stretched and yawned loudly. There was a fresh breeze blowing in through the open windows. It smelled good … fresh … so much better than the air in the stalls. Despite being cramped up on the seat, I'd slept better than I had since we arrived at Hastings Park … better than I'd slept since we left home … maybe even better than I'd slept for a few weeks at home before we left. I didn't know why I'd waited so long to come here to sleep, but I had a pretty good idea where I wanted to sleep tonight.

"Good morning," Sam said.

I was startled. I hadn't realized he was awake. "Good morning."

Sam stretched. "Sleep good?"

"I had a little trouble getting to sleep," I admitted, "but once I drifted off I slept like a log."

"Let's go to the mess hall. We can eat, throw some water on our faces and head out — that is, if you're still interested."

Sam and his father had been in another part of the crowd last night watching as the RCMP led the man away in handcuffs. We'd talked about what had happened. It certainly raised doubts in my mind, but they were more than outweighed by my need to know — even more so after my conversation with my father. Working at the base, Jed might know more than just what was happening with our house.

"I still want to go out … but I'm not really hungry," I said.

"Funny, me neither."

"You?" I asked in amazement.

"It happens. But I think I should force myself to have a meal," Sam said with a smile. "So let's just stop off and have a quick bite."

"That would be okay."

"But just a quick bite. We have to leave before one of us gets smart enough to change his mind."

"I didn't think you had any doubts," I said in amazement.

"You'd have to be an idiot not to have any doubts. Especially after last night. It's different hearing about people getting caught and then seeing somebody who did get caught."

"Then why are you doing it?"

"I can't very well let you go out there alone. Besides, I think these buttons are the ace in the hole we need to get away with it." Sam paused. "Here, take one and slip it in your pocket," he said, handing it to me.

I looked at the button. "I Am Chinese." What would my father think about me wearing this … actually, I knew what he'd think. He'd be almost as upset about me pretending to be Chinese as he would be if he knew I was sneaking out of the park. I stuffed it into my pocket.

"Do up the windows," Sam said.

I did up one window while he rolled the blanket into a rough ball and stuffed it behind the seat. I put the pillows back there as well, while Sam did up the other window. He then opened the door and climbed out. I followed behind him and closed the door as quietly as possible. We weaved through the vehicles, aiming away from the grandstand where the guards would be sitting.

"Here, this will hold you until we get to the mess hall," Sam said as he handed me a candy bar.

"Thanks, but I'm not that hungry, remember?"

"This isn't about hungry, this is about tasty. Eat it."

I ripped open the top with my teeth and took a bite. It was sweet and sticky and partly melted. The cab of the truck was cooler than the building, but had still been hot enough to melt the candy to the wrapper.

Wordlessly we moved along the path. There was dew on the grass and we moved silently across the meadow. For a few seconds I couldn't see guards or fence or buildings or gate. Then I caught sight of the fence off to the left that marked the end of our world. Following along it with my eye I could see the gate. The wooden railings were down to stop vehicles, not that anybody was trying to come or go at this early hour of the morning. The only movement was on the street paralleling the fence. It seemed like there was always traffic there.

We cut off away from the fence. I felt a sense of relief moving farther away. Our path was leading us right by the Forum, the school. It was still too early for any of the children to have arrived, but I saw that the windows and doors were wide open. And as we got closer a woman appeared, broom in hand, sweeping dirt out of one of the doors. A billow of dust rose up into the air.

"I'm surprised my sister isn't lined up waiting to go in," Sam said.

"Yours too? My sisters loved it!"

"The way she talked was like she had been at a party instead of at school. Go figure," Sam said.

My attention was suddenly caught by the sound of a truck. A big army vehicle, the type that had brought us here, rumbled noisily around one of the buildings. It was quickly followed by a second one. It was slowly bumping along the path, coming straight toward us.

"Maybe going out to pick up more people," I said.

"Could be. I hear there's over three thousand people here now."

"But I thought some had left already," I questioned.

"Some did, but more came. Those stalls were only open for a few hours."

We stepped well off the path to let the trucks pass. The first one moved by and I saw that it wasn't empty. The metal tailgate was up, but the back flap was open to reveal faces, Japanese faces, peering out the back.

"They must be leaving … but why so early?" I questioned.

"Maybe they need the space or maybe because they're sending them so far away," Sam said.

"Do you think they're going to the mountains?" I asked as the second truck passed by, revealing more faces.

"Maybe even to Alberta."

"To the fields," I said.

"Three days by truck to get there, I heard."

"That would be awful. It was bad enough being bounced around in the back of the truck the few miles from the docks to here," I said.

"And it's not like they're going to some Garden of Eden. My father said they were being put right in the fields to plant sugar beets. He says it's one of the worst jobs in the world, but they can always use another Japanese diesel."

"What's that?"

"A Jap with a wheelbarrow. Has your family decided where they want to go?"

"Decided? I think maybe the mountains. My father still hasn't decided."

"Then it could be New Denver, or Slocan or Tashme."

"I've heard of a couple of those. Do you know where they are?" I asked.

"In the interior, up in the mountains, is all I know."

"I was thinking Alberta wouldn't be too bad," I said.

"Then you're thinking wrong."

"If it's so bad, why would anybody go there?" I questioned.

"Some are farmers or gardeners, so they want to do that sort of work."

"Yeah, but at least everybody could be together," I said.

"What do you mean?"

"Going to the mountains might mean the men going someplace else for at least part of the time. They're putting them on work crews to fix roads and bridges and things. Where is your family going?" I asked.

"Probably farther east. Maybe even Ontario."

"I thought they were just sending prisoners out there."

"That's northern Ontario. We'd go to Toronto."

"Why would you want to do that?" I questioned. The farther away you went, the harder it would be to get back home.

"My father has some business connections out there. They might even let him go out there to try to arrange things."

"And you could do that? They'd let you just go and live in a house?"

"They don't have enough places to put us anyway, so if somebody can find a place for themselves that's outside of the restricted areas, then they don't care," Sam explained. "My father said that maybe it isn't the best place in the world to be, but it might be the least worst choice we get."

We stood and watched as the trucks slowed down at the gate. A soldier walked first to one truck, and then to the other. The gate was raised and the trucks lumbered away. Wherever they were going, they were now gone from here at least. I'd have to talk to my father again about where we were going. Maybe he didn't know about going out east … it wouldn't be so bad either.

"Let's eat," Sam said. "We better get in line before all the kids head for school."

We hurried off toward the mess hall. Entering, it was obvious that we were already too late. There was a fair-sized line, with lots of kids amongst those waiting to be served. More than half of the tables were already occupied. I looked around for my family. While I recognized a few people from my village, my family wasn't there. We both grabbed trays, plates and utensils. Despite the length of the line, I was surprised by how fast it was moving.

I looked way up ahead, trying to see what was for breakfast. I was hoping for eggs. I watched as the server scooped out a big spoonful of oatmeal. The old Japanese woman being offered the food shook her head and then turned her plate upside down. I guess it didn't look any better up close than it did from a distance.

She shuffled over to the second server and did exactly the same, refusing the food that was offered. Finally she moved to the next woman, and for the third time refused the food that was offered. She walked away, nothing on her tray but the overturned plate. Either the food was so awful she'd lost her appetite, or she wasn't hungry … but if she wasn't hungry, why did she wait in line in the first place?

Then I noticed that the man two back from her had passed by the first server without taking food. His plate was upside down as well. He too stopped at each server but refused the food that was offered. That was strange. I watched him walk away with his empty tray.

"Did you see —" I started to say.

"Yeah, I saw," Sam said, cutting me off. "I just don't understand."

Before we reached the front of the line, another half-dozen of the thirty people ahead of us did exactly the same thing. And as each left without food, they took a place at one of the tables, and sat silently staring off into the distance. That was even stranger. If they weren't going to eat anything, why didn't they just leave?

"Oatmeal?" the woman asked.

"I guess so," I said hesitantly, looking closely to see if I could see why so many people had turned it down.

"Good!" she said as she spooned out a huge quantity that overflowed the bowl and splattered onto the tray.

"And for you too?' she asked Sam.

"Not for me," Sam said as he took his bowl and turned it over.

I didn't know what shocked me more, Sam refusing food, or what he had just done with his bowl.

"Hummmp," snorted the server. "Suit yourself."

"Why did you do that?" I asked Sam out of the corner of my mouth as we shuffled forward.

"I don't like oatmeal."

"But why did you turn your bowl over?"

"I saw the other people do it. Did you notice how angry that woman got?"

"It was hard not to —"

"Sam, are you part of this too?" It was Betsy, the woman who got Sam his newspapers. She was carrying a big, steaming pot of something.

"Part of what?" Sam asked.

"People refusing to eat."

"We noticed. But why are they doing it?" Sam asked.

"It's a darn foolish idea that some darn foolish people are doing. Can you imagine, refusing to eat the food we prepare. Do either of you think this food is so bad?" she asked.

"Always tasted good to me," Sam said. "I like the food here."

His answer didn't surprise me, and it wasn't just that he was being polite. While people like my grandmother barely ate at all, Sam always went back for seconds of everything.

"We work darn hard preparing and baking and cooking and serving! Do you think it's easy making three meals a day for over three thousand people?"

"I'm sure it isn't," I agreed. Were there really that many people here?

"And maybe it doesn't taste the same as if we were cooking for a few people around the table in our kitchen, but we try our best. First, it was just a few old ladies."

She couldn't mean my grandmother. True, she only picked at her food, but she was still eating some of it.

"Now it seems like every meal there's more and more of them. They stand in line, refuse to take anything to eat, and then just go to the tables and sit there. Does that make any sense to either of you boys?" she asked loudly.

I was painfully aware that almost all the other sounds in the mess hall had stopped, and everybody — the people serving, those waiting in line and those already sitting down — was staring at us and listening. The line ahead of us had continued to move forward while we were holding up everybody else behind us.

"And do they think by not eating they'll get the food they want?" the woman continued. "Even if we wanted to, we couldn't get all those different foods. And rice ... who eats rice for breakfast?"

"Well ..." I started to answer.

"Let's keep things moving," came an angry male voice.

I turned around to see a couple of soldiers striding across the floor toward us.

"Are these two causing you trouble?" one of the soldiers asked.

What two? Who was he talking about? He couldn't mean us, could he?

The soldiers stopped practically right on top of us, and my stomach did a flip.

"Not these two; we were just talking," Betsy explained. "They're here to eat, not cause trouble … not like some people!" she said loudly.

"Yeah, we're just eating," I said anxiously, holding my tray up for them to see the pile of oatmeal, to confirm my words.

"Then get moving, you're holding up the line," the older of the two ordered.

"Come on, Sam," I said, nudging him forward.

"No," he said, shaking his head. "I've suddenly lost my appetite."

He turned to one of the soldiers. "Here, take this," Sam said, and he handed the man his tray, turned and walked away.

The soldier looked shocked as he stood there holding Sam's tray. He was only slightly less surprised than me, though.

"Ummm … I'm not that hungry either," I said as I placed my tray on top of Sam's.

"Thanks … thanks a lot," I mumbled.

Before the soldier could even react, I had turned and run after Sam. Every eye in the whole place was on me as I quickly picked my way through the crowd. Sam was already outside before I caught up to him.

"Why did you do that?" I asked. "You like the food here."

"Maybe I do, but I don't like being ordered around by a couple of old donkeys who think they're so important because they're carrying guns!"

Sam pulled out a package of gum, unwrapped a piece and stuffed it in his mouth, adding to the wad he was already working.

"You got the letter?" he asked.

"Right here," I answered, tapping my pants pocket.

"Then let's go."

•••

I scouted up and down the fence as Sam slipped underneath the wire. There were no guards, nothing to be seen except for the cars flying by on the road. Sam stood up and dusted himself off. I dropped to my knees, spun over onto my back and pulled myself under. I quickly got back to my feet. There was a gap in the traffic in both directions — there didn't seem to be nearly as many cars as the last time — and we raced across the street, not even stopping when we reached the other side. We kept moving, trotting along at a fair pace, until we reached the little side street we'd been on when we snuck out the first time. Feeling safer, we started walking.

"We better put on our buttons," Sam said as he pulled his out of his pocket.

I did the same. Carefully I pinned it on my shirt. "I Am Chinese."

"How far do we have to go to mail the letter?" I asked.

"I don't know this part of the city very well, but there should be either a post office or a letter box not too far away. Let's go down this way."

We turned onto a smaller street that ran parallel to the major road.

"Wouldn't it be better if we were out on the big street … you know, more chance of there being a mailbox?" I asked.

"Better chance of seeing one, but a better chance of being seen. I figure we go a few blocks on this street before we head back out to the busier one. Make sense?"

"Perfect."

"Just relax, and just remember, act like we belong here."

"I'll remember, but I don't think there's any way I'm going to relax until we get back under that fence."

This street wasn't nearly as busy, but there was still a lot of activity. Aside from the occasional car, there were people sitting on their porches or working on their lawns and gardens. At two houses there were men in their driveways, hose in hand, washing their cars. On several occasions we saw people on the sidewalk up ahead, coming toward us, and we crossed to the other side of the street. I tried not to make eye contact with any of the people we passed. I just looked straight ahead, hoping they didn't notice us but certain that we were being watched by everybody we came near.

At first I thought it was just my imagination, but there really did seem to be an awful lot of people around. There were so many more people than the first time we — wait a second, today was Saturday! Of course there were more people out! That also explained why there were so many fewer cars on the street outside the park.

Having traveled five or six blocks, Sam turned us back onto the main street. Looking back, I could just make out what looked like the corner of the park. It would be good to get it completely out of sight — of course, that also meant we had to travel farther back before we were safe.

I looked up. A man and a woman were coming down the sidewalk in our direction. She was pushing a stroller and he had a black dog on a leash. As we got closer, the man shortened his hold on the dog's leash and shifted him over to the other side. I was grateful for that. I didn't like dogs very much. I made way for them by moving slightly off the sidewalk and onto the grass. Sam stepped out onto the edge of the road.

"Hello," I said as we passed.

"Um, yeah, hi," the man answered hesitantly.

There, that wasn't so bad —

"Why did you do that?" Sam hissed at me out of the corner of his mouth.

"Do what?"

"Talk to them."

"I was just trying to be friendly."

"Don't be friendly, be Chinese."

"Come on, Chinese people must say hello."

"Not to white people they don't," Sam said.

"But there are some Chinese families in Rupert, a couple of the kids are in my school, and they talk to —"

"This isn't Prince Rupert. I don't know what goes on up there, but down here everybody keeps to their own kind."

"Then what do you think I should do when we pass people?"

"Keep your head down and look at your feet," Sam said. "We want them to see your button, not your face."

"Why don't we cross over to the other side instead?" I suggested.

"It's too busy to keep zigzagging back and forth."

Of course, Sam was right. The street was becoming much busier. The houses had started to give way to small stores, and there were many people out on the street. Right up ahead, the traffic was stopped at a light. The cross street held even more traffic than the one we were walking along.

"I know where we are now. There's a post office a couple of blocks down this way," Sam said quietly. "And Tadashi … keep your mouth closed."

I wasn't planning on arguing with that. I'd keep my mouth shut and my eyes open, but looking down at the ground. We came to a stop and waited for the light to change.

A young woman with three children stopped beside us as we waited. I glanced at them carefully out of the corner of my eye so as not to be seen looking. My attention was caught by the sound of a vehicle gearing down and the squeaking of brakes. I had a rush of fear as a large, olive-colored truck stopped right beside us. It was unmistakably an army vehicle, probably coming from the park. Had we been discovered? Had it come for us? Were they looking for us? The light changed, and in a cloud of exhaust smoke and a grinding of gears, the truck started off. With that my heart started beating again.

Walking along, I couldn't help being reminded of Prince Rupert. Not Prince Rupert before the war, but how it was when I left. There were cars parked at the sides of the street, people strolling along the sidewalk, walking, talking, pushing strollers or pulling grocery carts full of their purchases. It all seemed so friendly and safe and familiar. It was hard to believe that I wasn't allowed to be here ... or anywhere except the park.

"Here we are," Sam said.

We'd stopped in front of a large building. It had stone columns, and a series of cement steps led up to the door. Above the door, engraved in the rock, it said "Royal Canadian Post Office."

"Do you see the letter drop? It's right there by the front door," Sam said.

Slowly I climbed the steps. I had the eerie feeling that I was being watched, and that all the eyes on the busy street were on me. I stopped and turned around. People strolled along the sidewalk or stood talking. Cars and trucks whizzed along or waited for the light to change at the end of the block. Nobody was looking at me. I reached the letter drop, hesitated for a split second and then released it, allowing the letter to fall the first few feet of its trip to my friend.

I turned and hurried down the steps. I couldn't help but wonder what Jed would think when he read my letter. And what would he write in his letter back?

Sam was sitting on a bench, and I stopped beside him. "Let's go."

"Do you know that the bus that passes by here goes right to Stanley Park?"

"No, I didn't know."

"Have you ever been to Stanley Park?" Sam asked.

"You know I haven't," I said. I also knew what he was getting at. "And today isn't going to be the first time."

Sam smiled and stood up. "I guess you're right. But it does feel good to be out, doesn't it?"

"It does … but we have to get back to the park."

"You're right. It just reminded me of things — you know, what it used to be like," Sam said. "Let's go."

We started back, retracing our footsteps along the street. It was lined with stores, and I looked in the windows as we passed. I had to admit that it all did look friendly and interesting and harmless. Going to Stanley Park wasn't a good idea, but maybe we could stop around here for a minute.

"You thirsty?" I asked Sam.

"Thirsty and hungry."

"Maybe we could stop in at one of these stores and get a drink. My treat."

"That sounds like a good — hey, watch it!" Sam yelled as a boy walked between us, bumping into both of us.

"Who are you to tell me what to do!" the boy demanded. He was about our age and size — and white.

"Is somebody bothering my little brother?" came a voice from behind us.

I turned around. There were three more boys, a few years older than us, standing there. They were all smirking, and I could just tell by their postures and expressions that they were looking for trouble.

"Nobody picks on my little brother," the biggest of the three said as he came toward us threateningly. "Especially not people that don't belong here!"

How did he know we were Japanese? Had they already called the police? They moved in closer and I could feel the hair on the back of my neck stand on end.

"Now get back to where you belong! Get back down to Chinatown!"

Chinatown! He thought we were Chinese! I felt like laughing out loud!

"Sure we'll go back … we don't want any problems," I said. "We'll go right now."

I tried to take a step away, but one of them blocked my way.

"Where do you think you're going?" he demanded.

"Um … back … back to Chinatown."

"Chinatown is that way!" he said, pointing in the opposition direction from the way I was headed, which was back to Hastings Park. "Do you think we're idiots?" he demanded.

"No … I just … I mean … that was the way we came," I stammered.

"Well, that ain't the way you're going!"

He grabbed me roughly by the arm and pushed me back in the direction I'd just come with such force that I almost toppled over. The other three started to laugh.

"Gum?" Sam asked.

"What are you talking about?"

"Does anybody want a piece of gum?"

"We don't want any of your chink gum!" another of them snapped.

Sam shrugged. "It's not chink gum. It's good gum." He pulled a package out of his pocket. "Because I know I can use another piece. This stuff in my mouth is getting stale. I better get rid of it," Sam said.

He then spat out the wad, hitting the biggest guy right in the middle of his forehead!

.16.

"Aaagggh!" he screamed as he brought his hands up to his face and the wad of gum dropped to the ground.

Before anybody could even react, Sam punched him in the stomach and he groaned loudly, exhaling a burst of air. As he doubled over in pain, Sam brought his knee up and connected with the guy's face. He collapsed into a crumbled heap on the ground, blood spilling from his nose and mouth.

"Who's next?" Sam screamed as he bounced forward, his fists held high in front of him.

All three of them backed away. They looked shocked —and scared.

"What's wrong, don't you want to make the chinks go away?" he yelled. Sam jumped toward one of them, making him stumble back out of the way.

"Come on," Sam said as he grabbed me by the arm. "We're leaving."

They moved out of our way as Sam dragged me past. I expected one of them to lunge out or do something, but instead they made more space for us.

As Sam released his grip on me, I realized that we'd drawn a crowd. I'd been so focused on our four attackers that I hadn't looked beyond them. There must have been at least two dozen people who had stopped and were staring. Now all the eyes on the street *were* on us.

"Don't look back, just keep walking," Sam said.

"But —"

"And shut up," he said, cutting me off. "Save your breath, you're going to need it."

What did he mean by that? We quickly passed by stores, cutting through people on the sidewalk. I felt like there were eyes burning into our backs.

Rather than going straight at the lights, we turned to the left. I was relieved when we made the turn because we were now out of view.

"Why are we going this way?"

"To get out of sight faster. Come on!" Sam said, and began running.

I started to sprint. Sam, as always, was moving faster than I could. He disappeared down the first side street — the street we'd traveled partway before heading to the main road. At least I understood what he was doing. I dug down deeper and made the street a dozen seconds after him. I was relieved to see that he'd started to walk. I stopped when I reached his side.

"I wanted to make sure they wouldn't follow us," Sam explained. "We couldn't very well go back under the fence with them watching."

"I guess not. Do you think that guy's okay?" I asked.

"Don't know, don't care. I didn't start anything … just finished it. So what do you think? Was I right when I said I can handle myself?"

"No question about that; you cleaned his clock."

"Yeah, I did. Would have taken the others if they'd been stupid enough to try me. How about you?"

"How about me what?"

"Are you any good with your fists?"

"I can take care of myself."

"Have you had to very often?" Sam asked.

"A few times," I answered. Of course, that included play fights and arguing with my sisters. I hadn't actually ever been in a fist fight. Words usually worked.

"I wasn't sure about you. You looked like you were just going to walk away after he shoved you."

I felt myself flush. He was wrong, though. I wasn't just going to walk away — I was prepared to run.

"I thought it was better to get away — you know, not cause a scene," I said.

"It wasn't us who caused the scene," Sam said. "It was them when they stopped us and then shoved you."

"But it wouldn't be them that got in trouble if the police came. It would have been smarter to just try —"

"I'm tired of smart!" Sam snapped, interrupting me. "And I'm tired of people pushing me around. Aren't you tired of it?" he demanded.

"Of course, it's just that what —"

"That's the thing I just can't get over at that camp," Sam said, interrupting me again. "It's almost like nobody cares. They make us leave our homes, put a fence around us, make us live in stalls, and nobody does anything. Everybody just bows their heads, smiles and goes along with it. Like last night in the men's barracks. Why did everybody, hundreds and hundreds of men, just stand there and watch while a few policemen took somebody away?"

"What do you think they should have done?" I asked.

"I don't know … maybe stop them … maybe something, anything, instead of just standing there like cattle. Maybe that's it. It's okay for them to make us live like cattle because that's how we're acting, like dumb, stupid cows being herded around."

"People *have* done some things."

"Like what?" Sam demanded.

"Well … I heard they sent somebody to talk to the government, and people met with the commander of the camp to complain about things."

"That's right. Talk. That's all they do is talk. Talk, talk, talk!"

"What do you think we're supposed to do instead of

talking?" I asked.

"I don't know. Refuse to do things, disobey the orders, argue or fight with them! Maybe punch somebody right in the nose!"

"Like that would help."

"It helped today. If I hadn't stepped in they would have pounded us."

"You don't know that. They might have just let us walk away."

"Crawl away, you mean. They might have just let us crawl away. I'm telling you, I'd rather have to be carried out fighting and screaming and kicking than crawl off like some dog with my tail between my legs! You know, the only people in that whole camp who are doing anything more than just talking are those old people."

"What old people?" I questioned.

"The ones this morning who aren't eating. It seems like a pretty stupid way to fight back, but at least they're doing something — more than the rest of us are doing!"

Before I could answer, I heard a car engine roaring up the street behind us. We both turned in time to see two cars racing toward us. One squealed to a stop, its front wheels bouncing up onto the sidewalk a few houses past us. The second skidded to a stop behind us. Suddenly all four doors of the first car flew open. Five men scrambled out. A shudder shook my whole body as I recognized one boy, now holding a blood-stained towel to his face. It was the guy Sam had knocked down, and he'd come with more friends. There was no question what they wanted.

I heard the sound of car doors slamming and turned around to the car that was behind us. Another four men got out of it and started toward us. We were trapped!

"This way!" Sam screamed as he grabbed me by the arm.

His scream unfroze me, and I ran along beside him up the driveway of the house. We shot past the building and into the backyard. Behind me I could hear yelling and swearing and footsteps charging up the drive after us. Driven by fear, I was able to stay with Sam, and we both hit the fence at the end of the yard at the same time and were over in a single bound. We'd traveled no more than two dozen steps when I heard the metal fence groaning under the weight of our pursuers. We scrambled across the grass, hitting the gravel drive of the next house at a dead run. Running past the second house, I caught a glimpse of a surprised woman staring at us out of the side window. Once we hit the street, Sam grabbed me by the arm again and aimed me along the sidewalk. I chanced a glance behind me — they weren't there. Then the first guy broke free from behind the house, followed by another and another! They were still coming, and I felt a surge of fear push me to run faster.

Side by side, we ran along the sidewalk, cars whizzing by. Up ahead I could see the park, the fence surrounding it and the baseball diamond in the distance behind it. If only we could get to the fence, we'd be safe — or, at least, get to the part of the fence where the hole was. That was still a long way off.

"We're losing 'em!" Sam said.

I looked back. He was right! They were way back and looked like they were slowing down. There was no way I was going to slow down until I was under the fence and halfway across the park.

"Cross over," Sam yelled as he darted onto the street.

Blindly I followed behind him through a gap in the traffic. We skipped forward around a truck and kept on moving. Again I looked back. There were five of them. They were strung out over a long distance, some crossing the street, others still on the far side and one already on the same side as us. It didn't matter how many there were, though — they weren't going to catch us. Hopefully we could pull away even farther, so they wouldn't notice us going under the fence. If they *did* see us, would they be crazy enough to come in after us?

"Geez!" Sam screamed as a car raced by and bumped up onto the sidewalk, squealing to a stop and blocking our way. We skidded to a stop as the doors of the car opened and three guys jumped out. I already felt like somebody had punched me in the stomach. I swiveled my head to see our pursuers had closed in and the first was almost on top of us. He slowed down and the next two caught up to him. I struggled to catch my breath. My pulse was racing.

Desperately I looked around for a way out. We couldn't get over the fence. The strands of barbed wire on top of it would rip us to shreds. There was no way over it. Behind it, in the distance, the baseball game was going on ... why couldn't I have been there? The only way was the street ... we had to dodge the cars. I took a step toward the street, but Sam put a hand on my shoulder.

"Nope," he said, shaking his head. "We're not running any farther."

"But ... but ... we can't fight them ... we can't win," I stammered.

"We can't win, but we're going to fight them. Get rid of this," Sam said as he pulled the "I Am Chinese" button off my shirt and then took off his and stuffed them both in his pocket.

"Cover my back and I'll cover yours."

They came forward slowly. They knew there was no place to go. There were eight of them, three blocking one side, and five the other. We retreated until the fence was right at our backs.

"Payback time, chinks!" yelled one of them, the one who'd started it all. He threw the bloody towel to the ground.

"Yeah, you're both going to get a beating!" called out another.

"Does it always take eight whites to take on a couple

of chinks?" Sam screamed back.

For a split second they hesitated, as if they were thinking over what Sam had just yelled. Could it somehow …?

"Get 'em!"

They charged at us! I swung my fist wildly, connecting with the first man's face with a thud. Almost immediately I was knocked backwards. I bounced into the fence, lost my balance and fell to the ground. I screamed as I felt a searing pain shoot through my side and then absorbed another shot to the head. Another blow bit into my side — I was down and being kicked! I tried to scramble to my feet, but I was smashed hard back to the ground. I rolled up into a ball and tried to cover my head with my hands and arms.

Over top of everything I heard the sound of the metal fence being smashed, and there was yelling … in Japanese … but why … and who? I tried to look, feeling the sting of another blow, and another, and through teared-up eyes I caught the blurry outline of somebody scaling the fence … why would they climb the fence? My eyes fell shut … I felt like I was sinking into the ground … even the blows stopped hurting … why was everybody yelling so much? I strained to open my eyes. There were people, it seemed like dozens of people, screaming and yelling and swearing and punching … why were they punching each other? Sam couldn't be fighting them all …

I suddenly felt myself being pulled up by powerful hands. Why didn't they just leave me alone? I stumbled and staggered, unable to stand. I was held on both sides.

"It okay, Tadashi."

"Sam?" I asked. I tried to focus, but I couldn't.

"Toshio."

"Toshio?" I asked in amazement. I looked over. He was holding me up under one arm. "But how …"

"The fence. We climb fence."

I tried to look around. My head was spinning, and

my stomach lurched violently as I turned. There were men and boys, Japanese, standing all around us. There were ten or twelve or twenty or … I don't know how many of them there were. The whites were gone. Their car was gone. Where was Sam?

"Sam!" I yelled out.

"Here, I'm here," he said.

I turned around and was shocked by what I saw. The whole side of his face was covered in blood, as well as his shirt, which was ripped and practically torn right off his body.

"Now that was a fight!" Sam said. He was beaming, a smile breaking through the blood.

"Your face … you're hurt."

He grabbed the tattered remains of his shirt and wiped off some of the blood. More flowed freely from his mouth and nose. He spat and a mouthful of bright red blood stained the ground.

"I've had worse," he said. "Are you okay?"

My whole body either hurt or felt numb and I still thought I might throw up.

"I'm okay," I said, realizing that my jaw hurt when I answered.

"Did you see them run?" Sam asked.

"I didn't see anything, nothing."

"It was like in one of those cowboy movies, you know, where the calvary comes charging over the hill, except this time it was over the fence!" Sam stopped and spat out more bloody saliva.

"But how did they get over the fence?" I asked.

I turned around and saw the answer. There were blankets strewn over the top of the fence, covering up the barbed wire. For the first time, I noticed that there were lots of people standing on the other side of the fence. I guessed that everybody who was either playing or watching the baseball game was now on one side of the fence or the other. As I stood there watching, a couple of men started to scale the fence to get back inside the park.

"Hurry," Toshio said. "Have to get back."

I knew he was right. Maybe two boys slipping under a fence wouldn't be noticed by the passing cars, but a brawl involving this many people couldn't help but draw attention. Had one of the passing cars stopped at the main gate, or pulled over to a telephone booth and called the police … I knew what would happen if we were found outside the park.

"Let's go," I said. I took a tentative step and winced in pain. I brought my hand up to my side. The whole right side of my chest hurt — the place where I'd been kicked repeatedly. I tried to take a deep breath, but a stabbing pain, like something digging into my lungs, stopped me.

I grasped the fence with my hands. I looked up at the top and my head felt whoozy. I didn't know if I could scale it.

"Climb," Toshio said as he stood at my side.

"I don't know if I can."

"Climb, now!" he barked.

That sounded more like the Toshio I knew, always giving people orders. Sam was already halfway up, and others were dropping to the ground on the other side.

"Please … have to … please … Tadpole," Toshio said.

I didn't know what surprised me more, his gentle tone of voice or him calling me by my nickname. Nobody but my sisters and Jed ever did that.

"I'll try."

I reached up and wrapped my fingers around the coils of the fence. I dug in the toe of one shoe and heaved myself up. Pain shot down my right side. I grimaced, but held on.

"Hurry up!" called out voices from the other side of the fence.

"There isn't much time!"

"Come on, climb!" called out a third.

I used my right hand to hold on while I reached up with my left. I pulled myself up. It didn't hurt nearly as much using that arm. Grabbing the fence securely with that hand, I very slowly lifted my right hand. Rather than a shooting pain, it was only a dull ache. I repeated the same thing, again and again, limping up the fence. There were two men perched on the top of the fence, the blanket beneath them, and they reached down and pulled me up. I had to bite down hard and clench my teeth to avoid screaming out in pain. My feet slipped down the fence, and for a split second they slid as I tried unsuccessfully to get my toes into the fence. One toe and then the other dug in. Lowering myself was better, not nearly as painful.

I looked up and saw Toshio reach the top. He was the last one over … he'd stayed behind with me … why had he done that … why had he even come over in the first place to help me and Sam? There couldn't be anybody in this whole park he liked less than the two of us.

The men at the top grabbed the blankets and tore them off the barbed wire. The bundled blankets fell to the ground and the men scampered down the fence, reaching the bottom at the same instant I touched down.

An older gentleman was barking out orders in Japanese. He was yelling for everybody to get back into the bleachers to watch the game, and for the players to start the game. Quickly the crowd followed his instructions. I understood what he was doing. He wanted everything to look normal if soldiers or police came. So people could say, "Fight? What fight? We're watching baseball … are you sure there was a fight? Oh no, we didn't see anything … you must be mistaken."

The old man stopped me. "Doctor see you, and you," he said, pointing first at me and then at Sam. "And you, and you and you," he said, aiming his finger at three others who were also cut and bleeding. "All go to infirmary to see doctor … Japanese doctor."

I hadn't been to the infirmary, but I'd heard that there were two doctors and some nurses, all Japanese living in the park, who were caring for people. I didn't want to see any doctor, but maybe I should. Either way, we needed to get away. If soldiers were on the way, it would be hard to hide the fact that we'd been in a brawl.

"Go, different ways … not all together," the old man ordered.

That made sense. We shouldn't walk through the park like some sort of parade. He sent the three injured men off. Two of them headed in the completely wrong direction.

"Can you walk?" Sam asked.

I nodded my head. "I can walk … slowly."

We'd started to walk away when I noticed that while almost everybody had moved away, Toshio was lingering behind.

"Hold on a minute," I said to Sam.

I limped over to Toshio's side. "Thanks for helping," I said.

He nodded his head.

I wanted to say something more, ask him why … why did he come to help me and Sam, and, maybe even more, why did he help me over the fence after the fighting was all done? If he just wanted a good fight, and that seemed like Toshio, what did staying with me have to do with any of that?

"Japanese help Japanese," Toshio said quietly, answering my unspoken question.

"Thanks … I mean it."

"Go before soldiers come," he said, then turned and walked away toward the baseball game, which had already restarted.

.17.

"Ooowwh! That hurts!"

The doctor released his grip on my jaw. "Open your mouth as wide as you can."

I opened it partway, until the pain stopped me. The whole left side of my face was swollen and the pain was radiating out of that side. He looked inside my mouth and again took my jaw in his hand and moved it, this time more gently. It hurt, but this time I was ready and didn't scream out.

"I don't think it's broken, just a bad bruise. I could take an x-ray to be certain. That is, if I had an x-ray machine we could use."

"So I'm okay?" I asked.

"Do you feel okay?" he laughed.

"No, not really." I wasn't as dizzy anymore, but I still felt like throwing up and my side hurt every time I tried to take a breath.

"When you were hit in the head … was it punched or kicked?"

"Both — at least, I think so."

"Did you lose consciousness?"

"What?"

"Did you black out?" he asked.

"I don't think so."

"Feel dizzy, want to throw up, are you shaky when you stand?"

"All of those." I actually *had* thrown up on the walk over, and for a minute or so afterwards felt a little bit better.

"Remove your shirt, please."

I tried to move my arm, and a jolt of pain shot up out of my side and into my head. I was happy that I didn't cry out, but the doctor must have been able to see from my expression how much it hurt. He undid the buttons and helped me slip the shirt off.

"Lift up your arms and take a deep breath," he ordered.

"I'll try."

Tentatively I raised my arms. The pain stopped me before I had gotten them to shoulder height.

"Big breath," he said.

"I can't. When I do it feels like —"

"You're being stabbed by a knife," the doctor said, interrupting me. "I didn't think you'd be able to."

I nodded my head.

He gently lifted my right arm and started to touch my side, poking and prodding with his fingers, beginning at the bottom. I clenched my teeth and groaned in pain as he hit a tender spot.

"That's one."

He moved up farther and this time I couldn't contain the pain and cried out.

"That's two."

He moved up again and I readied myself. I almost laughed when he pressed in and it only felt sore. He continued walking up my rib cage with his fingers like it was a ladder. With each step up, the soreness faded away. That had to be good.

Next the doctor took the stethoscope from around his neck, placed the two pieces in his ears and held it to my chest.

"Breathe as deep as you can, until the pain gets too much. Keep taking those breaths until I tell you to stop."

I inhaled and he listened, and then he moved it over and listened again. He did this a few more times.

"Stop," he said as he removed the stethoscope from his ears and hung it back around his neck.

"Well?" I asked.

"You have a head injury, a badly bruised jaw, possibly with a slight fracture, and two broken ribs."

"Broken!" I exclaimed.

"But you have good air intake and your chest is not flailing. I'm going to tape up your ribs and you're to take it very easy for the next week, maybe longer."

I felt a rush of relief, like a weight had been lifted from my shoulders. Unfortunately, the weight was still on my chest.

"When should I come back to see you?" I asked.

"You don't understand … you're staying here."

"Here? But you let Sam go!" I protested.

Sam had been examined by the doctor first, while a nurse had packed gauze into my nose to stop it from bleeding and then cleaned me up.

"He wasn't as badly hurt. I imagine he didn't fall down as many steps as you did."

"I didn't fall down any steps," I said in confusion. Didn't he know what had happened?

"You look surprised," the doctor said. "I guess you hit your head so hard when you fell that you don't even remember how you were injured."

"But … but …"

He started to laugh. "You fell down a set of stairs — at least, that's what I'm putting in the medical files," he explained. "I couldn't very well put down that you had been in a fight, especially one outside the park, that is possibly being investigated as we talk. I heard it was quite the brawl."

"I don't know. I couldn't see much of it from the ground," I said reluctantly.

"That would explain your injuries. Your ribs and jaw, and those marks on the side of your face, look like the damage that would be done by somebody kicking you."

"Lots of people were kicking me. I don't know what would have happened if people didn't come over the fence to help us."

"You might have been beaten to death."

He was probably just being dramatic, sort of lecturing me about getting in fights.

"Another well-placed kick or two, and one of those ribs could have pierced a lung and you could have bled internally. Possibly bled to death."

His words hit me like another shot in the head.

"You mean …"

"Yes, you could have died," he said.

I exhaled loudly. "But I'm okay now … right?"

"You'll be fine, but with rib injuries there's always a danger the patient will develop pneumonia. I can't have you going off to sleep on the floor of some damp stall. You'll stay here in the infirmary."

"But what about my parents? I didn't want them to …" I let the sentence trail off.

"To know you'd been in a fight?"

I nodded my head. "But in the report you're going to say I fell down stairs."

"That report is for the administration here. Them we lie to, parents we don't. Understand?"

"I understand." I felt badly for even thinking about lying to them. What sort of person did the doctor think I was?

"I want you to move both arms away from your sides. It may help if you use your left arm to cradle the right," the doctor said.

I followed his directions. It did help a little to hold my right arm with my left hand. The doctor took a roll of adhesive tape from a tray beside him. He started to apply it to my left side.

"But it's the other side that's injured."

"Who do you think is the doctor here?" he asked.

He slowly wrapped the tape around my back, under my arm and across my chest. After several wraps, the sharp pain in my chest eased to a dull ache as the injured ribs were held in place.

"I hope you don't mind me asking, but what was so important to make you and your friend leave the park?" the doctor asked.

I hesitated. I really didn't want to tell him about the letter. "I guess mainly we just wanted to get out ... be free for a while."

The doctor had started back around with a second piece of tape. "I can understand that. If they didn't let me out to check on patients that have been transferred to the hospital I think I'd go crazy."

He cut off the second piece after making a complete loop and then started back around for a third time.

"This is to immobilize the site of the injury. To stop the ribs from moving. How does it feel?"

"Very tight ... but it does feel a little bit better, I think."

"Good."

"Could I ask you a question?" I asked.

"Certainly," the doctor replied.

"Do you like what you're doing?"

"Being a doctor?"

"Yeah, do you like being a doctor?" I asked.

"It is a fairly rewarding profession. Why, is it something you're interested in pursuing?"

"I thought I might. I just don't know about having to go away to Japan to school," I answered.

"It was difficult, but until things change there's no choice. There still isn't a medical school in all of Canada that will admit an Oriental." He paused. "Funny, before all this happened, I really thought it might be different by the time somebody your age got around to being old enough to apply. Shows you what I know. But then again, if some of the rumors I hear are true, it won't be as big a shock for you as it was for me to go to school in Japan."

"Why not?" I asked.

"Because you'll already be living there."

My mouth dropped open, and I think he could see the shock on my face.

"I'm sorry, I shouldn't have said that. Just another stupid rumor about us all being shipped to Japan. Nothing to it at all, I'm sure," he said, shaking his head. "That's just my frustration talking. There's lots of frustration. We all feel it. In the last four weeks I've had a lifetime's worth of experience in dealing with this sort of injury. Slip your shirt back on."

"Have a lot of people been falling down stairs?" I asked as I carefully slipped my arms back into the sleeves of my shirt.

"Every day at least one, and sometimes a lot more. You put this many people, this many men, together in one place, all packed in tight like sardines in a can. You give them nothing to do all day, and then you add alcohol, and you can't help but create conflict." He paused. "But even worse is what they've taken away from us," he said.

"You mean like the houses and the fishing boats?" I asked.

"It's not the possessions, but what they mean. What does your father do for a living?"

"He's a fisherman."

"There are lots of fishermen in here," he said. "You have to understand that being a fisherman is more than what your father *does*. It's a big part of what he *is*. Me, I was a doctor."

"You're still a doctor," I argued.

"You're right, technically. They still let me do some

parts of my job, seeing people here, but it's different ... let me see if I can explain."

He slowly walked across the room, rubbing his chin with his hand, thinking. He came back and sat on a high stool beside the examination table.

"I saw patients in my office and in their homes. Mostly Japanese, but some Chinese, even some whites. Doesn't matter. They all trust me, call me 'doctor', or even 'sir'. Respect me. I have a big house. Wife and kids, four kids. A car. A nice car. Enough money. Respect in the community." He paused and his expression changed. "And then this all happened, and me and my family are sent here, along with everybody else, and you know what I realized? None of it mattered. In the end I'm not a doctor, or a respected member of the community, or a property owner, or even a husband and father. All I am is a Jap." He paused again. "But enough. You weren't brought to hear me rant. I'll send somebody around to let your parents know you're here."

"When they come, could I be the one to tell them what happened?" I asked.

"It might be better."

"I just think they should hear it from me."

"Certainly. What is your last name, Tadashi?"

"Fukushima."

"Fukushima? Does your grandmother live with you?"

"Yeah, and my mother and ... why?" I asked. I was overcome by a terrible fear.

"Come," the doctor said, walking away.

I carefully climbed off the examination table and limped after him. The pain in my body made it hard to keep up with him, but I was pushed along by the uneasiness in my head. I trailed behind him as he passed beds filled with people. The doctor stopped and pulled back a curtain. My entire family stood around a bed, a bed occupied by my grandmother!

"Tadashi, we were looking for you everywhere and …" Midori stopped talking. "What happened to you?"

I could tell by the look on her face and the expression of my parents that they were shocked by my appearance. Even though the nurse had cleaned up the blood, I knew I still must look awful.

"He's going to be all right," the doctor said.

"But, but … what happened?" my father questioned as my mother ran over and threw her arms around me. I grimaced in pain.

I took a deep breath — at least, as deep as I could take. "I was in a fight … outside the park. But how is grandmother?"

"Same, sick. She's so weak she couldn't get out of bed."

"Influenza. Same strain that's spreading like wildfire across the park," the doctor said.

"Is she going to be okay?" I asked in a whisper.

The doctor nodded his head. "She'll be fine in a few days, a week at most."

"Fine now," my grandmother said. "Go back home." Her voice was just a whisper. She didn't sound fine.

"I'm going to leave you all alone. I'm sure you have much to discuss," the doctor said. He pulled the curtain closed behind him as he left. I wasn't looking forward to trying to explain to my father why I had left the park.

•••

I started as I woke up in the darkened room. My grandmother was standing over me, and I felt reassured and confused at the same time. Where was I? As I tried to sit up, the pain in my side reminded me.

"Go to sleep," my grandmother said softly.

"Why aren't you in bed?" I asked.

"Checking on you. Fixing covers," she said as she tucked in my blanket.

"I'm fine, but you need to get back into bed."

She ignored me, continuing to tuck in the loose edges of my bedding. She then sat down on the edge of my bed. Even in the dark, she looked so thin and frail. The sound of coughing filtered through the curtains that surrounded and separated our two beds from the rest of the patients. At my grandmother's insistence, they'd put both of our beds in the same space, so close together that they were practically touching.

"You need to go back to bed," I said again.

"Later." She reached up and stroked my head. It felt good, reassuring. It brought me back to a time when I was little and she used to do that every night after my mother had put me to bed.

"Like your father, Tadashi. Sit and stroke his head when he boy. Now he is man and his son is nearly man." She chuckled softly. "My time is near."

"What do you mean?" I asked in alarm, although I knew in my gut exactly what she was saying.

"Old."

"You're not that old!" I protested.

"Look at my hands," she said as she stopped stroking my head and held them before my eyes. "Old woman's hands." She turned them over. They were as tiny as the rest of her, wrinkled and old.

"Will die."

"But the doctor says you're getting better!" I protested.

"Not yet, but will happen. You die too."

"I'm not going to —"

"Everybody die," she said with a shrug.

"Of course … but not for a long time. A long, long time."

"Time," she said, shaking her head. "I remember Tadashi as a baby, and your father as a baby … and me … little girl." She was staring off into the distance. "Time goes."

"But not yet, not today."

She shook her head. "Not yet. Soon. And then ashes."

I knew what she meant. After she died she wanted her body to be cremated, burned until all that was left was ashes. That was how Buddhists took care of their dead. Right now, though, I didn't want to hear any of this. Why didn't she just go back to bed?

"You just baby when grandfather die."

I was less than two years old and could only remember him from the pictures we had.

"Beautiful, in forest. All day and all night. Pretty fire. Sitting, standing, watching … eating foods … his favorite foods … shrimp, nuts … taking sips of sake." She paused again. "You were there."

"I was?"

"Everybody there. All family. All village."

I guess that shouldn't have surprised me. I'd only actually been to one other cremation, but I knew that all members of the family would be present, as well as friends and neighbors. It was funny, but if you could forget for a second that there was a dead body burning in the fire it had more of the feel of a picnic — outdoors, eating, drinking, tears but also lots of laughter and talking, and, of course, the gigantic bonfire to warm your hands.

"For me, like husband." She paused. "Then ashes need go home."

"Father will make sure they get back to Japan," I said, although I didn't know how he'd do that — not, at least, until the war was over.

"No … not Japan … *my* home. Sikima. Village. Our home. Together with family. Family together."

"But I thought Japan would be home for you," I said in disbelief.

"Japan *was* home. Canada *is* home."

Canada was my home, but hers? Especially after all that had happened?

"I did not know either," she said, obviously aware that her answer had surprised me. "When close eyes I dream of home … our village … our home … Sikima. That is where ashes go."

I thought it might be easier to get them to Japan, but I wasn't going to say anything. What was the point?

"Don't be sad," she said.

"I'm not …" She was right, though; I was feeling very sad.

"I tell story to help you sleep."

"It's the middle of the night and we need to get to —"

She put a finger on my lips to silence me. "Story, then sleep. Okay?"

"Okay, but only if you promise to get back into bed to tell me the story."

She nodded her head. She shuffled the few feet and climbed up onto the high hospital bed.

"Get under the covers," I ordered her.

She chuckled and pulled the blanket over her. "Story now?"

"Yes, story now," I answered.

"A boy in forest … in jungle. Gathering food when he sees a tiger. And tiger sees him."

I hadn't heard this story before.

"Boy runs. Tiger chases. Just as tiger to get him, the boy falls down a cliff!" she said, her voice rising.

"Sshhhhhhhh!" I hissed, not wanting her to wake up the whole hospital.

She giggled like a little girl and then nodded her head. "Fall, fall, fall, and then, grab branch," she whispered. "Look up, tiger looking down. Look down … very far … and tiger at bottom!"

"How could the tiger get to the bottom?" I questioned.

"Other tiger, second tiger."

"There are two tigers?" I was trying to think how this story was going to help me get to sleep.

"And boy hang by branch. Cannot go up or die. Cannot go down or die. Looks beside. And he sees it."

So there was going to be a happy ending — he was going to escape.

"Sees a strawberry."

"A strawberry?" I questioned. How would that help?

"Big, fat, juicy strawberry. He reach out and grab strawberry and put in mouth. *Sooo* good, *sooo* tasty, better than ever." She paused. "Now go sleep."

"Go to sleep? You mean that's the end of the story?"

She nodded her head.

"But he's still hanging there, surrounded by tigers … he's going to die!"

"All will die. All."

"But there has to be more …"

"Think," she said softly. "Think."

"I don't under —" I stopped as it suddenly hit me. At least, I thought I understood. "The story isn't about death, but about life. The part between the tigers. We're all going to die, but we have to enjoy whatever happens in between. Whether it's hanging from a branch or living in a cattle stall."

I could see her smile in the dark. "Good night, my little boy."

"Good night," I answered.

I turned over and pressed my eyes tightly shut. She was old, and we all had to die. Of course, I knew that. But, please, not here … please, not now, I prayed.

.18.

"So how long are you going to pretend to be sick?"

"Sam!" I called out as I got off my bed and stood up. "They're letting me go today."

"About time. I can't believe they kept you in here for three days," he said as he sat down on the edge of the bed. "I didn't even think you were that badly hurt."

"Neither did I ... at first," I said, putting a hand on my still-taped side.

"Next time you're in a fight, try to hit them *more* with your fists, and *less* with your face and side."

"I'll try to remember that."

"Say, where's your grandmother?" Sam asked, gesturing to where her bed used to be.

"They let her go yesterday."

"So she's better?" he asked.

"Still weak, but doing a lot better. She's holding down food and drinking."

I think Sam liked my grandmother, and she liked him. Whenever he'd dropped in to visit, they'd talk and she'd make a big fuss over him. He didn't have grandparents, so I think he found it different and maybe even a little embarrassing at first, but then he just liked it. The last visit, he'd spent more time talking to her than he did to me.

"Do you want me to wait around until they release you?" Sam asked.

"No, that's okay —"

Just then one of the nurses pushed through the curtain. "Hello, Tadashi."

"Hi."

"I see you have your friend here to escort you home."

"I can go now?"

"Right now. We need the bed."

"Great! I can be dressed and gone in ten minutes."

She laughed. "It sounds like you didn't enjoy your stay."

"No, I'm just happy to be better."

"Dr. Izumi wants you to come back in three days to see him. But if you feel any back pain or start coughing badly, come back sooner, okay?"

"I will … for sure … and thanks, thanks for everything. I really appreciate what everybody did," I said.

"That's quite all right," she said, and smiled. "And do us all the favor, both of you, and don't go falling down any more stairs."

"You can count on that!" I said.

"Weeeelllllll," Sam said, drawing the word out. "It all depends. Sometimes a set of stairs comes right up to you and you just don't have any choice but to go down them."

"Try and take the elevator for a while," she suggested.

"I'll try," Sam agreed.

She left and I finished dressing and tying up my shoes. I couldn't believe how happy I felt to be leaving. Strange, I was one of the few people in the whole place sleeping in a bed and I was glad to be going back to a mattress on the floor of a cattle stall. I guess what my grandmother always said was right — it didn't matter where you were as long as you were with your family.

"It's almost lunchtime," Sam said. "Are you hungry?"

"Not really."

"Even better. Let's get to the mess hall."

His answer made no sense, but it didn't matter much to me. I was just happy to be leaving, and my family might even be there now eating.

We left the infirmary and crossed over the park toward the mess.

"Did anybody ever question you about the fight?" Sam asked.

"Well, Dr. Izumi said a few things, and both the nurses —"

"No, I mean like the soldiers or RCMP."

"No, nobody like that," I answered, with some alarm. "I didn't even know they'd heard about it."

"Everybody heard about it. It was in the newspapers," Sam said.

"You're joking, right?"

"No joke. There was an editorial in the paper about security in the park and how some of the Japanese had stormed the fence and attacked some innocent —"

"Innocent! They started it and —"

"And they're white," Sam said, cutting me off. "Who do you think the newspapers and police are going to believe?"

I didn't answer, which of course said it all.

"The editorial went on about how there should be every effort made to relocate us as soon as possible and more security should be added so more whites don't get injured."

"Some of them got injured?" I asked.

"Of course. A few of them limped away in a lot worse shape than you were in."

"Did anybody question you?" I asked.

"Not me, but they did make some inquiries all around the park. They were sniffing around. I heard they were threatening to ship out to Angler anybody they found."

"I guess we won't be going out again," I said.

"No question about that. Even if we weren't caught, my father threatened to personally kill me if I even tried." He paused. "That reminds me, what did your parents say about you going out of the park?"

"Not much. My father said we'd talk about it after I healed. So I guess I'm going to find out soon enough."

I looked up ahead. "Look at that lineup!" I said to Sam. It extended right out the door of the mess hall.

"Yeah, it's been like that since supper yesterday."

"Have that many more people arrived?" I asked.

"More every day. The number is up to almost three thousand five hundred."

"Wow, that's a lot of people. Maybe we can come back later when the line has thinned out a bit," I suggested.

"Don't worry, it'll move fast."

"But I hate waiting in line, and I'm not even hungry."

"Like I said, that's good that you're not hungry."

"You want to explain to me how not being hungry is good?" I asked.

"You'll see."

I would have pressed Sam for an answer, but I knew him well enough to know there was no point. At least he was right about the line; it did seem to be moving very quickly. We were almost inside the mess hall already. I wondered if they'd made some changes to accommodate the extra people since I was in the infirmary. They must have added more servers or be doing something different to explain the speed. Of course, looking back I could see that it was a good thing we were moving quickly because the line behind us was growing even more rapidly than we were moving forward.

"I wonder what they're serving for lunch," I said.

"It doesn't matter," Sam replied.

"Why doesn't it matter?"

"You'll see," Sam answered with a smile.

I was becoming much more than a little bit curious. Between Sam not answering questions and him practically pushing me into the mess hall to begin with, there must be something worth seeing.

"Here," Sam said, passing me a tray.

"Thanks."

I grabbed a bowl and plate and put them on my tray. The bins holding spoons and forks were empty.

"There are no utensils," I said.

Sam shook his head. "It doesn't matter."

"What do you —" I stopped myself as Sam started to chuckle to himself.

I craned my head around to try to see to the front of the line. I couldn't see anything out of the ordinary. I caught glimpses of the women behind the counter — there didn't seem to be any more of them than before — they were standing there with their arms folded across their chests and ... they didn't seem to be serving anybody, just standing there.

I turned my attention to where everybody was sitting. There didn't seem to be an empty seat. People were crowded around the tables, and ... strange, nobody seemed to be talking, they were just sitting there silently staring ahead ... nobody seemed to be eating! In front of each person there was a tray, and on the tray was an overturned bowl or plate. I scanned row after row. There was no food! Nobody was eating!

"I said you'd see," Sam said, realizing by my expression that I'd finally caught on.

"There's not a person in the whole hall eating!" I said in amazement.

"There's not a person in the whole *park* who's eating from the mess. Not one," Sam said. "It's a food strike."

"But how?"

"It all started with those old people. They refused to eat, protesting that they wanted proper food, maybe even Japanese food."

"Protesting like we saw the other day — the day we left the park?"

"Yeah, it had been going on for a few days already at

that time. But then some other people our age joined in … I was one of the first," Sam said, beaming. "And then some other people joined in, and then our leaders, people like Mr. Wakabayashi, organized it so that everybody in the whole park got involved, starting with supper yesterday. Isn't it amazing!"

"But people have to eat!" I protested.

"Some people haven't stopped. They've set up a special place where the old people can get some food, mainly rice and other Japanese stuff. And of course anybody who's sick and in the infirmary is still eating."

"Like me. Is that why I didn't know about this?"

Sam nodded his head. We were almost at the front of the line. Sam put down his tray on the ledge and then noisily slammed his plate and bowl upside down. I did the same, except not as dramatically. We slid the trays past the silent and sullen serving women. Overflowing bins of steaming potatoes and tomato soup and buns stared up at us. I still wasn't even hungry, but I couldn't help thinking that things did smell good.

We came to the end and picked up our empty trays. There now wasn't even a single seat to be seen, and we joined a line of people leaning against the far wall. I looked around for my parents or sisters. I didn't see them.

"A place will soon open up for us to sit," Sam said.

No sooner had he finished his sentence than the people at a whole long row of tables at the back of the hall stood up and started to move away. We took seats at one of the vacated tables.

"So we just sit here and look at our plates?" I asked.

"For fifteen minutes. We sit for fifteen minutes and then we go. That's what everybody is doing."

"Wouldn't it be easier if we just didn't show up at all?" I suggested.

"Easier for them, maybe. It isn't a protest unless they can see you, and they can't see you if you don't come."

I guess that made sense.

For the first time I also noticed something else. There were soldiers positioned around the mess hall. I counted them ... ten of them.

"Sam, do you know why there are soldiers here?" I asked.

"They were here at breakfast this morning. I think we have them worried."

"Worried about what?"

"They're scared that the food strike might turn into something more."

"Something more? Like what?"

"I don't know. Maybe a food riot. There's a lot of anger pinned inside this fence."

"I know, but ..."

"But everybody's too Japanese," Sam said, completing my thought.

"Yeah."

"A few days ago I would have agreed with you. Now I'm not so sure. Something could happen."

"Maybe. But how long can this go on? People need to eat."

"We will eat. Everybody is having supper tonight."

"And that's the end of the food strike?"

"No. Like you said, people need to eat, but there'll be another strike at lunch or maybe breakfast the next day. It'll be a surprise announcement."

"Why a surprise?"

"So that they have to bring in food and prepare each meal. So that they don't know when we're going to stop eating. To take control," Sam explained.

"And we'll just keep doing that?" I asked.

"Until they give in to the demands."

"What demands?"

"For better food," Sam said. "Maybe even Japanese food."

"But you don't even like Japanese food," I said.

"No, I don't," Sam answered. "But you know what I like even less? Being told what I have to do or what I have to eat … and I think other people are getting tired of it too."

.19.

"There's no reason to be nervous," Sam said as we walked.

"I'm not nervous ... well, not very nervous."

"You're just going to pick up a letter."

"I know, and I should be happy." My name had been posted on the board amongst those people who had received mail. It meant I had to go to the main administration building.

"It has to be from your friend, right?" Sam asked.

"I can't think of anybody else who'd be sending me mail."

"I hope it's from him ... I wouldn't want that trip outside to have been for nothing."

We stopped in front of the administration building. The palms of my hands felt sweaty. I knew this was just about getting mail, but part of me wondered if there was more to this. Had they somehow found out that I was one of the people who was involved with that brawl outside the fence and were tricking me like this to get me here? Of course, that made no sense, but fear seldom had anything to do with sense.

The building was a hub of activity. It sat just inside the park, directly behind the main gate, and there was a steady stream of soldiers and vehicles that went back and forth from the building to the entrance.

"Do you know where exactly I'm supposed to go?" I asked.

"It's this way," Sam answered. "I was here with my father to pick up mail a couple of times."

Sam motioned to the side of the building and I followed. Rounding the corner of the building it was obvious where I had to go. There was a line of Japanese extending out one of the doors.

"Is there anyplace in this whole camp that doesn't have a lineup?" I asked.

"Not that I've seen. I'm going to wait over there," Sam said, pointing to an empty bench shaded by a big tree.

"You're not coming with me?"

"Why, are you expecting a really heavy letter?" Sam sauntered off and flopped down on the bench.

I shuffled along quietly. I couldn't help but think that the Japanese were just about the best people in the world at lining up. Of course, we'd all had plenty of practice around here, but we seemed to be so naturally polite and quiet. I would have loved to have seen somebody not be so polite — maybe complain out loud, or swear or push and shove, or even butt in.

"Next!" called out a voice.

I moved over to the woman behind the open counter.

"Name?"

"Fukushima, Tadashi."

"Which of those is your last name?" she asked.

"Fukushima. My first name is —"

She held her hand up. "It's hard enough to remember one name, so don't confuse me with the second."

She walked off, returning in thirty seconds with a box, which she placed on the counter in between us.

"Here you go," she said.

"Are you sure it's for me? I wasn't expecting a parcel."

"This your name on the top?" she said, spinning the parcel so the label faced me.

Instantly I recognized the handwriting. It was from Jed! "Yes, it is! Thank you!"

I picked up the parcel and left the building. I had to fight the urge to simply rip open the box right there. But I wanted to sit down beside Sam in the shade and open it.

"That looks interesting," Sam commented as I approached. "What do you think it is?"

"I don't know."

I sat down and pulled the tape holding the top closed. It came off easily, and I knew that the censors had already been inside, looking at whatever it was, before sealing it back up and passing it on to me.

I pulled out some paper that was stuffed in the top of the box as packing. There was an envelope and my baseball glove! Why would that be in there, and how did he even get it in the first place? I was positive I'd left it in my house. I grabbed the envelope and ripped it open. I pulled the letter out and unfolded it.

Dear Tadashi,

I was very happy to receive your letter. My family is all doing well and I hope everybody is good in your family. I have been working very hard in school. Do you go to school as well where you are?

I was going through all my old things and I thought you might like to have my old baseball glove.

I stopped reading and picked up the glove. This wasn't his old glove, this was my glove, the one I always used, the one that I left in my house when we had to leave. If I'd have known there was going to be a baseball diamond here, I would have taken it along with me. At least I knew he must have received my *real* letter because I hadn't mentioned anything about anything, including playing baseball, in the fake letter I sent from the camp. But why was he claiming that it was his glove?

*I still spend a lot of time in the forest. Sometimes I go
past your village. The weather has been good for early
summer, not much rain. I still work with my mother,
but not as much.*

Your friend,
Jed

"That's it?" I said in amazement. "I get beaten up to
mail him that letter and he doesn't answer a single one
of my questions?"

"Maybe he couldn't figure out how to tell you anything without tipping off the censors," Sam suggested.
"At least you got a baseball glove out of the deal," he
said as he picked it up. "Although it's not much of a
glove."

"It's a great glove!" I said, snatching it away from
him. I tried to slip it on my hand, but one of my fingers
couldn't fit in — something was in the finger hole. I
pulled out my hand and peered inside. What was blocking it? It looked like a piece of paper. What would that
be doing in there — unless … Hastily I pulled it out and
unfolded the tightly folded paper. It was another letter!

Dear Tadashi,

*We figured out a way to write you so the censors
wouldn't see it. I was really glad to get your letter. I'm
sorry about how things worked out and about where
you're living. Things here aren't the same without you.
School is more boring, although with all the Japanese
gone, the teachers now see me as being a good student.
Hard to imagine, me a good student. I spend more
time at home now that they hired a second cook.*

*My mom and Naani are okay. I still worry about my
father. He writes letters and tells us there's nothing to*

· 211 ·

worry about, but I know what he's doing is about as dangerous as you can get. I'm also very proud of him. I heard, not from him, of course, that he's an ace, which means he's shot down at least five enemy planes.

I keep an eye out for Eddy. I haven't seen him, but one of the guards is sure he saw him.

I'm sorry to be the one to have to tell you, but some of those rumors are true. I was out at your village two weeks ago. I was tracking a big buck. I got into the village and found some guys breaking into the houses. I chased them off, but they said they'd be back. I heard from the soldiers that looting has been taking place all over. Major Brown said the RCMP doesn't have the people to stop them. Anyway, I figured that though I couldn't stop everything, I could stop them from taking your stuff. I went and collected a lot of your belongings, things I thought your family would want. They're safe and I'll get them to your family as soon as you know where you're going to.

I'm really sorry for all that's happened. Please let your family know that most of the people, even people like Major Brown, figure what they did to you was wrong. I just hope it won't be wrong for too long.

Your best friend,
Jed

I put down the letter and took a deep breath.
"Sounds like he's a good friend," Sam said.
"What?"
"I hope you don't mind, but I was reading over your shoulder. He sounds like a good friend to do that for you and your family."
"He is a good friend."

"So what are you going to do? Are you going to tell your father?" Sam asked.

"I don't want to, but I guess I have to tell him what's happening," I said.

"And maybe the other people from your village," Sam added. "They have a right to know too."

"You're right … but I don't think I want to be the one to tell them. I'll tell my father and he can decide how —"

"Tadashi! Tadashi!"

I turned around at the sound of my name and saw Midori rushing toward me. Why didn't she just leave me alone for — there were tears running down her face and she looked panicked.

"What's wrong?" I demanded.

"It's grandmother. She's very sick — come quickly!"

"How bad is she?" I demanded.

"I don't know … Mother and Yuri went for the doctor, Father stayed with her, and they sent me to find you. I looked everywhere. At the baseball diamond and the mess hall and —"

"We have to go to her," I said, cutting Midori off abruptly.

I started to run. Sam was quickly at my side, and we left Midori behind as we dodged through the crowd of people. We cut off the path and went between two buildings. By now I knew almost every inch of the park and all the best ways to get from one place to another.

"I can't go on like this," I panted to Sam as I slowed to a walk. My ribs were feeling better, but as I was running I was struggling to take a full breath, and I felt a stabbing pain start to dig into my side.

"I thought she was doing better," Sam said.

"Dr. Izumi was there to see her the day before yesterday. He said she was doing much better. She's eating and holding down her food. She's able to walk around and she even looks better."

"But …"

"I don't know," I said. I wrapped an arm around my side and started to run again. Sam jogged at my side.

I felt my breath becoming more and more labored as we ran, and the little stabbing pain was getting sharper and starting to dig deeper into my side. Up ahead I caught sight of our building. I could run that far, but probably not much farther. There was a crowd of people standing outside of the big sliding door. Sam and I barreled past them and into the building. I stopped running, panting to catch my breath.

I suddenly realized that something wasn't right. Why was it so quiet in here? And where were all the people? The building was practically empty. Why would everybody leave the … A shiver ran up my spine.

I wanted to start running again, but stopped myself. Instead I walked, slowly, quietly, with respect, toward our stall. I turned the corner and saw my parents standing, my father with an arm around my mother, Yuri pressed against her side. My mother looked up at me and there was a look of pure anguish on her face. I felt the tears start to flow from deep within my chest and I knew without asking … my grandmother was gone.

.20.

She looked so peaceful lying there, like she was just asleep. She'd always liked to have a nap in the afternoon. That's all that was happening ... she was just lying down and in a little while she'd get up and then come with us for supper. If only. I turned and left the stall. My father stood there quietly talking to Dr. Izumi. My mother had taken my sisters to be with Mrs. Miyazaki in her stall in another building. She and my grandmother had been friends as far back as childhood in Japan. She said Mrs. Miyazaki would need them there. I think they needed to be with her as well.

I stood just behind my father.

"Thank you for everything, Doctor," my father said quietly, bowing slightly.

"I'm sorry. I didn't expect this. She was getting better, stronger."

"It was ... her time," my father said, his voice cracking over the last words. While everybody else had cried, he had tried to stand strong. I could see the tears were there, just beneath the surface, but he needed to be brave. I expected it. I even knew he might expect me to remain stoic too, but I couldn't help but let loose some tears, despite trying my hardest to contain them.

"Is your mother ... was your mother a Buddhist or Christian?" the doctor asked.

"Buddhist," my father answered.

"Then I imagine you'll want a cremation."

My father nodded solemnly.

"When I advise the camp authorities, I'll make sure they know the body is to be cremated."

"Thank you," my father said.

"I'll have them wait until after supper before removing the body," Dr. Izumi said.

"What do you mean, remove the body?" I asked, stepping forward.

"She must be removed in order for the cremation to take place."

"Moved to where?" I asked.

"To the crematorium, of course."

"What's a crematorium?"

"It's a special facility where the cremation takes place."

"It's a building … in the city?" I asked.

"Yes. And then they return the ashes for the family to dispose of them in accordance with the wishes of the deceased—"

"No," I said loudly, surprising myself not only with the force of the word, but the way it echoed around the silent and empty building.

The doctor took a step forward and placed a hand on my shoulder. "Tadashi, I know it is hard. Hard to believe she's gone and hard to say goodbye … but you must."

"That's not it," I said, shaking my head. "She's not leaving. Not to some building surrounded by strangers."

"The camp authorities will allow family members to be present and even hold a small ceremony with a priest and—"

"You don't understand! She didn't want that; she told me. She wanted all her family and friends to be there."

"Perhaps there can even be some sort of blessing arranged back here at the camp when they return the ashes," the doctor suggested. "I'm sorry, I don't know much about such things … I'm a Christian."

"No," I said. "She wanted to have the cremation in the woods, like her husband, my grandfather. Where we come from, there is no special building to do it … we just go into the forest … that's what she wanted."

My father gave me a questioning look, wanting to know how I knew what she wanted.

"She told me," I said, my voice hardly a whisper. "She told me a lot of things when we talked at night in the infirmary."

"I understand," the doctor said. "Often older people make requests, things they want, and then the family feels so guilty because they can't possibly fulfill that last request. Surely you understand the authorities won't allow you to travel up north to —"

"We don't have to travel anywhere. There's lots of open spaces here in the park —"

"You can't be serious," Dr. Izumi interrupted. "That just isn't done … not just because we're in this camp, but because we're in the city. The Japanese here in Vancouver, in all the cities, use the crematoriums … it just isn't allowed … there are laws!"

My father nodded to the doctor. "May I take a moment to speak with my son?"

"Certainly … thank you … thank you very much, Mr. Fukushima."

The doctor suddenly looked relieved, like he was happy to be free of this … that he was sure my father was going to talk some sense into me … and, of course, that was what he was going to do.

My father motioned for me to follow him into the stall. Seeing my grandmother lying there startled me — almost as if I had forgotten she was there. Part of me wanted to look away, but I couldn't. It was almost like if I looked hard enough, there'd be something — a slight movement, her chest rising, the sound of her breathing or coughing — that would signal that none of this was real, that somehow she was still alive.

"Tadashi … speak."

I took a deep breath. "We talked, a lot, those nights we spent together at the infirmary. She told me about grandfather and how he was cremated and how she wanted the same thing. It wasn't like the doctor said; she didn't make me promise or anything … it's just what she wanted."

My father slowly nodded his head, rubbing his face with his hand.

"Trouble … for the family. The authorities will object… maybe try to stop us … maybe punish us."

"How would they do that?"

"Send us away. Send me away. Possible."

"They can't do that!" I pleaded. "We have to stay together … we have to! Grandmother will understand if she has to go to a crematorium … I'm sure she'll understand."

He placed his hands on my shoulders. "Thank you for telling. Now it is my decision to make."

"Yes, Father," I mumbled, feeling like I was a little boy again. I realized that what I was suggesting hadn't been realistic … we couldn't jeopardize everybody because of something my grandmother had said … she said a lot of things, and I knew that she wouldn't have wanted anything that could have caused problems for us.

"Come," he said, and I trailed after him.

The doctor was at the far end of the aisle and came back to meet us.

"Well?" he asked.

"My mother … Tadashi's grandmother … will be cremated … here in the park with her family."

"But you don't understand how —" The doctor stopped himself in mid-sentence. "It doesn't matter what I say, does it? You've decided."

My father nodded his head.

"I think you better speak to Mr. Wakabayashi," Dr. Izumi said.

"He's not going to convince us to do anything differently," I stated defiantly.

"I didn't think he would even try to dissuade you," the doctor said. "But you'll need help, his help, to do this, and mark my words, there *will* be trouble."

•••

"Are you sure this is the plan you wish to pursue?" Mr. Wakabayashi asked my father.

He nodded.

"And that you are acting in accordance with the wishes of your mother?"

"Yes," I answered, stepping in since I knew better than anybody what she wanted, what she had said to me.

He pulled a handkerchief from his pocket and wiped the sweat from his brow. It wasn't hot in here at all ... he looked uneasy ... nervous. Then I realized why he was talking so much. Mr. Wakabayashi might be a powerful man and own half of the Japanese businesses on Powell Street, but even he was having second thoughts about what we were doing. That thought got me even more worried.

"The site has been prepared," he said.

It was the place I'd thought of earlier. It was a fairly large clearing, away from the buildings, beside the railroad tracks, partially hidden by bushes from the main part of the camp. It had one other feature that I liked — it was at the far end of the park, away from the administration building and the guard house. It wasn't the most pretty spot, but when the trains weren't rumbling by it was almost peaceful. I hoped my grandmother would understand it was the best we could do.

"And the body ... is it ready?" Mr. Wakabayashi asked.

Again my father nodded.

My grandmother's body had been bathed, and then she was placed in her best clothing. It was a dress and shawl that were her favorites, and little slippers. At first my mother wanted to put shoes on her, but Yuri had said she knew grandmother would rather have on her slippers because she always said they were more comfortable, and my mother agreed.

In her hand had been placed six coins. Those were to help pay for her passage into the next world. A clean white sheet had been placed underneath her, wrapped all around tightly and then sewn in place. Her head peeked out the top of the sheet.

"It's almost five o'clock," Mr. Wakabayashi said. "That means we have a little more than four hours until sunset. If the authorities don't notice before that, they'll certainly be able to see the flames then. By that time, though, I hope it'll be too late for them to try anything."

"What could they even try?" I asked.

He shook his head. "I don't know … maybe they might try to put out the funeral pyre."

"They can't … we won't let them," I said defiantly.

"We'll do everything we can," he said. "I'm prepared to talk to the commander at that time, reason with him, and try to convince him to allow it to continue. But you have to remember the circumstances under which we are living."

There was a silence, time to allow his words to sink in. Of course, what he said was right. What could we do if the soldiers, armed soldiers, tried to stop the proceedings?

"Could the family please proceed to the site?"

My father nodded and followed Mr. Wakabayashi out of the stall. I took a step to follow and then stopped. I looked back at my grandmother. She still looked like she was just sleeping. There was a peaceful look on her face, and I imagined she was having a pleasant dream.

A dream about home, about Sikima. Or maybe she knew what we were doing and approved of it.

All around her were flowers, real ones taken from the gardens and ornate, delicate paper flowers that had been crafted as an offering. On the wall was a picture, one I'd never seen before yesterday, of my grandmother. Beside her was a man, my grandfather, also impossibly young, and a little boy, my father. The picture was grainy and gray, taken when they were preparing to leave Japan. That was so long ago and she looked so young, and unsure and scared. It would have been a frightening trip, coming to a new country, having to learn a new language, not knowing anything. It was only in the past few weeks that I could even begin to understand how scary that journey into the unknown would have been.

I looked down at her again, lying there, looking almost serene. She looked so much more sure of this journey.

"Goodbye, Grandmother," I said softly, then turned and left the stall.

My father, mother and sisters were waiting. Everybody was dressed in their most formal clothing. I felt uncomfortable in mine — the collar of my shirt pinched my neck and the shoes just seemed a little smaller than the last time I wore them. My father motioned for me to come to his side.

We started walking. I was beside my father; my mother, with Yuri on one side and Midori on the other, walked behind us. Passing by each stall, I was aware of people standing there — silently. The whole building was so silent that I could hear the soles of our shoes against the cement floor as we walked.

I felt a sense of relief as we left the building. It was good to feel the warmth of the sun and the gentle breeze against my skin. I turned slightly to look over my shoulder and was shocked. A dozen paces behind us a procession of people had formed. It had two branches, one of which extended back into the building, while the other stretched along the entire length of the building and then disappeared around the corner! My mother and sisters had also looked back, and when my mother turned toward me I could tell by her expression that she was as surprised as me. Surprised but pleased. We continued to walk.

"Tadashi," my father said as we came to a junction in the path.

I knew without him asking that he was unsure of which way to go. I subtly motioned to the left and we proceeded. I knew a shorter way to get there — cutting between some buildings — but I thought it was better, somehow, more formal and proper, to stay on the path. Besides, was it right to lead all these people on a shortcut?

I turned around again to look at the people following behind us. I couldn't even see the end of the procession. How many people were there ... and what would the authorities think when they saw it? And how could they avoid seeing it ... a long thick parade of people snaking across the park? Suddenly I wanted them to all just go away. I was still hoping that somehow we wouldn't be discovered by the soldiers — or, at the least, discovered when they couldn't do anything about it. But now ...

We reached the last of the buildings. The railroad tracks were still hidden from view, but I could hear a train rumbling by. We moved through the bushes and entered the clearing. In the center was a large pile of wood, the funeral pyre. In the middle of the pile of wood was a green picnic bench, positioned so the body could be placed upon it. As we got closer, I detected a strong smell of gasoline and realized that the wood had been doused with gas to ensure that it would catch fire. We stopped about a dozen paces in front of the pyre, and my mother and sisters came up beside us.

I could hear people gathering behind us. I looked over my shoulder. The crowd was quickly filling the clearing. It was a fairly large opening, but it couldn't possibly hold all the people I'd seen in line behind us. As I watched, the crowd parted and two white-robed priests appeared. They were quietly chanting, saying prayers, and one carried incense. The smell was brought to us by the gentle wind, replacing the strong smell of the gasoline.

Close behind the priests came the men carrying my grandmother, still wrapped in the white sheet. The procession crossed the short open space between the edge of the crowd and where we stood. My father and I moved just off to the side to allow them to pass. The priests separated, one moving around the pyre in one direction, the second in the opposite way. Carefully, almost delicately, the men placed my grandmother on top of the picnic table. As the four men retreated, the two priests began chanting again, this time louder. Their voices were trapped by the crowd and echoed back at us. There wasn't another sound — not a whisper or cough, or the faint distant rumble of traffic, or a train, or even the call of a bird. It was like everything in the entire world had paused and was holding its breath, waiting, watching.

"Who is to light the fire?" asked one of the priests. He had already lit a small torch and was holding it at his side.

My father came forward and took the torch from the priest. As my grandmother's son he would be the chief mourner, and it would be his role to put the torch to the pyre and ignite it.

The priests retreated, leaving my father standing alone beside the pyre. He motioned for me to come to his side. I stepped forward, aware that hundreds and hundreds of people were watching my every move.

"Here," my father said, holding out the torch to me.

"But you should do it," I said. "You're her son."

"And you are her grandson. She would be honored … we both would be honored."

I nodded my head and carefully took the torch from his hand. I could feel the heat of the flame against my arm. I took a step forward and then hesitated. I looked back. My mother was standing with Yuri and Midori, an arm around each, their faces buried into her. There were tears streaming down her face. My father nodded his head, ever so slightly, but enough to let me know what I had to do. I turned and tossed the torch into the pyre.

Instantly there was a "whoosh," and a rush of heat pushed me back a step. I put my hand up to shield my eyes. The pyre was ablaze, fire shooting up everywhere. Fingers of flame were starting to lick up and over the edges of the green picnic table, but had not yet reached my grandmother. Above the fire was a thick black column of smoke. I followed it with my eyes. It soared high above us, straight up into the clear blue sky. There was no wind to disperse it, or clouds or darkness to disguise it. Anyone anywhere in the park would be able to see the smoke. It wouldn't be long until somebody came to investigate.

.21.

I looked at my watch. It was almost six-thirty, close to an hour since I'd thrown the torch into the pyre and still two hours before the sun would set and darkness would cover the smoke. The column of smoke was, if anything, thicker and blacker. Men were continually stoking the fire with wood — scrap wood found around the park, as well as broken-up pieces from benches and tables. I didn't know how the authorities couldn't see the smoke — they had to be coming. But somehow that thought didn't seem all bad. At least it gave me a distraction, another place to look.

I'd watched the white sheet catch fire. And then her clothing. And then my grandmother. I couldn't watch anymore. But there wasn't any need to look. Instead of staring into the flames, I scanned the crowd, looking for the first sign of the soldiers.

Somehow I'd expected the people to start to disperse once the pyre had been lit, but that wasn't the case. I didn't know if anybody had left. Maybe more had even come. Many had taken a seat on sparse grass that filled the clearing, as had my family. Some men sat in little clusters, playing cards. Others were eating. We'd been offered food and water. I'd taken a drink, but wasn't hungry — at least, not yet. I knew I'd probably feel different in a few more hours. We'd probably be here all night and probably at least until after lunch tomorrow. Maybe longer.

Twice Sam had come over and talked to me for a few minutes. He'd then retreat back into the crowd, leaving me with my family. I knew that Sam thought we were crazy for having the cremation here, in a park, in front of everybody. But I also knew he liked the idea of us doing something that would defy the authorities.

"They're coming," my father said.

"Who's ..." Both my mind and my eyes answered the question that I'd started to ask.

My heart rose up into my throat at the sight of the soldiers and RCMP officers. There were two RCMP officers and four soldiers. They picked their way through the crowd. People got up and moved aside to allow the column of men to pass.

My father and I both stood. I had to fight the urge to run away from the approaching men. They were moving purposefully, quickly, and the man in the lead looked angry. He stopped right on top of us.

"We cannot allow fires," he bellowed, "especially ones of this size, to be lit in the middle of this park. It is ..." His sentence trailed off. I think he had seen the remains of my grandmother's body and realized what the fire was.

"My good Lord," he muttered. "Who is responsible for this?"

"It is my —" my father started to answer.

"But we are all responsible," called out a voice, cutting him off.

It was Mr. Wakabayashi. I had long since lost sight of him and didn't even realize he was still here.

"This is your doing, Mr. Wakabayashi?" the soldier asked. Obviously, he knew who he was.

"I did not arrange, but I was aware it would take place."

"And you did not inform the authorities of your plan?" the soldier asked briskly.

"It was not my place ... nor yours."

"There are rules against such things, not just here in the park, but in society —"

"Perhaps in your society," Mr. Wakabayashi interrupted, "but she was not of your society, and neither are we ... are we?"

"I insist that this stop immediately!"

Mr. Wakabayashi looked at my father, and then at the pyre. He looked at the soldiers and police officers — all with side arms. He scanned the crowd that surrounded the clearing. There were hundreds of people. Now none of them were talking, or playing cards, or eating, or even sitting. Everybody was on their feet, watching and listening. Finally he turned once again to face the soldier — he was some sort of officer and clearly in charge.

"We would respectfully request that it be allowed to continue."

"I don't have the authority to approve this!" the soldier bellowed.

"Then please speak to your commander," Mr. Wakabayashi said.

"I shall." He paused. "And if we decide to intervene?" the commander questioned.

Mr. Wakabayashi didn't answer immediately. Everybody was listening. I looked beyond where we stood. The soldiers and police were anxiously looking all around them. The crowd was hushed, waiting for the answer.

"We request that you do not intervene ... for the sake of *all* involved," he said.

Of course, the "all" involved not just us and the rest of the Japanese, but also the commander and his men. Would he understand that?

"I have five men here," the soldier said. "A hundred more could be here within a few minutes if I so desired."

"That is understood," Mr. Wakabayashi said. "You

have the authority to arrange that."

"And we could forcibly extinguish the flames," the officer continued.

"You could … if you chose to do so."

Was he going to send somebody to get the extra men? Was he going to stop it? Or try to stop it?

"Mr. Wakabayashi, I will retire to speak to the commander. I will advise him that there is a bonfire and it has some religious significance, and that you will take responsibility for it not spreading … is that correct?"

Mr. Wakabayashi nodded.

"And I would appreciate it if you could also meet with myself and the commander … perhaps tomorrow at noon?"

"It would be my honor," Mr. Wakabayashi said, bowing slightly.

"Until then, good day, sir," the officer said. He turned on his heel and started off through the crowd, the other soldiers following after him.

•••

My father passed me the bag and I dug out a handful of pistachios and handed the bag back to him. I crunched one between my teeth, spitting out the shell into the mound of shells at my feet. My hands were stained red from the pistachios — I couldn't believe how many I'd eaten. They were one of my favorite things in the world … and one of my grandmother's favorites too.

My father and I had taken a seat on a bench some of the men had brought close to the fire. Eventually it would be added to the flames, but for now it was our place to sit. Behind us on the ground, huddled underneath some blankets, my mother and sisters were sound asleep. They'd been asleep for hours. I was surprised that I wasn't tired, although I would have welcomed a blanket over me. I was a little cold — at least, half of me, the back half that wasn't facing the fire, was chilly. I cracked open another pistachio.

"You can go lie down," my father said.

"That's okay. I don't think I could sleep."

He nodded.

As we talked, two men came into the halo of light thrown out by the fire. They were carrying between them a large branch. They brought it to the edge of the fire and then tipped it into the flames. It crashed down, spewing ashes and embers into the air. I watched as the embers drifted up into the night sky, flickering and floating and finally disappearing, absorbed by the stars.

The men were just a small part of the large crowd that remained. Most had long since gone away. Some, like the men gathering wood, were fairly young, in their early twenties, but there were a lot of old people, many from our village. They were staying to show respect, but I thought they were also here because they knew their time wasn't far away. It would be different for them than for somebody young, knowing that the fire would soon be for them. A shiver ran down my spine at that thought.

"I've been thinking about where we should go," my father said.

For an instant I thought he meant after death, and then realized he probably was referring to after we left Hastings Park.

"The abandoned towns in the mountains or Alberta are the choices. You favor one, do you not?" he said.

"Yeah, I was thinking that maybe —" I stopped myself. This wasn't the time for me to be disrespectful. It was my father's decision to make. "Whatever decision you make will be good."

"I hope that will be the case," he said. "But I do wish your opinion."

"I really don't know that much about either," I admitted. "I just heard that those who volunteered for Alberta were going soon … and I also hoped that we could be together."

"Alberta," he said in a voice barely audible. "I am a fisherman, not a farmer."

I nodded my head.

"I have heard it is very rough … hard, hard work, but yes, we could all be together," he said. "Together is important, but maybe not the most important thing."

I wanted to jump in and correct him. It was the most important thing, especially now, especially for my sisters. With grandmother gone they needed the rest of us to stay together. I held my tongue. Instead I stared into the fire.

"Hard times," my father said. "Very hard. And hard decisions still to be made."

.22.

I heard the crack of the ball against the bat and saw a glimpse of it screaming toward me. I charged back and to my right, following it, following it, reached up and felt it smack into my glove for the last out of the inning! There was a roar of response — cheers and groans of disappointment all mixed together. I tossed the ball to the shortstop, who rolled it toward the pitcher's mound.

"Great grab," Sam said as we trotted in toward the infield together.

"That's what happens when you have a quality glove," I said teasingly.

"Don't get me started about that — hey, isn't that your father?"

Sam was right. My father was standing beside the bleachers. That was strange; he'd never had any interest in baseball whatsoever. Why was he even here …

"Don't worry," Sam said reassuringly. "I'm sure it's nothing."

Sam was right about me being worried. I just hoped he was right about it being nothing.

Over the last few days, since my grandmother's cremation, I'd been nothing but worried. Worried that the authorities were going to do something to us or that something was going to happen to somebody else in my family.

Sam joined the rest of the team on the bench and I

jogged to my father's side.

"We need to talk. We are leaving," he said.

"Today … now?" I asked, my voice hardly a whisper.

He shook his head. "Tomorrow."

"Hold on, please," I said. I walked over to Sam. "Could you get somebody to take my spot in the lineup?"

"Sure, no problem." He paused. "What's happening?"

"We're leaving. Tomorrow. My father needs to talk to me."

"Do you know where you're going?" Sam asked.

I shook my head. "He didn't tell me yet."

"Okay. I'll come by your place right after the game … okay?"

"Sure, I'll see you then." I hurried to my father's side. "Do mother and the girls know already?"

"They're packing now."

"I should go and help them and —"

"No need. There is not much to pack. They pack. We talk."

We started walking. I waited for him to start talking.

"I've heard more about Alberta," my father said. "Things are very hard."

"I know." I guess that meant we were going into the mountains and he was going to a work camp. I just hoped that he could come back and spend time with —

"Tomorrow morning we leave for Alberta."

"Alberta!" I said in shock.

"Is that not what you wanted?"

"Yes, I just didn't think …"

"It is my decision. Whatever the conditions or consequences, they rest on me. Understand?"

"Yes … of course … yes, sir."

"I have heard we will all be working the fields, perhaps even Yuri."

"We can all work."

We walked on, not talking, my father thinking.

"It is not too late for other options," he finally said.

"You mean the ghost towns and work camp?"

"It would be easier for your mother and sisters."

"Grandmother would want us to be together."

My father laughed. "Then I guess it is decided. I'm to be a farmer instead of a fisherman … but I am no fisherman now either … not without a boat."

I'd shared the contents of the letter from Jed. There was nothing in there that he hadn't known. But he also told me other things, worse things. It wasn't just that people were destroying or stealing some of our things, but that the government was taking all of our things. All of the things that had been left behind — houses, cars, belongings and boats.

My father suddenly stopped walking. He was staring into the distance. "I think about my boat. I heard stories. The boats are all tied together, uncared for, not tended to. All rotting away in the water. If only I'd known."

"Known?" I asked.

"What was going to happen. That my boat would be left to rot away or sold out for pennies. If only I'd known."

"But even if you knew you couldn't have done anything about it," I reasoned.

"Oh yes, I could! I could have sunk it! Sent it to the bottom! If I was standing on my boat right now I'd scuttle it!" he said defiantly.

"Even if you did that … even if you could do it right now … what would it change?" I asked.

My father shrugged. "We would still be away from our home. Your grandmother would still be gone. We would still be going farther away … but somehow … somehow, it would be a little better."

"Do you really mean that?" I questioned.

He nodded his head. The expression on his face left no doubt what he believed.

I took a deep breath. "What if we could do it?"

"Do what?"

"Sink the boat."

"That is just a wish … it cannot come true," my father said.

"I just want to know. If you were standing on the boat right now, would you pull the plug and send her to the bottom?"

"Yes."

"Then how about if we go and do that … tonight."

As soon as I said the words I regretted them. What a stupid thing to say. Was my father going to yell at me or think I was being a silly little boy or —

"Tell me … how could we do this?"

•••

"Look, even if I get you the truck, do either of you even know where the Annieville Dyke is?" Sam asked.

"No, but there are maps. Is it far?"

"Not far at all. I've been there dozens of times on pick-ups from the fields just around there."

"Then you could tell me how to get there," I reasoned.

"It's not that simple. It's one of those places you go where you don't remember the names of the roads, you just sort of know which spots to turn and which roads to travel. And even if you could find your way up there what makes you think you could even find your boat? Aren't there hundreds and hundreds of them up there?"

"Twelve hundred."

"Even worse. It would be impossible to find your boat."

"My father says he can find it. He said he'll be able to 'smell' it when he gets close."

"That's crazy! I can't believe your father has agreed to do this," Sam said in amazement.

"It was his idea to sink the boat."

"Come on … you're joking. Right?"

"I couldn't believe it at first either. I don't really understand it, but that's what he wants to do. He said the only way it can remain his boat is if he sinks it. Does that make any sense at all?" I asked.

"I don't know."

"It's like your father's trucks, the ones they made him put here in the park. It must bother him that they're going to take them away from him."

"He's angry. Very angry. I think it bothers him more about the trucks than about losing our house or even us having to live here," Sam said.

"I understand that."

"You do?" Sam questioned.

I nodded my head. "The trucks aren't just what he *owns*. They're what he *does*. Just like the boat for my father. He's a fisherman; that's not just what he does, but who he is. Understand?"

Sam scrunched up his face and scratched his head. "Not really," he admitted. "What time do you have?"

I looked at my watch. "Twenty after three."

"I've got twenty-two minutes after three," he said, showing me his watch.

"Why did you ask me if you're wearing a watch?" I questioned.

"I didn't really want to know what time it is. I just wanted to know that our watches were pretty much in agreement as to the time. I'll meet you and your father at the hole in the fence at eleven. The truck will be there."

•••

It felt good to be out in the cool night air. It also felt good to be away from the stall. I'd had even more trouble than usual sleeping there the last few nights. I was so used to having my grandmother just a few short feet away. A few times I'd woken up in the middle of the night and listened for her breathing and looked for her sleeping shape, not remembering for a few seconds that she was gone ... gone.

We'd all be gone soon enough. This was our last night in the stall, in the park, and while I was grateful for that, there were still so many questions that couldn't be answered until we got there. My worst thought was how each step of the way, from our house to the boat to this park, things kept getting worse. Then again, how much worse could they get than living in a cattle stall?

I hadn't said much to my mother about why I had to leave. I simply told her I had to meet my father. That was the truth. Both he and I figured it was better if she didn't know. There was no sense in worrying her. As well, I guess we figured she wouldn't understand. I had to admit that there were more times than not, when I was bouncing this plan around in my brain, that I didn't really think I understood. If the government was going to buy the boat, like the rumors said, wouldn't it be better to just take the money?

I arrived at the place where my father and I had agreed to meet. I'd have to lead him to the spot where we'd go under the fence. There was no sign of him. That wasn't like him to be late — and we really couldn't afford to be late. Sam had been insistent that the truck would be there at exactly eleven and that he couldn't guarantee it would wait more than a minute or two. I understood. While there weren't any more soldiers guarding us now, they were guarding us differently — many more around the outside of the park, along the fence, and not so many on patrol inside. The newspapers had been filled with scare stories about what would happen if all of us Japanese escaped Hastings Park, so they'd put more guards on the fences. That meant that whoever was driving the truck couldn't wait too long or he'd be spotted. Sam had said he didn't think we could get there by ourselves, but not to worry because there'd be a driver. I wondered if it was somebody Japanese who was still living in Vancouver.

What was keeping my father? I knew he couldn't have forgotten or lost track of the time. Maybe he'd had second thoughts and decided that the whole idea was just too crazy or dangerous … but he would have got word to me. He wouldn't just leave me standing out here waiting if he wasn't coming.

There was a third possibility; maybe he'd been caught outside his building by one of the guards. It was true that most of the sentries were on the perimeter of the park, but some still circulated through the — I stopped at the sound of footsteps. Maybe it was him … or maybe it wasn't.

I took another step backwards so I was farther off the path. I could still peer out but I was even less visible, buried in the shadows and shielded by the branches of the bushes.

The footsteps were getting louder. It had to be him. Carefully, still completely hidden, I looked out. I could see the outline of somebody coming up the — my heart jumped into my throat when I caught sight of a second darkened outline, and then a third and a fourth!

It was a whole patrol coming!

I shifted even farther back into deeper cover and then cringed as a tiny twig snapped underfoot. They couldn't have heard that … or could they? I couldn't hear footsteps anymore. Had they stopped right beside my hiding spot?

Then there was a whistle … it sounded like my father's whistle. Was he coming from a different direction and hadn't seen those men on the path? Another whistle … this time I was sure it was from the path. Had those figures passed?

"Tadashi!" I heard my father call out in a loud raspy whisper.

I stumbled out of the bushes, tripping, and — I stopped, stunned. It was my father, along with Mr. Yamamoto, Mr. Hirano and Mr. Nakayama, three men from our village.

"What are they doing here?" I mumbled.

"We hope you do not take offence," Mr. Yamamoto said, bowing slightly.

"No ... not offense ... I just don't understand what you're all doing here."

"They are accompanying us," my father answered.

"If you do not object," Mr. Yamamoto added.

"No, of course not! But why would you all want to come with us to ... um ... come with us?" I didn't even want to say the words "to sink my father's boat." It wasn't that I didn't think he'd told them, but I just couldn't bring myself to say it.

"We wish to do the same as your father," Mr. Hirano said.

"You mean you want to ... to ..."

"Scuttle our vessels," Mr. Nakayama said.

"Send them to the bottom," Mr. Yamamoto agreed, while both my father and Mr. Hirano nodded solemnly.

"When your father told us of your plan we asked his permission to take part," Mr. Yamamoto said. "You look surprised."

"I guess I am. I didn't expect my father to even agree with it, let alone others."

"There were many others. Dozens and dozens wished to do the same."

"You're kidding!"

"Kidding?" Mr. Hirano asked. "What is kidding?"

"Nothing. I just mean I didn't expect that."

"Your father said there would not be room for more than a few. There is room?" Mr. Yamamoto asked.

"Sure, Sam said it was a big truck so there's no —" I stopped and looked at my watch. It was less then ten minutes to eleven. "We have to hurry or we'll miss the truck!"

I turned and started to run to the fence. The four men hurried to keep up to me. They were making a tremendous racket, their feet slapping against the path as we ran. If there were any guards around, they couldn't help but hear. Turning off the path, I was relieved at how the grass softened their steps.

I could tell by the breathing of the men behind me that they were struggling to keep up, but nobody would ever say anything. I stopped just before the fence, taking refuge in a clump of small trees and bushes, the only cover close to the perimeter. The men stopped beside me. I took a few more tentative steps and then, still hidden, peered out in both directions.

I'd never been here at night and was amazed at just how bright it was. The light from the street lamps didn't just illuminate the road, but haloed in the park. The entire fenceline was bathed in light. I could clearly see along the section of fence. I looked around for Sam. He was nowhere to be seen. Luckily there were no sentries either. Of course, if a guard did turn the corner, he'd be able to easily spot us as we moved along the fence.

I looked beyond the fence. There was also no waiting truck. Actually, there were no vehicles visible except for a set of headlights, approaching but still far away. A second set of lights appeared behind the first.

I quickly retreated to the safety of the bushes. My father and the other three men were all squatting down, resting, not talking, waiting.

"I didn't see the truck." It was now a couple of minutes after eleven, and I hoped it hadn't come and gone already. "When we go under the fence —" I stopped as the sweep of headlights cut through the bushes, bathing us in a swath of bright light for a split second before the car raced off. I readied myself for the passing of the second car. I could hear the engine, louder and rougher running than the first, but where were the lights? Instead came the high-pitched whine of brakes. Was that the truck?

"Stay here ... I'll look," I ordered as I got up. I was struck by the fact that not only was I giving orders to these men, but that they were listening.

I looked out. There was a truck parked in the curb lane, its lights off. It was parked just down the way — right by the hole under the fence. It had to be Sam ... didn't it?

I stepped out from the cover and felt exposed. I had to fight the urge to jump back into the trees.

"Hurry up!" Sam hissed. He was pressed flat against the outside of the fence. I hadn't expected him to be on the other side of the fence already.

I let out a whistle — the same tone my father always used — and then ran toward Sam.

"Where's your —" Sam stopped. "Geez, who are those other men?" he demanded.

Instead of answering, I dropped to the ground and quickly pulled myself under the fence. Somehow I thought it was better to give him an answer once I was on his side of the fence.

"They're from our village. They're coming."

"To sink their boats?" Sam asked in disbelief.

"That's what they want to do. Can they come along ... do you mind?"

"One, four, ten ... we're in the same amount of trouble no matter the number of people. Let's just get going. Fast!"

I turned around. Mr. Hirano, Mr. Yamamoto and my father were on our side of the fence, while Mr. Nakayama was wiggling his way underneath.

"Tell them to get into the back of the truck!" Sam ordered. "You come up in the front with me!"

I would have liked to have had my father sit up front too, but I knew there wouldn't be enough space for him as well as me, Sam and the driver.

"And tell them to hurry!" Sam called out. "There are cars coming!"

I looked past the four men and down the road. There were three sets of lights, still in the distance but coming fast. Any one of them could be a police car or military truck. But even if it wasn't, whoever it was could very well report us.

"Hurry," I screamed. "Into the back!"

The four men scrambled to the truck. The vehicles were coming fast but couldn't possibly close the gap before the men got into the truck. The truck engine sprang to life as I offered a hand to Mr. Hirano, who hoisted himself into the back of the truck. Mr. Yamamoto practically leaped into the back. My father and Mr. Nakayama followed close behind.

"Come on!" I heard Sam scream.

I rounded the side of the truck as the first headlights reached us. I grabbed the door, flung it open and climbed up into the truck. I hadn't even managed to pull the door completely closed when I was thrown against the back of the seat as the truck lurched forward.

"That took too long," Sam said.

I looked over. It was only me and Sam, and he was at the wheel of the truck.

"Where's the driver?" I demanded.

"I'm the driver."

"But you can't drive!"

"Of course I can drive," he said as the gears ground together noisily and the truck jerked and rocked before gaining speed.

"It sure doesn't feel like it."

"You want to take over?" Sam asked, taking both hands off the wheel.

"No!"

"Then button it," he said as he grabbed the wheel again.

"I'm sorry. It's just that I was expecting somebody else to drive."

"Like who?"

"I don't know … maybe the person who usually drives the truck."

"He would of done it if I asked him, but I couldn't do it."

"Why not?"

"He's white. Can you imagine what would have happened if he got caught?"

"What could they do to him that they haven't done to us?" I questioned.

"Maybe put him in jail," Sam said quietly. "I wasn't going to take a chance on taking anybody else away from their family."

"You're right. That wouldn't be fair."

"Besides, I'm not that bad a driver, am I?" Sam asked.

He did seem to be doing okay. We were staying on the road, straight and even and at about the right speed.

"I drive all the time."

"Your father lets you?" I asked.

"Sure," Sam answered. He stared straight ahead out the windshield like suddenly the road was interesting.

I knew Sam well enough to know that a short answer like that meant he was either lying or, more likely, only giving me part of the truth. For somebody who was so good at talking he wasn't very good at lying — at least with me.

"So your father is okay with you driving the truck … on the road … at night?"

"Car or truck, day or night, road or on a farm lane, it's all the same."

"So you're saying?"

"He wouldn't be happy about me driving. Then again, he wouldn't be that happy about us using the truck."

"You mean he said no."

"No, he didn't say that."

"Did he say anything?" I questioned.

"Good night … see you in the morning … something like that."

"As in, you didn't ask him, right?"

"Something like that. But it's better that he doesn't know."

"And how do you figure that?"

"At least this way if we get caught it doesn't involve him."

"I guess that makes sense. But maybe you shouldn't have done it. I don't want you to get into trouble."

"Too late for that. Besides, I didn't have a choice."

"How do you figure that?" I questioned.

"You're my friend. You needed the truck. End of story."

"Thanks, Sam … thanks."

We drove along in silence. Occasionally the lights of an oncoming car appeared down the road, got bigger and passed us in a flash. Each time I held my breath for that split second. Worse, though, were those vehicles that came up from behind us. They came alongside and slowly passed us, having the opportunity to look up and through the windows. It only happened a few times, and I couldn't see into their vehicles so I figured they couldn't see us inside ours, but it was a terrible feeling.

"Has your father decided where your family is going to go?" I asked.

"He's still trying to arrange for us to go out east."

"To Ontario?"

"Hamilton."

"Where's that?" I asked.

"Close to Toronto … a long way off."

"I guess that makes Alberta seem a lot closer."

"Closer, yeah, but … better?"

That was more a statement than a question. We'd heard nothing about Alberta that didn't indicate it would be hard. The only question was how hard.

"It's going to be okay. Besides, it doesn't matter whether it's Ontario or Alberta or wherever, as long as we stay as a family," I said.

Sam geared down and the truck slowed. We passed a road sign, but I wasn't able to read it. Sam slowed the truck more and turned onto a narrow, gravel road. Though there were no lights, I could see that ditches lined both sides, and beyond were planted fields. A few isolated lights in the distance marked houses set well back from the road.

"I was wondering," Sam said. "Do you think you could give me your friend Jed's address?"

"Sure, but why would you want it?"

"It's the only way you and me can stay in touch," Sam said.

"I don't understand."

"You're gone tomorrow and you don't know where you're going, right?"

"Yeah?"

"And by the time you get there and write me here at the park, assuming the censors even let it get through with an address, I might be gone. So we both write to Jed, and he writes back and passes on the others' address so we can exchange letters."

"That makes sense," I agreed.

"You do want to stay in touch, don't you?" Sam asked.

"Of course!"

"'Cause I figure after all we've been through we should write."

"I'd like to do that."

"Maybe we could even visit some time."

"Alberta to Ontario is a long way."

"None of this is forever. Who knows, someday we may even be neighbors."

"Neighbors? Me and you?"

"Why not? About the only thing I've learned from all this is that you never can predict what's going to happen," Sam said. "Could you have predicted any of this?"

"I guess not," I had to admit.

Sam geared down and the truck slowed almost to a stop. All at once the road went pitch black — Sam had shut off the lights.

"Why did you do that?" I asked in alarm.

"We're almost there."

"We are?" I looked all around, waiting for my eyes to adjust to the darkness. Soon I could see that there were still open fields on one side, while on the other the land had given way to water. We crept forward.

"Can you see where you're going?" I asked, peering through the windshield.

"I can see enough. Besides, I can't risk us being seen — wow!" Sam said as he brought the truck to a complete stop. "Look at that!"

Off to the side, backlit by the moon reflecting off the water, were boats, more boats than I'd ever seen, more boats than I'd ever imagined I'd ever see in one place. And somewhere out there was our boat.

"I'll be back in three hours," Sam said. "Is that going to be enough time?"

"I'm not sure. Do you think you can give us a little more time?" I asked.

"Can't," he said, shaking his head. "By the time I drop you all back at Hastings, and then drop off the truck and get back myself, it'll be almost daybreak."

"I understand. We'll be here. What are you going to do?"

"Drive a bit. Maybe find a place where I can sit with the truck that's a little more private than here."

"Okay, we'll see you at three ... and Sam, thanks."

"That's okay," he said. "And good luck."

I closed the door as quietly as I could and leaped down off the step and onto the ground. I scurried off the gravel road as the truck's engine came to life with a roar. In the still of the night that sound could probably be heard for miles across the flat land and open water. I stood and watched as it headed up the road. Within a few seconds it faded into the darkness, although the sound of the engine continued to cut through the night. At least we wouldn't have any trouble hearing the truck coming back.

Standing on the edge of the road, I could see a number of wooden docks extending into the water. A couple of small boats were bobbing up and down, tied to the nearest docks. I could see the darkened shapes of my father and the other men as they headed out onto one of the docks. By the time I caught up with them, Mr. Hirano was already sitting in a rowboat. The other two men climbed down into the boat with him, while my father bent over and untied the ropes that held it to the dock.

"Get in," my father said, without looking back.

"Can we all fit? Is it big enough?"

Mr. Hirano snorted. "As long as nobody takes too big a breath."

That wasn't the reassurance I was looking for.

I climbed into the small space in the bow. My father pushed off, and the whole boat rocked and rolled as it glided away from the dock. Mr. Yamamoto and Mr. Nakayama, side by side in the middle seat, took up the two long oars and began to row us toward the dark shapes of the fishing boats about fifty yards away. Luckily, it was completely calm, as there wasn't more than three inches of gunwale above the waterline.

"Tadashi," my father said.

I turned around to face him.

"Do you have a knife?"

"A knife! Why would I need a knife?" I asked in alarm.

"To cut ropes."

"Oh … no, I don't." As far as I knew, nobody in the camp had a knife, not even to eat their meals with.

My father passed something to Mr. Hirano, who passed it forward to me. It was a large knife, secured within a leather sheath. I pulled it out of the sheath. Light glistened off the blade. I gently ran a finger along the edge. It had been recently sharpened. I pushed it back into the cover and shifted my weight so I could put it in my pocket, but it was too long, so I tucked it down my pants.

In my mind I started to try to figure things out. There

were around twelve hundred boats and five of us. We had three hours, less the time it would take to row across to the boats and back again. We probably had two hours to search. It wasn't much time. And we still had to have time to sink the boats. All without attracting the attention of the guards.

I looked up. We were practically in the shadow cast by the nearest boat. I could now see how the boats were moored. A series of pilings ran parallel to the shore, spaced about fifty yards apart. The pilings ran in three or four rows, each row about twenty-five yards farther from shore. The fishing boats were moored to cables strung between the pilings, side by side and nose to nose, a bit like cattle feeding from each side of a trough. The boats were packed so tightly that it looked like once we got onto the first boat, we would be able to make our way right through the fleet by climbing from the stern of one of the longer boats in one row onto the next row.

The oars were pulled out of the water and we glided forward. I reached out a hand to cushion us as we bumped against the bigger boat. I got to my feet and reached up to steady the little rowboat so that the others could climb out. Starting with Mr. Hirano, they quickly climbed onto the deck of the larger vessel.

In rapid Japanese my father and the men described their plan. Staying close together, separated by no more than one boat, they would move from vessel to vessel. They were certain that all their boats, all the boats of our village, would be tied together or close together, so if they found one, they would find them all.

I looked at my watch. There was barely enough light to read the dial. It was almost twelve-thirty. We had only two hours left to search.

●●●

Of all the things that had happened over the past months, I couldn't think of anything that seemed as unreal as what I was now doing. I tried to stay low as I walked along the length of the boat — it wasn't one that I recognized. Off to my side I could just make out the silhouette of one of the other men, maybe it was even my father, moving along beside me on another vessel.

The boats were all tied with very little space between them. In places, they had old car tires hanging over the side as bumpers, but sometimes the tires were just sitting uselessly on the deck. I had to fight the urge to put them over the side. I could only imagine the damage that would be done if a storm blew up and the vessels were bounced wildly on the waves.

I moved as quickly as I could from boat to boat, looking for something familiar, something that spoke to me of my village. Around me, I was only sometimes aware of the movement of some of the other men.

•••

I stopped again to look at my watch. More clouds had rolled in and there was less light to read the dial. It looked like it was almost quarter past two. Behind us was row after row of boats, boats we had searched without success. In front, an even greater expanse of vessels stretched out. And somewhere nearby there had to be guards, whose job it was to watch over this fleet. Of course, we hadn't seen anybody, but we knew they had to be there. Most likely they were on shore, huddled around a woodstove in a shed, or perhaps even sleeping. If they were anything like the guards at the park, we had nothing to fear from them. Then again, why would they need to be vigilant? It wasn't like anybody would even suspect that anyone would come here to sink boats.

Regardless, time was passing, quickly. Even if we did find the boats, would we have time to sink them, travel back over all the other vessels, locate the rowboat, get back across and find Sam? I looked back, trying to pick out the point of light on the far shore that marked where the rowboat had been tied up. I didn't see it. Maybe it would be best to just give up and — I heard a whistle. The hairs on the back of my neck stood up straight. That was the signal we'd agreed on if somebody came across one of the boats.

I turned my head and tried to figure out where it had come from. My father had been off to my right and — the whistle came again. Definitely off to the right side, and up ahead. That was the direction I'd have to go.

I felt a surge of renewed energy. I leaped over to the next boat, my feet slipping as I landed on the deck; I grabbed the bulkhead to regain my balance. I crossed over the deck and climbed the railing. There was no open water between that boat and the next, and I just stepped onto it.

Up ahead I caught sight of movement on one of the boats. I froze, thinking it might be a guard, but almost instantly realized it had to be one of us — nobody else would be out here in the middle of the night, jumping from boat to boat.

I walked along the length of the vessel and then was startled as a figure stood up right in front of me. I jumped backwards in shock before I realized it was Mr. Hirano.

"Sad shape," he said. "Taking on water below."

"Has my father found our boat?"

"All boats. All four. Almost side by side. Your boat is there," he said, pointing up ahead.

They all looked pretty much the same in the dark, but there was something about that boat just two in front that was unmistakable. I cut from one to the next and then landed on the deck of our boat. My father came out of the bridge. In his hands was an ornate vase. I'd forgotten that we'd had to leave things on board when we left for the park.

"For my mother," he said.

For a split second I didn't understand what he meant. Then I understood. Her remains, her ashes, were now in a plain wooden box. This would be a better urn.

Of course, there were other things on board that we could have taken. Things we could use, things that we owned and should rightfully come with us. But I also knew that there wasn't any possible way to take anything more on that little rowboat. Nor would we be able to take much more with us on the trip to Alberta.

"Almost everything else … gone."

"What do you mean?" I asked.

"Taken. Someone opened the boxes. Took things, broke things. Hardly anything left."

I didn't know what to say, but why would I expect anything different here than at our home? It was like vultures swooping down on the remains of our lives.

"My boat," my father said, shaking his head sadly. "Look how she was kept."

I couldn't tell much in the dark, but I couldn't imagine how it wouldn't be in bad shape.

"She might have sunk all by herself, if we did not come along."

"What do you want me to do?" I asked.

"The ropes. Cut those that are attached to that boat, and that one," he said, pointing them out. "Those aren't ours to decide. But leave her tied to Nakayama's vessel. The two ships can keep each other company on the way down."

"And what are you going to do?"

"Pull the main plug. Now go … hurry … not much time," my father said as he turned and left to go below deck.

I pulled the knife out of my pants and then removed it from the sheath. I sank it into the first rope. The line was waterlogged and soft, and the blade cut quickly into the fiber. I sawed it back and forth until the line snapped in two, one end falling into the water. I worked my way along the side of the boat, stopping at a second line. It was tied with a badly made knot, and given time I could have easily untied it. Instead I cut the line with a sweep of the knife.

I looked over at Mr. Nakayama's boat. I couldn't be sure, but it looked like it was starting to list to one side. Could it be taking on water that quickly?

"Come, Tadashi," my father said quietly.

I went to his side. "What do we do now?"

"There is nothing more to be done. We have to get back to shore."

"Shouldn't we wait here to make sure it goes down?"

He shook his head. "They will sink, but it will take time. More time than we have."

I looked again at my watch. He was right.

"And I need to leave," he said quietly. "I … I don't wish to be here when …" He let the sentence trail off.

In the dim light his face betrayed no emotions. He looked like he was simply studying what was happening.

My father turned to me. "It will soon be gone … and we need now to be gone as well so that we are free to start … again."

.24.

Dear Jed,

I am writing to you from Alberta. We are living on a sugar beet farm. Things are hard but they are going as well as can be expected. I am still not sure what I can write and what I shouldn't. I know we have been through a lot, not just the past few weeks here, but over the last few months. Maybe things are finally going to start to get a little better. The family that owns the farm seem like good enough people. We live in a little house on their property. The work is hard and we work long hours, but the food is good.

Just before we left Hastings, my grandmother died. It was hard for everybody. In the end, after everything is settled, I'll be coming back up to Sikima. That was where she wanted her ashes scattered. She said it was her home. I wish it was still my home, but I don't like to think about that too much. Who knows? So much has happened that I don't know what might or might not be possible someday.

My grandmother always said, 'shikata-ga-nai'. It means it can't be helped. I don't know if any of this could have been helped. I know that sometimes I get very sad, and other times very angry. It doesn't change anything, or even make me feel any better. It's just the way I feel and I can't help that either.

What I do know is that I'm grateful for the few things that didn't change. Thank you for the things you did for me and my family. It means a lot, not just to me but to my whole family. I'm also grateful that my family is still together. This may not be where we want to be, but at least we're in the wrong place together. And someday ... who knows ... They can take away a lot of things, but they can't take away my hopes and dreams for the future.

Your friend always,
Tadashi

afterword

I found this a very difficult novel to write. I've written historical fiction before. And in writing this type of novel, you're both guided and constrained by the realities of what actually happened. While this helps in giving direction to the storyline, it also keeps an author from exploring other interesting or intriguing options because they aren't realistic possibilities. While a certain amount of license is allowed — after all, it is fiction — it isn't permissible to change or misrepresent major facts of history. In *Caged Eagles*, however, I did take some liberties. For example, I decided to have a death and cremation scene set within the confines of Hastings Park. The historical record indicates that there were no deaths during the use of the park, and it is unlikely, even if there were, that a cremation would have taken place.

A further complication came from the fact that I was writing from the perspective of a person whose cultural heritage I do not share. Though in other novels I have written from the perspective of characters who were part Native Canadian or female, somehow this was different. When I first contemplated writing this story, I spoke to a number of Canadians of Japanese descent. Some were very encouraging of my efforts, while others thought I had no right to write this book, not only because I wasn't of Japanese descent, but also because I didn't experience life in the camps first-hand. For them it wasn't just cultural, but experiential.

In the end, the opinion that mattered to me most was that of a woman of Japanese descent who not only was interned, but whose literary skills I greatly admire. She basically said, yes, you can do it, but you better do it well. Starting out to write any book is pretty scary, but this was downright frightening. After much thought I decided to go ahead with this project. I knew I would risk some upset and resentment.

I hope that people will at least read *Caged Eagles* before making a judgment. Rather than seeking to stir up animosity, I am trying to help a new generation of Canadians, of all backgrounds, understand a neglected and sad time in our history. As well, I see this story as being more than just about Canadians of Japanese descent. It is a story about Canada and is relevant to Canadians of all backgrounds. I hope that by understanding what happened we'll all be more willing to stand against any future injustices.

Lastly, I think this book was most difficult because I felt a sense of helplessness. I knew from the first word that there could be no happy ending, or sense of redemption, or saving grace that would make everything better. I was writing about an injustice, certainly one of the greatest injustices perpetrated on citizens of this country over the past hundred years. And while I was free to document it, I wasn't free to change it. At times I had to stop writing because I found myself in tears. Other times I turned away before the tears came. In the end, I wasn't able to save Tadashi or his family. I wasn't free to change anything, only to watch and document it. I'd like to believe that, as a country and a culture, we're beyond such blatant acts of racism, discrimination and injustice ... but I read the newspapers ... I watch television and listen to the radio ... and sometimes I just don't know.

Eric Walters